FEAT OF CLAY

Also by Keith R.A. DeCandido
from eSpec Books

The Adventures of Bram Gold
A FURNACE SEALED

The Precinct Series
DRAGON PRECINCT
UNICORN PRECINCT
GOBLIN PRECINCT
GRYPHON PRECINCT
TALES FROM DRAGON PRECINCT
MERMAID PRECINCT
PHOENIX PRECINCT
MANTICORE PRECINCT (forthcoming)
MORE TALES FROM DRAGON PRECINCT (forthcoming)

Other Titles
WITHOUT A LICENSE
TO HELL AND REGROUP (with David Sherman)
SYSTEMA PARADOXA: ALL-THE-WAY HOUSE

Anthologies
THE SIDE OF GOOD/THE SIDE OF EVIL
THE BEST OF DEFENDING THE FUTURE
THE BEST OF BAD-ASS FAERIES
FOOTPRINTS IN THE STARS
BEST LAID PLANS
DEVILISH AND DIVINE
A CRY OF HOUNDS

FEAT OF CLAY

Keith R.A. DeCandido

Pennsville, NJ

PUBLISHED BY
eSpec Books LLC
Danielle McPhail, Publisher
PO Box 242,
Pennsville, New Jersey 08070
www.especbooks.com

ISBN: 978-1-956463-43-9
ISBN (ebook): 978-1-956463-42-2

Interior Design: Danielle McPhail, McP Digital Graphics
Cover Art and Design: Mike McPhail, McP Digital Graphics

Acknowledgments

MANY THANKS TO ALL THE AMAZING PEOPLE AT ESPEC BOOKS: DANIELLE Ackley-McPhail, Mike McPhail, and Greg Schauer, who were kind enough to take over this series. Also, naturally, my agent, the magnificent Lucienne Diver, who keeps the paperwork mills grinding.

There are many folks who helped make this book better, most especially my wife, Wrenn Simms, and The Mom, GraceAnne Andreassi DeCandido, who edited the manuscript (both of these amazing women are professional editors of many years' standing, which are handy things to have in a wife and mother). Also huge thanks to ToniAnn Marini, Meredith Peruzzi, and Matthew Holcombe for so many reasons.

Additional gratitude for various bits of inspiration and/or research and/or assistance: Kevin J. Anderson, Laura Antoniou, Michael A. Burstein, Nomi S. Burstein, Michelle Corsillo, Carol Greenburg, Ian Hanley, David Mack, the late great Dale Mazur, Rebecca Moesta, Peter J. Wacks, Marie Whittaker, and the spectacular reference works published by the Bronx Historical Society, including the histories written by Lloyd Ultan with Gary Hermalyn, and also John McNamara's wonderful *History in Asphalt: The Origin of Bronx Street and Place Names*.

Thanks to Mary Fan for inviting me to the *Bad Ass Moms* anthology, which inspired me to create Yolanda Rodriguez for the story "Materfamilias." Thanks also to the aforementioned Danielle Ackley-McPhail and John L. French, the editors of *Devilish and Divine*, for whom I wrote a second Yolanda story, "Unguarded." Also thanks to all my Patreon supporters, for whom I wrote the vignettes that appear in the back of this book. If you want to see more of this sort of thing (I do monthly vignettes featuring my various and sundry original characters, not just the ones in Bram's world), please consider supporting me at http://patreon.com/krad.

In 2010, I worked the Decennial Census as a crew leader, and in 2020, my aforementioned wife did likewise. During both, we got to meet some amazing people and see some wonderful parts of our home borough. That 2010 work I did was what inspired me to start this series with *A Furnace Sealed*, and the 2020 work Wrenn did helped inform the writing of this second book in the series. So the final thank-you goes to all the government workers and all the people of the Bronx, especially in 2020, when a global pandemic (among other things) made it one of the most difficult Census operations in history.

ALL THE VARIOUS SYNAGOGUES IN THIS BOOK ARE FICTIONAL, THOUGH they are all located at addresses that have synagogues at them. However, there is no intended relationship or similarity between the fictional temples in this book and the real ones in the same locations.

In addition, while most of the geography is accurate in this novel, Seward Place is a wholly fictional cul-de-sac.

I SAT AT THE DESK OF MY OFFICE, ACROSS FROM THE LITTLE PISCHER WHO had killed my parents. He wanted to hire me.

The technical term for that is chutzpah.

Okay, strictly speaking, Joshua Roth didn't kill my parents; the golem that he had animated a dozen years ago had done that. Still, he was hardly my favorite person in the world, what with his actions being responsible for making me an orphan at eighteen.

I'd never met Roth before today. My mind had created this image of him in my head: tall, curly haired, big bushy beard, and a permanent sneer on his face, wearing a white shirt and black pants, but not a yarmulke, for some reason.

So I was really surprised to see that it was a short, chubby guy with a receding hairline, and a plaid yarmulke bobby-pinned to his thinning brown hair sitting in my guest chair. He was wearing a T-shirt from a Shakespeare in the Park production from a few years back and jeans with a hole in the left knee.

I hadn't been using this office much lately. Most of my business as a Courser—a supernatural hunter-for-hire—was done via phone and e-mail these days. But I justified to myself the notion of keeping the office as a maildrop, at the very least. The big-ass pile of mail I'd pried out of the overstuffed mailbox by the front door that looked like it was entirely catalogues and political flyers made that idea patently ridiculous.

At least the air conditioner still worked, which was good, as it was pushing ninety outside. Still, for this I didn't need to be paying such exorbitant rent…

Roth finally broke the uncomfortable silence. "Look, Mr. Gold, first of all, I need to say something *really* important."

I held up a hand. "For the love of all that's holy, do *not* apologize."

"But—"

"*Don't.* There is absolutely *nothing* that you could say that would make it right. You said you had a job for me?"

Roth just sat there for a second, his mouth hanging open. "Mr. Gold, I *really* need to—"

"I could give a damn what you think *you* need, Mr. Roth."

He actually smiled timidly. "You can call me Josh. Or Joshua."

"No, honestly, I can't. And I can't hear your apology, either. I don't care if you've been rehearsing it for a dozen years, I can't hear it. I *won't* listen to it. You see, if you apologize, then I have to at least consider the possibility of forgiving you, and I'm nowhere near ready to do that yet."

"Um, okay." Roth swallowed and shifted uncomfortably in his chair. "I guess I should tell you what the job is?"

"Not a bad start." It was certainly a better start than the one he'd been planning. I wanted to know what, exactly, I'd be turning down.

"So first of all, I need to tell you that the spell that Wardein Zerelli ordered to be cast on me *really* works. I have absolutely no idea how to create one of those—those things. I can't even say the word—I can't even *read* about it." He held up both hands before I could interrupt. "Before you ask, I didn't try to read about them on purpose, I was reading a story on the web about Prague. When the story got to talking about the—the thingie that was created in Prague back in the day, the whole article turned to gibberish."

"Good," I said emphatically. Back then, the Wardein of the Bronx had been Mike Zerelli. Roth's punishment when he was found out was having Ampuero cast on him: a spell that can eliminate particular memories, in this case everything he knew about golems.

"Anyhow, the point is, I *really* didn't do this."

"Do what?"

"Animate the thing. But *somebody* did."

My stomach had been doing somersaults since Roth had come in, and it was just starting to calm down when he said that, and then it went crazy again. "Somebody animated a golem?"

Roth nodded. "I caught sight of it lurking outside the synagogue twice, but it ran off before I could get near it both times."

"And you didn't animate it?"

"I told you, I *really* can't!"

I closed my eyes and counted to ten, then blew out a long breath. It almost worked.

"All right, I'm guessing you want to hire me to find out who did animate it?"

"Yeah, because it's *really* not me, and I don't want anyone *thinking* it was me. I need you to find out *who* did it. I mean, I think I know why."

"Oh?"

Again, Roth nodded. "I don't know if you remember, Mr. Gold, but the whole reason why I animated the— Why I did what I did back then was because of some attacks on Jews in the area."

"I remember," I said tightly. "I also remember that you screwed up and sent it after some kids who had nothing to do with it."

"Right." Roth shrunk into his chair. "I was such an idiot. But anyhow, someone else could be doing this for the same reason—to protect us after the thefts at the synagogue. I mean, the whole point of them is to protect us, right?"

I nodded. All the legends of the golem, most notably the Prague-based one about Rabbi Loew creating the golem in that Czech city in the sixteenth century, centered on protecting Jews.

There was something else he had said, though, that was more important. "There've been thefts?"

"Yeah. Isn't the rabbi your aunt? Didn't she tell you?"

"She is, yeah, and no, she didn't." Which wasn't all that surprising. I'd been a mess the last few months, and Rabbi Esther Lieberman, my father's sister, was always the type to help other people with their problems rather than burden people with hers. (Of course, if you *didn't* have any problems, then Esther would burden the hell out of you.)

"So, I guess what I need is to give you money, so you'll hunt it and stop it from doing whatever it's doing? Like that Haitian guy did to me?"

"That would be the process, yeah." After the golem killed my parents, Esther hired a Courser named Hugues Baptiste to find out who animated it—he's the one who tracked Roth down. After I finished medical school, Hugues took me on as an apprentice.

"I gotta ask, Mr. Roth—why me?"

"Excuse me?"

"There's dozens of Coursers in the Bronx, including the guy who found you twelve years ago. So why me?"

"Look, Mr. Gold, I know that what I did back then was inexcusable, unforgivable, awful, horrible—name the crappy adjective. But I *really* have changed since then. And I *really* want to do what I can to make up for it. And I know—" he added quickly "—that I can't *actually* make up for it, but I still have to try. Hiring you is one way to do that. If I have to pay someone to do this, I'd rather it was you I paid than any of those other dozens of Coursers you're talking about. Does that make sense?"

It did, but I couldn't bring myself to say that. Instead, I told him what my fee was and how much I'd need up front. I didn't always charge an up-front fee, but for this schmuck? I wasn't a hundred percent convinced he hadn't found a way to blow past Ampuero and animate the golem himself and this was his way of screwing with me.

He pulled out his phone and sent me the fee electronically, which my phone then told me was in my account. Gotta love modern technology.

"Do you need anything else?" he asked.

"I'm gonna need to go where you saw the thing first. It was at Esther's synagogue?"

"Yeah."

"All right, I'm having dinner with her tonight, as it happens, so I'll talk to her about it and then check out the temple itself tomorrow."

"My email address should be attached to the payment," he said, getting up from the guest chair, "so if you have any questions, that's the best way to get in touch." He went to the door, opened it, then turned back around. "Mr. Gold?"

I just looked at him expectantly.

"I *really* am sorry about your parents. I was trying to help people, but—" He shook his head. "I'm sorry. Really."

With that, he left.

I sat in my office chair for a good long while after that.

Chapter 2

After spending however long it was sitting and staring at the door Roth had walked out of, I finally decided to go through the huge pile of mail that had built up since whenever I'd been here last. Which was probably when I met the Reverend Daley from St. Stephen's Church. He'd hired me to track down a lamprey sucking the energy out of people in Marble Hill.

Most of the mail was what it appeared to be on first glance: junk. It was all ads for things I didn't need, political flyers urging me to vote for candidates who'd already won or lost their elections, and a whole helluva lot of catalogues.

And one hand-written envelope, sent by someone named Bartholomew Jackson, whose return address was on Briggs Avenue here in the Bronx.

It was only postmarked a month ago, so it hadn't been here *that* long, but it hadn't been here that short, either. I wish this Jackson guy had called or e-mailed.

The letter was also handwritten, which was a novelty.

"Dear Mr. Gold:

"My name is Bart Jackson, and I'm hoping you can help me. Every once in a while, I see what looks a lot like a dragon in my back yard. I've called the cops, but they never see it, and I think they think I'm a crazy man. But I know what I saw.

"I heard that you were the type of person who could help a man out who has a dragon in his yard. I didn't know there were such things as people who could do that, but I didn't know there were such things as dragons, either. The Lord truly does work in mysterious ways.

"Please, Mr. Gold, if you could help an old man out, I'd be very grateful to you."

He'd signed it and put his phone number under his signature.

Reaching into my pocket, I pulled out my phone and called the number. It rang four times, and then I got a voicemail message. "This is Bart. Either I can't come to the phone right now or I don't feel like talking on the phone right now. Say your piece after the beep, and I'll ring you back when I feel like it."

I chuckled, and then, after the beep, said, "Mr. Jackson, this is Bram Gold. I just now got your letter — sorry to take so long to get back to you, but I don't use my office much these days. Anyhow, I'll be happy to look into your dragon problem. Please call me back so we can set up a time to meet." I left him my number and then hit END.

I also couldn't remember the last time I'd taken on a new client. What little Courser work I had been doing lately was routine stuff from regular clients — mostly Miriam Zerelli, Mike's daughter, who had taken over as the Wardein of the Bronx after the car accident that had killed her father. That same accident had left her wheelchair-bound. Miriam was also my best friend since childhood, and she was good about throwing work at me: wrangling a sprite here, stopping a dangerous ritual there.

But the cases had been few and far between the last four months.

This was mostly an issue due to a rapidly dwindling bank balance. I had emergency money in savings and had actually had to dip into it a couple of times to pay the bills. The occasional regular client and my medical work was barely covering my day-to-day.

Of course, I was also paying rent on this place that I never used, and on top of that, I had an empty one-bedroom apartment in my house that I could easily make available for rent.

But that required going into the apartment and cleaning it out.

And being reminded of who lived there before.

After my parents died, I sold the apartment they owned in the huge building that overlooked the Henry Hudson Parkway. Once I got my MD, I bought a three-story house on Johnson Avenue that was split into three units. I lived in the three-bedroom apartment on the second floor and converted the matching third-floor apartment into a combination doctor's office and Courser workout space. Mind you, the only patients I saw in the former were fellow Coursers and spellcasters and various non-human creatures and the like.

And then there was the ground floor, which had a garage and a one-bedroom apartment. For the first year, I'd rented that apartment to a fellow doctor who needed a place, but then she'd seen me bring home an injured duende I'd captured, and she moved out within four weeks.

After a couple of years of the place being empty, I finally gave it to my cousin Rebekah—Isaac and Judy's kid. A student at Manhattan College, she'd needed to get out of the house before she and Uncle Isaac killed each other. I got free apartment cleaning out of it, since she would play housemaid for me in exchange for no rent.

Oh, and she borrowed a bunch of my books. And taught herself magick. And tried to free an old Wappinger god named Malsum, attempts that resulted in several maimings (including someone I care a great deal about) and about a dozen deaths, including all four of the immortals that were then living in the Bronx.

Yes, my cousin killed immortals. Talented young woman she turned out to be.

Unlike Joshua Roth, though, she wasn't exactly repentant, and so she got herself banished to the Nagashima Dimension.

And I hadn't looked in her apartment since.

Aside from me as a Courser, my family didn't really deal in the realm of the magickal, the mystical, and the things that go booga-booga in the night. Some knew about it, like my parents and Aunt Esther. Others, though, refused to acknowledge it. Among those who had taken up residence in the state of denial were Uncle Isaac and Aunt Judy.

Which, unfortunately, meant we had to lie to them and say Rebekah was missing.

Still, I needed to go through her place and find all the stuff she'd used in her little murder campaign and give it to Miriam to take care of. Plus, I had to put the rest of her stuff in storage. Isaac and Judy had absolutely refused to do any of that, as they thought it was admitting that their daughter was dead, and Uncle Isaac in particular couldn't bring himself to do that. So it was all on me.

Once I finally cleared the place out, I could rent it, preferably to someone in the game, so I wouldn't have a repeat of my fellow physician freaking out over a duende.

But that required entering it.

I was startled out of my reverie by the buzzing of my phone.

Looking at the display, I recognized the number that was calling me as the same one that was written at the bottom of Bartholomew Jackson's letter.

Accepting the call, I put the phone to my ear. "Hello."

"Mr. Bram Gold? This here's Bart Jackson."

"Thanks for calling me back, Mr. Jackson."

"Thank you for callin' me at all. I gotta admit, the letter I wrote was a long shot and I figured I came up craps. So it kinda blew my mind when I got back from PT and heard your voicemail."

"Well, I usually respond faster to calls or emails — like I said in my voicemail, I don't use my office much these days."

Jackson chuckled. "I'm just old-fashioned, Mr. Gold. Letter in the mail strikes me as more official, I suppose. Besides, most folks these days don't answer phone calls from people they don't know."

"I'd never get any new clients if I did that, Mr. Jackson."

"Good point."

Doctor instincts kicked in, then. "If you don't mind my asking, Mr. Jackson, what're you in physical therapy for?"

"Had my hip replaced a couple months ago. My own damn fault — eighty-year-old men shouldn't be goin' for a walk in the park in the rain, and that's a fact."

"Yeah, but you should be done with PT pretty soon, then, right?"

"Just another week, or so they tell me."

I leaned back in the chair and smiled. Don't know what it was, but something about just shooting the breeze with this codger was relaxing. Which was a nice palliative after wanting to jump out of my own skin the entire time I was with Roth.

But I needed to get down to business. "So tell me about this dragon, Mr. Jackson."

"I'll tell you, Mr. Gold, I thought it was a snake at first, but as the Lord God is my witness, they do *not* make snakes this big. I've seen plenty in my years, but never a snake that was this huge — or this *red*."

"When did you last see it?"

"Remember when it rained last week? It was in my yard then. That's when I usually see the thing, when it's raining."

Big red snake sure sounded like a dragon. Or maybe some other kind of supernatural creature. Either way, it was definitely Courser business.

Look at me, two new clients in one day!

"Tell you what, Mr. Jackson, why don't I come by your house tomorrow morning? I can check out your yard and see if there's any evidence of a dragon beyond what you've seen, and if there is, we can talk about my fee."

"I would surely appreciate that, Mr. Gold. You can come by today if you'd like. After PT, I'm all done for the day."

Shaking my head, even though he couldn't see that over the phone, I said, "Can't do today, I've got a full plate, but I'm good for any time tomorrow."

"I ain't goin' nowhere tomorrow, neither, so come by whenever's good for you. I'm always awake at sun-up, so if it's daylight, I'll be around. I'll have my checkbook ready."

I chuckled. I had one client who always paid me by check, and she was about the same age as Jackson. Everyone else paid me electronically—or sometimes in cash, though that had only happened a couple of times.

After ending the call, I checked the phone to see that it was one-thirty. I had somewhere to be at two. I went to the bathroom to wash up, then shut down and locked up the office.

I headed out into the sweltering heat and humidity. First, I stopped at a bodega on Broadway to grab a quick sandwich, before catching the bus for a run up the hill to Katie Gonzalez's house.

I'd mentioned before that Rebekah's attempts to free Malsum from his prison resulted in several maimings and deaths. Katie was one of the former.

Four people had sacrificed their mortality to maintain the spell that imprisoned Malsum, but after Rebekah'd killed three of them, the spell was weakened enough that Malsum started to be able to influence this world. Since Malsum was a wolf-god, that meant he could control wolves, dogs—and werewolves.

Katie was one of four werewolves who lived in the Bronx. We'd managed to corral the other three and pen them up in Miriam's basement. By the time we'd been able to get in touch with Katie, she'd already been possessed by Malsum, whereupon she'd ripped out the throat of one Courser and got herself shot by another.

She'd been in a coma for about three weeks, and when she'd awakened, she'd been catatonic. While technically conscious, she barely responded to any stimulus, wouldn't talk, wouldn't engage.

What had worried me while she was in the hospital was that Katie didn't have any family left alive. Her parents had also been werewolves, and they'd been killed a while back on the night of the full moon.

But, as it turned out, she'd made Miriam her medical proxy. Which meant that the wardein was empowered to check her out of the hospital and hire a full-time at-home nurse.

Me, I was just glad that she'd woken up and gotten herself checked out before the next full moon. Explaining a patient turning into a hairy mutt would've been fun.

Miriam had hired a woman named Candi O'Rourke to be Katie's nurse. Candi fed her, bathed her, gave her the meds she needed (she was still recovering from a major gunshot wound and subsequent surgery), and did as much physical therapy as you could do with someone who wouldn't move much on her own.

And once a month, Candi brought her to Miriam's and put her in one of the dungeons in the basement of her house on Seward Place. But when it came time to transform, she just went from being a human being who stared into space all day and didn't say anything and didn't move to a wolf who stared into space all night and didn't make any noise and didn't move.

The reason why I was visiting her? Well, we'd sort of been dating. And by "sort of," I meant that she'd asked me out after I'd spent the better part of two years not realizing that she was flirting with me. Miriam often hired me to keep an eye on the local werewolves each full moon, letting them run loose in an isolated dog run overnight and keeping them safe. The Bronx had a number of such runs in parks, sufficiently off the beaten path, especially late at night.

Katie and I had had a single coffee date, and we were going to do more, but then Rebekah and Malsum happened.

The blessedly air-conditioned bus took me up Riverdale Avenue. By the time we got to my stop, I'd inhaled my sandwich. I hopped off the bus and walked the two blocks to Katie's small house, tossing the paper the sandwich had been wrapped in into a wireframe garbage can along the way. I went through the small gate in the middle of the white fence that surrounded the house and rang the bell.

After a minute, Candi unlocked and opened the inner door and stared at me through the screen door. She was short, dark-haired, with a permanent scowl on her face. "You know, Bram, it would be easier if I just gave you a key."

We had this argument every time I visited. "I don't feel right having a key without Katie's permission."

She rolled her eyes. "I live here too, now. And you have my permission to not make me have to get up and walk over to let you in every damn time you show up."

"I'll think about it." I walked past her into the large living room, enjoying the cooler air that filled the house and evaporated the sweat that had been pooling on my flesh just from the two-block walk from the bus. I remembered Katie mentioning once last summer that she was grateful that she had spent the money to put central air conditioning into her hundred-year-old house.

I glanced at the staircase that led to the second floor and Katie's bedroom. "How is she?"

Closing the door behind her and locking it, Candi said, "She seems to like cooking shows."

I turned to look at her. "Does she even cook?"

"How the hell should I know? I've only known her since she's been catatonic."

"Well, what does she have in her kitchen? Pots and pans? Food?"

Candi snorted. "Please, I tossed everything in the fridge and nuked it with bleach when we first brought her home. I didn't look all that closely at it. Matter of fact, I wish I'd worn a hazmat suit. But that's not the point. The point is, she *likes* watching the cooking shows. Sometimes she almost comes close to smiling."

"Wow." That actually warmed my heart some.

"She's having her post-lunch nap right now, but you can go sit with her."

I nodded. "Thanks, Candi."

"I gotta go do some shopping, so can you stay for an hour or so?"

"Absolutely."

Candi nodded, grabbed a purse off the sofa, and went out through the door.

First, I went into the kitchen, as I found my mouth was incredibly dry. Candi always kept a filtered pitcher of water in the fridge, so I poured myself a glass. The ground floor of Katie's small house just had a big living room and an equally big kitchen that also had a small dining-room-type area to one side, plus the staircase, with a small half-bath wedged in under it.

After I finished the water, I climbed up the stairs.

The house had two bedrooms and a full bathroom up there. Katie had converted one bedroom into an office, since she worked from home. She had rather crippling social anxiety, so she hardly ever left the house even before this whole mishegoss. She'd been working to overcome it slowly, though. In fact, she'd told me that asking me out was one such step on that road.

Now that home office was Candi's bedroom.

Katie was asleep on the queen-sized bed in the master bedroom. The blazing sun was streaming in, providing tons of light through the white lace curtains. Since that window's view was of the second floor of the big apartment building next door, the privacy of those curtains was kinda necessary. Facing the bed was a fifty-two-inch flatscreen TV mounted to the wall.

A big, well-used easy chair was next to the bed, and after four months, it pretty much conformed to my butt, I'd sat in it so much. Before I plunked myself down, I grabbed the book I'd left behind when I was here last.

"Hey, Katie," I whispered to her sleeping form. "It's Bram."

She kept sleeping. I opened the book, which was a copy of *Franken-stein, or the Modern Prometheus* by Mary Shelley that Miriam had given me. Prior to Rebekah and Malsum, Katie had been posting on social media about how there were certain books she wanted to read, and *Frankenstein* had been one of them.

So I'd been reading it aloud to her when I visited.

But she was asleep now, so instead I fondled my phone for a bit.

After a while, I heard a small moan from the bed, and I put the phone down to see her head moving back and forth.

"It's okay, Katie," I said.

She started thrashing around on the bed.

"It's just a bad dream. You're all right. I'm here to protect you."

I stayed seated in the chair, keeping my tone calm. She'd had nightmares before, and this was the only method that seemed to work. I'd learned the hard way not to try touching her. I'd spent more than a week having to explain the shiner she'd given me.

"Everything's okay, Katie. You're fine. Just a dream."

Sure enough, she stopped thrashing, started breathing normally, and eventually just lay there, staring at the ceiling.

"Sorry that's what woke you up," I said.

As usual, she didn't acknowledge me, just lay there, blinking occasionally.

"I took on a couple new clients today. One was a guy who wrote me a letter, believe it or not." I proceeded to tell her Jackson's story, ending with, "And I only saw the letter because I had to meet the other new client at the office."

And that was when I realized that I had never actually told Katie the full story of how and why I had become a Courser…

Chapter 3

So I decided to tell Katie about the absolute worst week of my life.

It was the end of the second semester of my first year at Harvard. I'd just finished my Inorganic Chemistry final. After collecting my phone from the basket that Doctor Chadwal made us put all our electronic devices in before tests, I went out into a beautiful spring day in Cambridge, Massachusetts, heading back to my dorm.

Hilariously, that had up to that point been a particularly happy day. Inorganic Chem had been my last in-class final for the semester. I just had to write a six-page paper for my Shakespeare class about the character significance of the duel scene in *Hamlet*. I'd already come up with the title of the essay — "Duel Personalities" — and while I hadn't actually written any of the essay itself yet, I still had two days to email it to Professor Robare, and then my English lit requirement would be taken care of, and my first year of undergraduate work would be completed.

I'd made it through two semesters of pre-med without burning out, flunking out, or running screaming to communications, English, underwater basket-weaving, or philosophy, like roughly fifty percent of the people who were pre-med the previous September. I was ready to hit my sophomore year running, well on my way to becoming Abraham Goldblume, MD, as my parents had intended.

But I was also ready to go home to New York for the summer. Cambridge was nice, but the bagels up there sucked, as they did everywhere outside the Big Apple.

As I walked down Oxford Street toward Harvard Yard and my dorm at Thayer Hall, I turned my phone on to find three voicemail messages and a text from Aunt Esther, which just said "CALL ME."

First, I played the voicemails.

"This is a message for Abraham Goldblume. This is Detective Lyd Toscano from the 50th Precinct in the Bronx. I don't know if you remember me, but we met at Mike Zerelli's place a few times. Look, I'm sorry to have to be the one to tell you this, but I'm afraid that there's been a terrible accident. Your parents are both dead. It looks like the ceiling fell in from the apartment on top of their office and — well, it's not pretty. We're still trying to figure things out, but you need to call me back ASAP."

"Abraham, it's Aunt Esther, call me back *now*."

"Hey, Bram, it's Mike Zerelli. I, ah — I have some really awful news. Both your parents were killed, and it looks like it wasn't an accident. Somebody set something loose that they shouldn't have."

And all of a sudden I wasn't so happy anymore.

I just stood in the middle of Oxford Street, unable to move, unable to speak, barely able to breathe.

My parents couldn't be dead.

But they were.

Somehow, I convinced my feet to start moving, and I went back to my dorm. My roommate had already gone home for the summer, so I could call Aunt Esther in peace.

I honestly don't remember any of that phone conversation. Or much of anything immediately after that. I mean, intellectually I know I emailed Professor Robare to tell her I might have trouble getting my final paper done, and why. I also know that I must have packed a bag, and then got my Maxima out of the parking lot and drove across Massachusetts, through Connecticut and Westchester County into the Bronx and home.

Except it wasn't home anymore. Not in the same way.

Home was Mom and Dad.

I hadn't known what to expect, but at least the apartment was okay. Doctors Mordechai and Rachel Goldblume practiced medicine in an office on the ground floor of a huge apartment building in the Riverdale section of the Bronx. We also lived in a three-bedroom apartment on the nineteenth floor of the same building.

They wouldn't let me into the office — it was a crime scene, still — but Aunt Esther *and* Mike and Miriam Zerelli were all waiting for me in the apartment.

As wardein, Mike was in charge of all magickal activity on the peninsula that was also the northernmost borough of New York City. Miriam—his daughter and my best friend—was also in her first year of college, but she'd stayed local at Fordham University.

As soon as I walked in the door, Miriam stood up and hugged me hard. "I'm so sorry, Bram."

I didn't say anything, I just held her.

When we finally stopped hugging, I asked, "What the hell happened, Mr. Zerelli?"

Mike ran a hand through his thick, dark hair. He was tall, skinny, and had an air of authority that I usually only saw in my professors at Harvard. "I'm honestly not sure, but *something* odd happened here. We're going to be hiring a Courser to investigate this. Right now, the cops are ruling this as an accident, but no way their ceiling collapsed on its own."

I nodded. I'd known about the supernatural since I was a little kid, and I'd even sat in on some of Miriam's training, since she was in line to eventually take over as wardein from Mike. So I knew that some kind of creature could've crashed through the ceiling.

Which led me to another question. "Did they— I mean, were they—" I shook my head. "How'd it happen? Did they go to the hospital, did they die right away, what?"

Aunt Esther finally spoke up. "We don't know for sure. All we know is that their nurse heard a noise, went into your father's office, and found a big hole in the ceiling, and the bits that used to be the ceiling were either on the floor or in the window. Your parents were under one of the parts on the floor, unfortunately."

"And that's the weird part," Mike said. "All the windows had bars on them, and I can't imagine a collapsed ceiling would break through the window *and* the bars like that."

"O-okay." That didn't really help as much as I was hoping it would.

Mike's phone rang—it was Detective Toscano, asking if I was there yet. I nodded, and said I was okay with talking to her.

The next few days after that were a whirlwind. I was an only child, and now I had to deal with the arrangements for the funeral and every other damn thing. Thank G-d that Jewish custom is for a closed-casket funeral, because their bodies were, um, not in the best shape after being crushed, and nobody should have to see that. I did have to see it—well, okay, I didn't *have* to, but I *wanted* to. Esther told me not to, Toscano told me not to, Mike told me not to, but I had insisted on seeing the bodies in the morgue.

Aunt Esther hired a Courser named Hugues Baptiste, and he talked to me at one point about my parents. His questions were pretty basic—a lot of them were the same ones Toscano asked me, honestly—and then he made the tactical error of giving me his phone number to call if I remembered anything useful.

Thing was, I didn't expect to remember anything useful. But I did now have the phone number of the guy responsible for hunting down what killed my parents.

And I used it.

A lot.

By the third day, Hugues had stopped answering my calls, and I was pretty sure he was erasing the (very lengthy) voicemails I'd been leaving him asking him for updates.

On the second day that we sat shiva, four days after Hugues was hired, he came by the apartment. I thought it was nice of him to pay his respects, but he asked to talk to me and Esther alone.

We went into my bedroom, and I sat on my unmade bed, while Esther sat at my desk, which was currently mostly empty, since most of the stuff I usually kept on it was in my dorm in Cambridge. For that matter, the walls were mostly bare, too, for the same reason, as I'd brought most of my posters with me to Harvard, and the bookshelves were half-empty.

The thing I remembered most was Hugues standing near the doorway, like he wanted to be ready to bolt from my presence as easily and quickly as possible. He was wearing a brown button-down shirt that was a slightly different shade than the brown button-down shirt he wore the last time I saw him, and it had stains in different places. The black slacks had the same stains, so it was probably the same pair.

"I got me some good news and I got me some bad news, okay?" Hugues said. "The bad news is, it was definitely something that killed your maman and your papa, because it also went and killed someone else—also an accident, like what happened here, but still."

"You said 'it'?" I asked.

Hugues nodded. "I did, yes, child. It was a golem, okay?"

"Excuse me?" Esther got up from my desk chair and stared wide-eyed at Hugues. "Somebody animated a *golem*?"

"Not somebody. Boy named Joshua Roth—he lives in the apartment on top of the Goldblumes' office."

Esther shook her head. "I know Josh, he's a good kid—and a member of our temple, for crying out loud. He's there every Friday. Why the hell did he—?"

"Some folks was vandalizing synagogues. Josh didn't think the cops were takin' it serious, so he got together some unused soil and some orange clay and some pure spring water and spoke himself the right incantations and, poof! There's his golem. He wanted to send him after the kids he thought were goin' after the synagogues."

"Wait, it wasn't kids," Esther said. "Lyd told me yesterday that they arrested a couple of old men—neo-Nazi alte kakers."

"Yeah, well, Josh ain't exactly overburdened with common sense, okay? He's a bright boy—the ritual to make a golem, that's some serious shit, real complicated—but it wasn't the kids he thought it was. Me, I figured the golem'd go after the kids anyhow, so I staked them out, and the monster showed up, and I took care of it."

"Thank you, Hugues." Esther walked over to him and shook his hand.

"Of course, Rabbi. I'll be sending you a bill for—"

"Who else died?" I asked.

That question seemed to catch Hugues off-guard. "What's that, child?"

"You said the golem killed someone else."

Hugues nodded. "Woman who was joggin' over on Palisade Avenue. Golem knocked a tree down that was in its way and it crushed the poor woman."

"Okay." I stood up from the bed. "Now what?"

"Now what what?"

"What happens to this Josh schmuck?"

"That be the wardein's problem, child."

"No, it's *my* problem, I wanna know what happens to this guy!"

"Abraham, calm down." Esther put a hand on my shoulder.

I shrugged it off. "What's Mr. Zerelli likely to do?"

Hugues shrugged. "I don't know, child. What's it matter? The wardein will dispense justice, that is the important part, okay?"

After that, Hugues left, and Esther and I went back out into the living room where there was an even bigger crowd than when Hugues had arrived: family, friends, patients. I barely acknowledged any of them.

I just sat on my stool and grunted and said bland "thank yous" to people offering condolences. Luckily, as both family and rabbi, Esther was there to pick up the slack, as she made sure all the food got put out on the dining room table, that people actually ate some of the food, and that nobody left without a Tupperware full of whatever food didn't get eaten to bring home, since there was no way I could eat all that stuff myself.

I just sat there on the stool.

I should've been thinking about a lot of things, like what to do with the apartment, like what to do about the office and the people who worked there, who were now suddenly unemployed, and so on.

Instead, I was only thinking about two things.

I had five more days of shiva to sit. After everyone left that second day, I went to see the Zerellis. As the chief mourner, I wasn't supposed to leave the apartment until shiva was done five days hence, but I needed to see Mike. Angry eighteen-year-olds suck at following tradition…

It was about a five-minute walk from the loud thoroughfare of the Henry Hudson Parkway service road to the quiet little cul-de-sac of Seward Place. Typical New York: you walk a couple blocks, and it's like you were transported to a different space-time continuum. My parents' place was in a huge apartment building near a bunch of other huge apartment buildings built in the 1970s alongside a busy highway. The wardein's late-nineteenth-century house was a giant manse at the end of a tiny dead-end street surrounded by trees and other big houses on the adjacent street. The old house dated back to when this peninsula was primarily farmland, a lot of it owned by Jonas Bronck.

The quiet was ruined by the sound of a Volkswagen Jetta pulling into the driveway next to the Escalade that was already parked. It was Miriam, probably coming back from Fordham.

"Hey, Bram," she said after shutting the car off and climbing out of it. Her long, dark hair was tied back into a long ponytail that went down to her butt.

"Hey, Miriam."

"What're you doing here?" The implied, *when you should be mourning your parents* was oozing out her pores, but she wasn't quite so rude as to say it out loud.

"I need to talk to your dad about the kid who animated the golem."

"No, you don't," Miriam said firmly. "Because you know he's going to tell you that it's not your concern. You're just a civilian, Bram, and he can't go telling you about how he punishes people who transgress."

"That little shit killed my parents!" I realized I was shouting even as the words exploded from my mouth, and I took a breath and looked down at the gravel driveway. "And some poor innocent lady."

"And Dad took care of it. That's all that matters." Miriam sighed. "Look, I can tell you this much, but you gotta promise never to let Dad know I told you."

"Of course," I said, grateful to Miriam for putting our friendship above common sense.

"Dad had someone cast the Ampuero spell on Josh Roth so he can't remember how to animate a golem ever again. He can't even really entirely remember what a golem *is*."

"That's *it*?"

"Bram, he—" She shook her head. "Roth felt *awful* about it. I only saw him when he first came to the house, but he was *miserable*. Trust me, you won't have to worry about him again."

"Uh huh." I didn't buy it, but I knew arguing wasn't gonna do me any good. "Well, I'm just glad Mr. Baptiste was able to catch him. I wish I could've done it myself."

That was when I decided I was gonna be a Courser.

◄—THE BRONX—►

At this point, I noticed Candi standing in the doorway. I guess she'd returned from shopping.

"Oh, hey, Candi."

"Whatever happened to that Roth guy? You ever see him again?"

I snorted. She'd obviously missed the beginning of the story when I mentioned that he was one of my new clients. So I filled her in on that bit.

Candi replied to this information with her mouth in an oval shape, squinted eyes, and her hands on her hips. "He hired *you*? What the hell for?"

"He says he's trying to make it up to me."

"Right, because your fee for being a Courser is *absolutely* enough to make up for getting your parents killed."

"Hey, look, I'll take his money. Besides, it's my aunt's synagogue. I'd take the case for that reason alone, never mind who's paying me."

"All right. Well, it's time for her meds and her bath, so I'm gonna have to kick you out, now."

I nodded. "Okay." I got up, moved the copy of *Frankenstein* from the foot of the bed back to the chair, and passed Candi as she entered the bedroom and I left.

She asked as I walked through the doorway, "How far did you get in the book?"

"I didn't."

Scowling, she asked, "How long were you babbling about that nonsense before I came up here?"

"A while, I guess."

I looked at Katie, who was still staring at the ceiling, showing absolutely no evidence that she'd heard a word I'd said.

Some days I wondered why I bothered.

Then I remembered how I'd been able to calm her from her nightmare. If I hadn't been here, and if Candi had been downstairs or out shopping, she wouldn't have had anybody, and might have hurt herself.

It was a nice way to talk myself into believing that she needed me.

Chapter 4

Since I had an infusion of cash from Roth, I decided to do some desperately needed shopping, which meant trips to both the supermarket for food and to Ahondjon's for various magickal supplies.

I went to Ahondjon's first, hopping in my battered old 2003 Toyota Corolla—which, thankfully, still had working air conditioning. The bad news was that it took me ten minutes to find somewhere to park. The good news was that it was a free parking spot, rather than a metered one, a block away from the shop.

I walked down alongside St. James Park. A mess of African-American and Latinx guys in tank tops and shorts were playing basketball games in two separate courts, while two middle-aged fellas were playing against each other in the handball court. I could see the sweat pouring off all of them even from the sidewalk, and I wondered what the hell they were thinking playing outside in this sweltering craziness.

The two hoops games had a bunch of spectators, most of whom huddled under the trees that bordered the courts, desperately seeking shade.

As I continued down the street, I saw lots of people sitting on the shaded benches chatting or fondling their phones. (The benches in direct sunlight were unoccupied, big surprise.) I continued to be amazed that anyone was outside today on purpose. My only plan was to get from one air-conditioned place to the next. I couldn't imagine why anyone would willingly be out in this for more than five minutes.

Dashing under the elevated 4 train that clattered overhead, I went into a newsstand-style store that sold papers, magazines, candy, lottery tickets, cigarettes, cigars, greeting cards, and the like. Nodding to the

Pakistani guy who sat behind the bullet proof glass at the register (one of these days, I really needed to learn the guy's name), I carefully moved past the tight shelves all the way back. Opening the door behind the greeting card racks, I went down the narrow, steep metal staircase to Ahondjohn's magick shop.

The man himself was hanging up the phone and cursing in his native Hausa as I walked in.

"Another satisfied customer?" I asked with a cheeky grin.

"Very funny, Mr. Gold. No, simply more nonsense from 'Madam Vérité'."

I winced. "Madam Vérité" and I had a past. She was really Bonita Soriano, a Dominican woman pretending to be Haitian who tried to bind the loa to her will a few months back. She'd only failed because it coincided with my cousin Rebekah's first attempt to free Malsum, which effectively torpedoed any attempt at a binding spell in the entire New York metropolitan area—an effect that hadn't worn off for another week after Malsum had been re-imprisoned. Miriam sanctioned Mrs. Truth after that—trying to bind gods was frowned upon by Miriam's superiors in the Curia, the international group that supervised all magickal activity around the world.

"She keeps calling me asking if I will sell her another Obsidian candle."

"Oy. She doesn't get what being sanctioned means, does she?"

"Apparently, she does not."

I shook my head. "Yeah, I've just been just letting her calls go to voicemail and then deleting the voicemails without listening to them."

"How do you know it is her calling?"

I rolled my eyes so hard I thought I could see my brain. "Ahondjon, you *do* get that there's this invention called caller ID, right?"

"For my cell phone, yes. You can do that with a landline as well?"

"Yeah, it's technology they invented in the 1990s."

"If you say so."

Sighing, I said, "Anyhow, I need some stuff. I've got a golem problem and a dragon problem, so I'm gonna need a Gans charm and some dragonsbane."

Ahondjon nodded. "Okay. You know for sure it's a European dragon?"

"I don't, no, but if it is, I wanna be ready."

"Fair enough, but dragonsbane is not inexpensive."

As he went to the shelves behind the counter to find what I needed, I sighed. Dragonsbane was hugely effective, but only against dragons from Europe. In fact, I used up the last of my supply of the stuff about six months back on a dragon that was hiding out in a school. The little pischer ate my watch, too, but the dragonsbane took care of it.

If Jackson's dragon was from Asia, though, the dragonsbane would be of absolutely no help. But Asian dragons were also generally *nicer* than European ones, so if that were the case, the big guns shouldn't be necessary.

I hoped.

Ahondjon came back to the counter and put a ziplock bag filled with herbs down in front of me. "Here's your dragonsbane. I am afraid that I sold my last Gans charm yesterday, and the new ones will not come in until next week some time."

"Dammit." I needed the Gans charm to track the golem. "Any idea where else I can go?"

Ahondjon gave me a sidelong glance. "You want me to help the competition?"

"Yeah, 'cause you got yourself a very unsatisfied customer. I need the Gans charm and I can't wait a week. You want me to stay an un-satisfied customer instead of, y'know, an ex-customer, then tell me where—"

"Fine, fine, Mr. Gold, this once, I will do you this favor." He picked up his phone and dialed a number. "Hello, Ms. Patel? It's Ahondjon. … Yes, I am well. What? … Yes, I know the woman, she has been harassing me, also. I am sorry she is bothering you. … Yes, Mr. Bram Gold stopped her from binding the loa."

Geez, was Madame Vérité annoying *every* magick shop in the city?

"Speaking of Mr. Gold, he is in need of a Gans charm, and I am sold out. Might you have one in stock? … I am simply functioning in the spirit of free enterprise, Ms. Patel and I am offended that you would think otherwise." Then he smiled, showing bright shiny dentures. "Very well, indeed. Thank you, Ms. Patel, I will pass that on to Mr. Gold. Be well. … Goodbye." He hung up and continued to smile at me. "If you go to Patel's on Vermilyea and 207th Street in Inwood, the proprietor says she has several in stock."

"Okay." That wasn't so bad, just a fifteen-minute drive from my house. Better still, I could take a bus, so I wouldn't have to deal with the nightmare of trying to park in Inwood. Parking there was even worse than it was around Ahondjon's place.

I paid for the dragonsbane, which Ahondjon put in a nice little paper bag, and I headed back upstairs.

The next stop was the supermarket, where I spent the better part of an hour, buying way too much snack food and not enough quality stuff that I could actually prepare and eat as a meal.

Luckily for me, most nights my main meal was covered. By the time I got back home, put all the groceries away, scritched Mittens, my Maine Coon, and also provided fresh food and water for said cat, it was time for me to head right back out again for dinner with my aunt and uncle.

Esther and Eli Lieberman had a nice apartment on Independence Avenue, a few blocks down from Esther's synagogue, and only a short walk from my place. They'd started inviting me over for dinner twice a week once Esther realized that I hadn't been eating healthy since Rebekah. Generally, I either cooked for myself—nothing crazy or complicated, just simple stuff that any idiot could cook, which was good, because I'm not just any idiot—or got takeout from one of the many restaurants near my house. I just hadn't been able to summon the wherewithal to cook, and my bank account had balked at too much restaurant takeout, so I'd been either snacking on junk food here and there or patronizing the local fast-food joints.

Of course, Esther found out. After a half-hour lecture on how, as a doctor, I should know better than to try to subsist on a diet of fast food, Twinkies, chocolate chip cookies, and coffee, she informed me that every Monday and Wednesday, I was having dinner with her and Eli. This was two hours after the lengthy text-message exchange with Miriam on a similar subject, which ended with Miriam insisting that she cook me dinner on Tuesdays and Sundays, and that we revive our old tradition of going to the burger place down the hill on Friday nights.

That they each picked different days of the week led me to believe that there was some collusion between my rabbi and the wardein—or between my aunt and my best friend, whatever—but I got good meals out of it five nights a week, so I couldn't complain, especially since I usually wound up with leftovers that covered Thursday and Saturday. Uncle Eli had been a gourmet chef, working at embassies and hotels and fancy restaurants over a several-decade-long career before retiring. Now he just cooked for family and friends. And while Miriam wasn't in

Eli's class—nobody was—she was pretty dang good at the fine art of yummy food preparation. And both had years of practice knowing what I liked to eat.

I yanked open the glass door of the big red brick apartment building where the Liebermans lived and stood in the vestibule for a few seconds, letting the central air conditioning wash over me.

When I finally opened my eyes, and wiped the evaporating sweat from my forehead, I saw the weekday-evening-shift doorman, Jamal, sitting behind the big fake-wood desk. You couldn't get to either of the two elevators, any of the staircases, or the first-floor hallways without getting past that desk.

Not that that was usually an issue for me, what with being a regular visitor and all, so I just nodded to Jamal, and started to walk past him—

—and then stopped when he said, "Can I help you, sir?"

Jamal had been working as a doorman in this building for about seven years. This was only the fourth time he called me sir, and the first three times were right after he started, and he couldn't remember my name. He also hadn't spoken that formally with me since those first few weeks.

"I'm fine, Jamal, I'm just going to have dinner with Esther and Eli, I—"

"That would be Rabbi and Mr. Lieberman in 5E?"

I looked around to see if there was a camera crew—or, y'know, anybody else, which there wasn't. "Jamal what the hell's—"

But Jamal was staring at the monitor on his desk. "I'm sorry, but there's nobody in the computer listed as visiting 5E this evening."

"I didn't even know you were supposed to do that."

Finally, Jamal's real personality peeked through as he smiled. "What did you think this computer was for?"

I shrugged. "I figured you just used it to play solitaire during slow shifts."

The serious face came back. "I'm sorry, sir, but I'm going to have to call the Liebermans. Can I have your name, please?"

This was really starting to freak me out. First, I'm reunited with the schmuck who got my parents killed, now this. "Abe Goldblume. I'm their *nephew*, in case, y'know, you forgot since I was here last two days ago."

More weirdness: Jamal didn't pick up the phone but put it on speaker. He *never* did that before when he called upstairs that I'd ever seen.

He entered a sequence of numbers that I recognized as belonging to Esther and Eli. Two rings, and then I heard Esther's voice over the tinny speaker. "Jamal? What's going on?"

"Rabbi Lieberman, I have an Abe Goldblume who says he's here to see you."

A pause, then: "Any particular reason why on his way up here he isn't?"

"I'm sorry, Rabbi, but building policy is that all guests must be in the computer, and I don't see anyone listed there. You're supposed to—"

"Are you kidding me with this?"

"I'm sorry, ma'am, but—"

"Since when does my own nephew have to be vetted? He's here twice a week *at least*."

"Ma'am, the policy of this building, as outlined to me *by my supervisors* is that *all* guests must be—"

"I'm coming down there." A click, and then a dial tone. Jamal hit the speaker button, which ended the call.

The other shoe had dropped in my head, as it probably did in Esther's, which was why she was coming down.

To prove the point, a door in the back corner of the lobby opened. I was fairly certain I'd never seen anyone actually use that door before. A short bald guy in a wrinkled button-down shirt and slacks came stomping out. "What the hell was that?"

"I did what you said, Mr. Horvat."

"I beg your pardon? When did I tell you—"

"You said that if someone wasn't in the computer to call the apartment. I did that."

Horvat waved his arms back and forth. "And now she's coming downstairs! You're supposed to get confirmation that the guest is supposed to be here, that's all!"

Jamal shrugged. "I can't help what she did, sir. I was just trying to get her permission, but she hung up on me and said she was coming down."

"I know. I heard." Horvat threw up his hands and started pacing behind the desk. "This is ridiculous. Things down here are worse than I thought."

I didn't like the sound of that.

The elevator dinged and the door slid open to reveal the stout form of my aunt. Five foot five with a short, sharp shock of semi-curly steel-gray hair, and wearing a white blouse and black jeans, Rabbi Esther Lieberman strode out of the elevator, pushing her black plastic-frame glasses up her prodigious nose. (She and I both shared the family hooter. Our noses tended to enter the room ten minutes before we did.)

As soon as she caught sight of the bald guy, she stopped short, stared at him, pushed her glasses back up her nose (they tended to start slipping back down her schnozz within nanoseconds of her pushing them up), and said, "Tommy? Are you the putz who's keeping my nephew from dinner?"

Horvat pointed at me. "This is your nephew?"

I decided to join this conversation that was more or less about me anyhow, though I was starting to realize that it was far more about the building. Putting out my hand, I said, "Hi, Abe Goldblume."

After a second, he returned the handshake. "Tomislav Horvat. I'm the new president of the co-op board, and I've been hearing complaints about how lax things are at the front desk."

Esther threw up her hands. "Lax? What, Tommy, you're worried people are gonna get nuclear launch codes if Jamal doesn't do a background check?"

"Please, Esther, you know it's not like that, but we have to have a record—"

"No, Tommy, we don't." Esther shoved her glasses up her nose, then put her hands on her hips, at which point I knew that Horvat was toast. "For starters, unlike you, my husband and I have been part of this co-op since before computers were even really a thing."

Horvat folded his arms over his chest. "Computers were invented before World War II."

"You know what I mean. The point is—"

"Oh, there is a point?"

Esther's glasses had fallen halfway down her nose, and she peered at him over the frames. "Yes, Tommy, there's a point. The point is, it's nobody's business who comes up to see me and Eli except for me and Eli."

"There are security concerns—"

"Yeah, there are." Esther shoved her glasses back up her nose. "You might recall that I'm a rabbi. People come to see me for reasons that are not only none of your business, but which are completely confidential, and should absolutely *not* be recorded on someone's cloud storage. What's more, Dr. Goldblume here is my nephew. He comes by us for dinner twice a week, and more besides. He's *family*. Family doesn't get to be screened by the apartment-dwelling equivalent of the TSA."

During this harangue, Horvat had slowly backed away from Esther, but she just kept moving closer to him. Jamal was also trying very hard not to giggle, and at one point developed a coughing fit.

"Furthermore, we're in Riverdale, which is one of the safest neighborhoods in the city. We haven't had any kind of break-ins or anything like that in ages."

"Says the woman whose own synagogue has been vandalized!" Horvat pointed an accusatory finger at Esther. "You of *all* people should be right here with me, making sure that the doormen actually screen the people who enter this building!"

"From people they don't recognize? Absolutely. So then they call upstairs, like Jamal did for my nephew here, even though he's known him for ages. But I will not stand for the entire building getting to know who has visited my home every day. That's a violation of Eli's and my privacy, it's a violation of our guests' rights, and it's, frankly, a rotten thing to do. Now, if you'll excuse me," she said while grabbing my arm a little harder than was necessary and then guiding me to the elevator, "I want to have dinner with my nephew here."

The elevator was still there from Esther's trip down, so it opened as soon as she pushed the UP button. I heard Horvat talking to Jamal as the doors closed on us after we entered.

"Can you believe this nonsense?" Esther asked, shaking her head, then pushing her glasses back up. "He's been a pain in the tuchas ever since he became president of the board. He was secretary for years, and we never heard a peep out of him, but now he's the president and he's got delusions of grandeur."

We arrived at the fifth floor and as we walked out into the hall, I said, "Well, he's got a point about security, especially with the synagogue being vandalized and all."

That was my subtle way of pointing out to Esther that I had to hear about what happened at the synagogue from a source other than my aunt who was its rabbi.

But instead of apologizing for this uncharacteristic oversight of information providing on her part, she said, "Maybe, but putting poor Jamal through that idiocy, he didn't need to do."

I might have had a reply to that, but as we approached 5E the smells of roasted chicken wafted to my nostrils, and I lost all power of speech.

Esther opened the door, which, in a weird quirk of New York City apartment design, led to the dining room. (This was an improvement over my own place, where the front door faced the bathroom door.) On the far end of the dining room from the front door was the kitchen, where I saw Eli chopping vegetables for a salad. The heavenly smells of roasted poultry emanated from the oven right to my eager nostrils and quivering taste buds.

Without even looking up from his chopping, Eli asked, "You find out why Jamal was being weird, or was I right and it was Tommy being a putz?"

"It was Tommy being a putz," Esther said.

"Soon as I heard Jamal was on speaker, I knew he was playing to someone, and Bram, it wasn't. How you doin', Bram?"

"Much better now that I'm inhaling your chicken."

"It's even better when you eat it."

"That's what I've heard. How soon till it's done, and I can prove you right?"

Now Eli looked up, sniffed, and said, "Four minutes."

Unlike Esther and me, Eli had an ordinary-sized proboscis, but what his nose lacked in size it made up for in accuracy. And that was with his thick, white mustache in the way, though it went nicely with his even thicker white beard, which came down to his sternum. He'd had to stay clean-shaven during his years as a chef for hygiene reasons, but the moment he retired he stopped shaving.

Competing with the olfactory wonderfulness of the chicken was the plate full of pickled herring on the table, along with horse radish and some bread that I knew came from Little Italy here in the Bronx. Hell, the chicken probably came from one of the butchers there, too. Sure, there were plenty of good Jewish grocery stores in Riverdale, but Eli did a great deal of shopping in Little Italy as well. "The Italians," he'd said once, "they know from food a little."

I sat down at the small round table. When they had more company than just a single nephew, they'd put a leaf or two in and it became a bigger oval-shaped table that just barely fit in the space. New York apartments don't generally do *big* dining rooms, when they even have them…

Popping some herring into my mouth, I chewed, swallowed, then said, "So I bet you're wondering how I knew about what was happening at the synagogue, since I *didn't* find out from the rabbi. I was hired to look into it—by Josh Roth, of all people."

Esther sat down next to me. "Yeah, I know that, Bram, who do you think told Josh to hire you?"

I nearly choked on my second piece of herring. I coughed for a moment, held up a hand to stave off Esther slapping me on the back, accepted the glass of water she poured for me from the crystal pitcher that was next to the herring, and then finally said, "What the hell are you doing talking to Josh Roth?"

Now it was my turn to have Esther peer at me from over her glasses, and I flinched. Thirty years of being her nephew, you'd think I'd have developed an immunity to that glare, but no. Every time she looked at me over her glasses, I was a six-year-old kid who just ate the last hamentashen without asking first.

"Remember what I said to Tommy downstairs about how people come to see me because I'm their rabbi?"

I blinked. "You're *still* Roth's rabbi?"

"Yup."

"Why?"

"Because none of your business."

Self-righteous anger was eating away at the scared six-year-old. "I think it's a little bit my business that you're giving aid and comfort to the piece of crap who got your brother and sister-in-law killed."

"I'm not. I'm giving aid and comfort to a scared kid who was devastated by a stupid thing he did that got three people killed, for which he's been trying to make up the last twelve years."

I reached for the glass of water, then put it right back down when I realized my hand was shaking. "So—so you told him to hire me?"

"He saw the golem first, and we all figure it's connected."

"You think maybe he saw the golem because he's the one who brought it back?"

Eli walked in from the kitchen carrying a bowl filled with lettuce and veggies of various shapes, sizes, and colors and covered in what smelled like his balsamic vinaigrette. "Didn't Miriam's father cast that spell on him?"

"Ampuero," I said. "And he didn't cast it, he hired a magick-user to cast it." Wardeins didn't manipulate magick, they just supervised it. "Thing is—the spell doesn't always work a hundred percent. When Miriam was questioning Rebekah before she—y'know."

Eli and Esther both nodded. They were fully aware of what really happened to my cousin.

"One of the options she gave me was casting Ampuero. The problem is, it isn't a hundred percent, so someone has to keep an eye on her regularly, and that had to be me, and I wasn't sure I…" I drifted off, as a few synapses belatedly fired in my brain. "It's you," I said to Esther. "You're the one keeping an eye on Roth."

"We're back at the none-of-your-business stage, but yes. I thought it was the least I could do for Morty and Rae."

Tears welled up in my eyes. Eli went back into the kitchen and opened the oven. Now the roasted-chicken smell was everywhere, and it was glorious.

"So you're making sure he stays away from golems?" I asked.

"Among other things. When he saw the golem, he was a little verklempt, I can tell you that."

I frowned. "Wait, you said he was the *first* to see the golem?"

Carving the chicken on the kitchen counter, Eli asked, "Just so I know, Bram, you gonna be five minutes behind the conversation the *whole* night?"

Unable to help myself, I chuckled. "I'll try to catch up faster, Uncle Eli."

"Good. It makes my wife cranky when you're stupid."

Esther rolled her eyes. "Don't listen to my husband. You make me cranky even when you're *not* stupid."

"*Thanks*, Aunt Esther."

"Don't get me wrong," she added, pushing her glasses up her nose, "you're being *incredibly* stupid right now. Yes, Joshua wasn't the only one to see the golem. Once it was corroborated by other people, I told him to call you. We need a Courser to deal with this, and I thought it'd be good for Joshua *and* for you if you handled it."

Whatever anger I'd had had melted away and I slumped in my chair while stabbing at another piece of herring. "Well, I guess I should ask about the break-ins, then."

"Not tonight. Tonight you're a mess, and aren't you at the hospital after this?"

"Yeah." I don't usually do two overnight shifts in a row, but one of the other MDs had called in sick yesterday, which was why I worked last night. Tonight would be my normally scheduled overnight, which was from ten p.m. to six a.m.

"So fine, after you play doctor, get some sleep, and then come by the synagogue tomorrow around lunch?"

Remembering Bart Jackson, I asked, "Can we make it later in the afternoon? I've got another client I gotta see first thing after I get up."

Esther's eyes widened. "Which client?"

"New one."

"Two new clients in one day? I'm impressed."

"Yeah," Eli said, "keep this up and people will think you do this for a living or something."

I swallowed my snotty retort to that when Eli came in with a serving plate covered in chicken parts, steam rising from the roasted bird. Now I could smell the spices, which Eli had rubbed under the skin along with grapeseed oil (it would normally be olive oil, but Esther was allergic to olives). My nose wasn't as refined as Eli's, but I picked out enough to know that this was Eli's "Simon & Garfunkel" chicken: he rubbed sage, rosemary, and thyme under the skin with the oil, and garnished the chicken in the oven with parsley. He'd also used carrots and celery as a support for the chicken in the pan instead of a rack, which meant there were roasted veggies infused with *eau de* chicken to go with the other food. Magnificent.

The conversation shifted after that, first to Eli enumerating every spice he put in the chicken—I called it, it was the Simon & Garfunkel version, plus kosher salt, of course—and then Eli confirmed another assumption, that he got the chicken at the butcher in Little Italy.

"I got a beef tongue while I was there, too," he was saying, "and Sal told me about the time he went to Italy and got to see St. Anthony's tongue."

Esther made a face and her glasses slid down her nose. "They saved St. Anthony's *tongue*?"

Nodding, Eli said, "And put it on display in a church in Padua."

Shaking her head and pushing her glasses up, Esther said, "I do *not* understand Catholics."

"Sal said it looked like a burnt piece of wood." Eli then looked at me. "Didn't you guys go to Italy for one of your August trips?"

I smiled with a tinge of nostalgia at that. Before my parents died, we used to go somewhere every August. They'd close the practice for a month, and we'd travel. We went to Spain, Japan, Australia, Germany, Greece, and closer to home, Vancouver, San Francisco, Chicago, and Atlanta.

And also Italy. "Yeah, we wandered all over Tuscany and Forli in a rental car. That was fun, especially with Dad insisting he could drive a stick-shift, and then proceeding to prove himself *incredibly* wrong and almost destroying the car's transmission."

"So Rae drove the whole time?" Esther asked.

"Oh yeah. And we're heading up toward Ravenna from Florence, and the GPS is saying it'll take two hours to go a distance that should only take half an hour at best. But there's no traffic, just a road with some squiggles here and there. Turns out one of those squiggles was a mountain, which we didn't realize until we'd been driving up in a circle for ten minutes on a skinny road with *no* guardrail. Mom and Dad were both convinced we were gonna die, while twelve-year-old me thought it was the coolest thing ever."

Eli chuckled. "Sounds about right."

"The view from on top of the mountain was absolutely breath-taking, though. We stopped at a rest area there so both Mom and Dad could get their hearts re-started. It was late afternoon, so the sun was starting to set, and the sky was about eighteen different colors at once, like an impressionist painting on top of this beautiful countryside of green hills broken up by the occasional village." I shook my head. "Damn, I miss those trips."

"You should take a vacation," Esther said. "You haven't taken one since before you went off to Harvard, have you?"

I shook my head. "I'm pretty sure my passport expired, and I just haven't really felt the need to travel."

"Need, it's not about," Esther said, peering at me from over her glasses again. "You're a big honking mess. Once you take care of this golem and that other client you mentioned, you're taking a vacation."

I thought the idea was stupid but wasn't suicidal enough to say so. Instead I mentioned the time we were in Greece and Dad insisted on going up Santorini's steps on mules, which led to Eli and Esther talking about their honeymoon in Mexico, and various other travel stories that got my mind at least temporarily off Rebekah and Josh Roth.

By the time I needed to head out so I could start my ER shift on time, I had consumed a ton of chicken, a half-ton of salad, and a mess of rice that I had no memory of Eli actually putting on the table, it was just kind of there. Armed with three Tupperwares full of leftovers, I headed out around nine, which was barely enough time to walk home, put away the food, feed and scritch Mittens, and drive over to Montefiore Hospital.

Luckily, work was busy, so I didn't really have time to focus on how crazy it was that Esther had been helping Roth all this time without ever telling me. And I still wasn't entirely convinced that Roth hadn't beaten Ampuero and re-created the golem himself…

Chapter 5

After a busy shift and an autopilot home, I collapsed in bed and proceeded to have bizarre dreams involving me and my parents walking up the mountain in the middle of Forli on mules, only to have a golem leap down from the mountaintop and knock us all over the edge.

I woke up in a cold sweat around ten-thirty. This didn't even crack the top fifty of weird dreams I'd had since my parents died. But in a lot of ways, the ones *about* my parents dying were the worst, and since that day at Harvard, it was always in the back of my mind.

Right now, of course, it was at the *front* of my mind…

But first things first. I'd only had four hours sleep and I was feeling shaky as hell, and operating a motor vehicle didn't sound like the best idea. Luckily, I live in a modern city with a robust mass transit system, so I decided I was going to depend on buses for the day's work.

First, I consumed a mug of black coffee and gave Mittens some food and water. Before the latter, I picked the gigunda Maine Coon up out of the basket he sometimes slept in on my bedroom floor and snuggled him for the better part of a minute.

Bless him, the fuzzy little moggie just purred while I held him against my face and chest.

Eventually, though, he got all squirmy, as he always does eventually, and I let him jump down onto the floor.

I guzzled a second mug of coffee and took a quick shower. I stared at myself in the mirror, noticing that I wasn't as skinny as I had been. A month ago, you could have seen my ribs sometimes when I inhaled, but you couldn't today. Maybe being fed by people who love me really was good for me!

Also my neat short black hair had somehow turned into an unruly mop of not-so-short black hair and the thin beard that I generally kept trimmed and neat was now a thick thatch of fur on my face.

Still, I no more wanted to operate an electric shaver than I did my car, so I let it go for today. But I made a mental note that I was guaranteed to completely forget to make a hair cutting appointment with the barber shop up the street, and to actually trim my beard once I regained stability, both physical and mental.

Which I was sure would happen any month now.

I guzzled down another mug of coffee while I got dressed in a simple black T-shirt and jeans. I had to use a different hole in my belt verifying that I was in fact getting some weight back. I gave Mittens a final scritch and headed out.

First, I went to the bagel place and got a fourth coffee, along with a poppy seed bagel with lox. Normally I just ate it plain, but I was gonna need a protein infusion this morning. I chewed on the bagel and gulped the coffee while walking—a feat of dexterity that was *almost* beyond my means this a.m.—while I cut through Ewen Park down the hill to the bus stop.

As I walked down the pathway, ducking under the massive mulberry tree, I stopped for a second and stared over at the dog run. The park was mostly a big hill that originally was part of the estate of a Civil War-era general named John Ewen, hence the name. They had put in a dog run on the only level ground in the park, where Ewen's house once stood.

It was there where Miriam let the local werewolves galumph about overnight during the full moon, under the watchful eye of a Courser. For the last four months, that *hadn't* been me, by my own request. I couldn't bear to do that job for Anna Maria, Tyrone, and Mark while Katie lay catatonically in Miriam's dungeon.

As it happened, this was the first time I'd walked through Ewen Park since that night when I discovered Warren Mather's body under the sycamore tree—the first of the immortals Rebekah had killed—while minding the four werewolves.

It hurt as much as thinking about my parents. Maybe even more so, if only because the wound was more recent.

After a moment, I continued down the hill. There were four buses that stopped at the corner of West 231st Street and Riverdale Avenue at the bottom of the hill, and I had my choice of two of those four that would bring me close to Bart Jackson's house.

The Bx10 won that particular lottery, and it also came about ten seconds after I was ready to melt from the combination of the heat, humidity, and all the hot black coffee I'd consumed. Thankfully, the AC was working on the bus.

Unfortunately, I'd forgotten about bus karma dynamics. Yes, the Bx10 came first, but the Bx1 would've brought me two blocks closer to Jackson's house on Briggs Avenue. This meant that I was drenched in sweat by the time I walked the five-and-a-half blocks from the bus stop to Jackson's house. This was why I wore a black T-shirt. Yes, I know, white T-shirts are more comfortable because they reflect the light as opposed to absorbing it, but it was over ninety degrees and humid as hell and the black hides the sweat stains. I wanted to present an at least vaguely professional look for the new client, assuming he didn't notice that I was gasping for breath…

The block was made up primarily of century-old two-story frame houses, some two-family, some single-family. Jackson's place was one of the latter. It had an overgrown postage-stamp garden in front, fenced in. I opened the gate and walked down the short pathway that was barely wide enough for a single person, and only then if that person didn't mind having their arms brushed by blooming rhododendron bushes.

To be fair, the poor guy had had his hip replaced recently, which meant he probably wasn't very mobile for the years leading up to that surgery. Taking care of a yard, even one as small as this, required either physical effort or spare cash. The former was right out with the hip problems, and the latter could have been an issue as well.

I had to hop up two steps to a wooden front porch that had two reclining lawn chairs on either side of a small plastic table. The doorbell was next to the screen door, and I rang it.

A few moments later, the red wooden inner door opened to reveal a stooped-over African-American man leaning on a black cane with his right hand. He had close-cropped white hair and sideburns and wore silver wireframe glasses.

"You Mr. Gold?"

"Yes, sir, and you must be Mr. Jackson."

He pushed open the screen door with his left hand. "It surely is a pleasure, Mr. Gold, and thank you for stopping by. Please, come on in."

I entered a hallway that was crowded with overstuffed bookcases and piles of old newspapers. The hardwood floor was stained and discolored, at least what I could see of it under the threadbare runner that ran across it. To the left was the doorway to the living room, which had a bunch of mismatched, battered old furniture all covered in papers, books, magazines, catalogues, and envelopes. An old-looking air conditioner was chugging away in the front window, keeping the place somewhat cool. It wasn't nearly as efficient as, say, the central air in Katie's house, or the fancy-shmancy ACs I had in the windows in my place, but it beat the hell out of standing outside.

To the right was a staircase that was equipped with a shiny new stairlift, which looked like the only thing in the house that dated from *this* millennium. He probably got it after he came home from his surgery.

He closed the front door and then reached into his pocket. "I've got your check right here, Mr. Gold, and—"

I held up a hand. "Hold off a minute, please, Mr. Jackson. Let me take a look first, make sure this is really a dragon. I don't want to take your money unless I know for sure it's Courser business."

"That's very Christian of you, Mr. Gold."

"I appreciate the thought, although I should *probably* tell you at this juncture that I'm Jewish."

Jackson laughed. "I apologize, but I don't think it'd be appropriate for me to say whether or not that was Jewish of you."

"Definitely not." I grinned. "So where did you see this dragon?"

"Follow me." He led me through the hallway to the kitchen at the back of the house. The living room AC didn't make it back here, and I was starting to feel the sweat re-form. The Formica counters had a gold squiggly pattern that was vintage 1970s, and the round fluorescent light on the ceiling had an old pull chain with a traffic light at the end of it. The sink was piled high and deep with dirty dishes, and various appliances covered what little counter space there was.

At the back of the kitchen was a sliding glass door, which led to another overgrown postage-stamp yard.

Using his cane, Jackson pointed at a privet hedge. "See that hedge there, Mr. Gold? That's where I usually see it. I tried to get a picture, but it kept movin' real fast—and I gotta tell you, I have a hard time making the camera on my phone work right."

"You see it more when it rains?"

Jackson nodded. "Under that privet hedge, like I told you."

"All right, I'm gonna take a look there."

I really didn't want to go back outside, but the kitchen was stuffy enough that it wasn't much of an improvement anyhow. I slid open the glass door.

Stepping on the dandelion-filled grass and over the root of a large oak tree that stood in a corner of the mini-yard, I got to the privet and pushed the branches aside.

Sure enough, there was an impression in the dirt underneath the hedge, and what looked like a filled-in hole.

With a sigh, I got down on my knees and started pushing away the dirt in the hole, but it was too loosely packed and fell right back in.

But I did find a small red object. I picked up it up and examined it after brushing the dirt off. It was definitely bright red, flat, with a sort of smooth, slimy feeling.

I clambered back to my feet and wiped my hands on my jeans. Looking at Jackson, I said, "Well, it definitely looks like *something* has been there, and it's something that likes to dig. But that could just make it a raccoon or a squirrel."

"Ain't no raccoon or squirrel, Mr. Gold, that's for *damn* sure. They don't make either'a them creatures so big. 'Sides, what I saw didn't look nothin' like either one of them things. No fur, for starters."

I walked back to the door and went into the kitchen, which was at least a little bit cooler than outside. "Yeah, and then there's this scale. Does this look like the same color as what you saw?"

Jackson took his glasses off and looked at the scale, which I held out in the palm of my hand. "That ain't the same shade of red, no. What I saw was brighter."

I nodded. If the dragon—or snake, or whatever it was—shed this scale, it was as likely as not to lose a certain lustre once it wasn't part of a living being anymore, so it being duller still made sense. "Can you give me any kind of description of the thing?"

"Like I done told you, Mr. Gold, I swear it almost looks like a snake. No wings, no legs, no breathin' fire, nothin' like that. But I saw its face a couple times. It's got horns and whiskers, almost like a Fu Manchu mustache kind of deal. I see that head, and I'm thinkin' dragon, crazy as that sounds."

"Crazy's kinda what I do for a living," I said with a reassuring smile. That description didn't ring any specific bells, but I wasn't exactly an expert on dragons, beyond the three or four I'd encountered already. And none of them looked like that—but there were also dozens of types of dragons.

"All right, Mr. Jackson, this scale alone tells me that there's definitely been a dragon here. Like you said, they don't make snakes this red. I need to do some research and figure out the best way to deal with this. Meantime, if you see it again, call me right away."

"I heard that. Thank you, Mr. Gold, you've put an old man's mind at ease. I don't mind tellin' you that I was startin' to think I was goin' nuts."

I grinned. "Well, I wouldn't rule that out entirely, either, but that doesn't mean you don't *also* have a dragon."

Jackson laughed again as he reached back into his pants pocket and pulled out a folded-over rectangle of paper. "Here's your check, Mr. Gold. I look forward to hearing from you."

I unfolded the check to see that it was made out to Bram Gold—which was fine, my bank account was listed not just in the name I was born with, but also "doing business as Bram Gold"—and for the amount I'd quoted to him.

Shoving the check into my own pants pocket, I thanked him and once again headed out into the sweltering awfulness.

Next stop was Patel's. My transit karma was doing well: a Bx34 was just pulling into the stop as I got there. I rode it down to Fordham Road, which is one of the busiest thoroughfares in the Bronx. At this point, I had to take a Select Bus, which they did for high-volume lines. You dealt with the fare on a machine at the stop and just got on the bus, which sped up the boarding process. It also made fewer stops.

Sure enough, the bus I took was packed. I wound up standing between a teenager with earbuds connected to her phone, and music playing loud enough that I felt the bass line in my rib cage, and a short guy who looked either Latinx or Indian who reeked of cigarette smoke. I was also standing over two seated women: an elderly Asian woman who was knitting what appeared to be a scarf and a dark-skinned woman playing a game on her phone.

The bus lurched down Fordham Road, making constant slowdowns and stops despite theoretically having its own dedicated lane. Getting over the 207th Street Bridge took an especially long time, and I honestly think I'd have made better time if I'd walked. Which wasn't really true, because the humidity would have melted me before I got six blocks, but still…

Once we got over the bridge, I got off. I still had three blocks to go, but there was a branch of my bank on the way, and I stepped into the bank's glorious AC long enough to deposit Jackson's check.

At the northeast corner of 207th and Vermilyea Avenue, there was a five-story building. Like a lot of buildings in the city, it was mixed-use. The top three floors were apartments, while the bottom two were commercial. The entire first floor at street level was taken up by a tapas restaurant, but there were several smaller businesses on the second floor: a nail salon, a real estate place, a dentist, and Patel's, identifiable by a sign that covered the store's one window.

I liked the idea of a magick shop that actually *had* a window, given how dark and dank Ahondjon's basement store was.

A gray metal door wedged between the tapas place and a tiny newsstand would lead me to the places upstairs. There were sixteen black buttons on the wall to the left of the door. I pushed the one that had a sticker that read PATEL'S in the same blocky type as the sign on the second-floor window.

At the dim sound of a buzzer, I grabbed the door handle and yanked it open. It revealed a narrow, poorly lit stairway made of uneven stairs that creaked under my weight.

So much for avoiding dark and dank…

At least until I hit the second floor. To the right, the staircase continued upward, while to the left was a filthy glass door. I pulled it open to reveal a nice brightly lit, if stuffy, hallway. I walked across the cracked linoleum floor, passing three thick metal doors to other businesses before reaching the one at the end of the hall that had the same PATEL'S sign.

I opened the door to a small, but bright and beautiful, space. The AC was kinda weak in here, but there was a ceiling fan which helped keep the air moving around, at least. A red-and-black patterned rug covered most of the hardwood floor, on top of which sat a tall desk with a stool, and three comfortable looking chairs. A large red curtain bisected the space, which also blocked half the window. I especially liked that the paint on the window was a type that allowed light in, but was still opaque enough to keep anything from being seen through it.

As I entered, a woman in a softly patterned blouse and slacks came through the curtain. She had a bright smile, brown eyes, and a red dot in the center of her forehead. This just had to be the proprietor.

"Can I help you?" she asked in a musical voice.

"You're Kawtha Patel?"

"I am."

"Well, you said you could help me when you talked to Ahondjon—he called on my behalf?"

"Yes, the Gans charm." Kawtha pointed to the ceiling with her index finger, then said, "Have a seat, I'll be right back."

She went back through the curtain. I sat down in one of the comfy chairs and immediately realized that it was going to take a crane to get me out of it. Or maybe a lot more coffee, as the main urge I felt as my butt sank into the soft cushions was that now was a great time for a nap…

"You're the one who got Yolanda Rodriguez into the game, right?" she asked from behind the curtain.

I smiled at that. Yolanda was a Courser who lived and worked in Washington Heights. I'd met her a bunch of years ago when her husband had come into my ER with his leg gnawed off by what was written on the chart as "possibly a bear," but which Yolanda had insisted was something else entirely. I recognized the teeth marks as being that of a wendigo and decided to tell Yolanda the truth—as much so she'd stop harassing the rest of the ER staff as anything.

Me and two other Coursers wound up hunting the thing down—Carlos Rodriguez hadn't been the creature's only victim—and Yolanda decided she'd found herself a calling. I didn't train her—you can't take on an apprentice until you've been a Courser for five years, and I hadn't made it that far back then—but we'd stayed in touch. We even did a few jobs together, most recently dealing with the annual haunting of the Dyckman House.

I also remembered something else about Yolanda: she had a dragon! That meant I could call her and pick her brain about the possible dragon I had to deal with.

To answer Patel's question, I said, "Yup, that was me. Haven't seen Yolanda in a bit, she doing okay?"

Patel came out from behind the curtain holding a small box. "She was just up here last week with her oldest."

"Kamilah?"

"Analia." Patel sat on the stool next to the computer.

Right, Kamilah was her younger daughter. Analia was the older one who trained at the karate dojo near my house. Yolanda also had a son, who I was pretty sure was an infant.

Patel started tapping on the keyboard and added, "She just turned eighteen, in fact."

"Wait, Analia's eighteen already?" Maybe the son wasn't an infant anymore.

Nodding, Patel quoted a price for the Gans charm that was twice what I was expecting.

I winced. "That's gone up a lot."

"The only magick user in this hemisphere who could make one died last year. Now we have to have them shipped in from overseas, either from Israel or Eastern Europe. That's probably why Ahondjon ran out of them."

With a reluctant sigh, I got up from the comfy chair and took out my bank card. Glad I deposited the retainer from Jackson, so this wasn't as devastating as it might be, but it was still a bigger dent in my bank account than I had expected.

Then it occurred to me that I could put it on Roth's invoice as an expense, which improved my mood tremendously.

"Can I get a receipt?"

"Sure. You want to enter our rewards program?"

My eyes went wide. "Excuse me?"

"Rewards program. It's like—"

"No, I know what one is, I just expect that sort of thing from Starbucks, not a magick shop."

Patel shrugged and smiled. "Well, why not? It's good to reward regular customers."

My response that I wasn't a regular customer died on my lips. This place was bright, shiny, and had a rewards program. True, it also had scary stairs, but at least they were above ground. It certainly couldn't hurt to do a little comparison shopping.

"Sure, sign me up." I gave her the information she needed—name, phone number, email address—and then I took my Gans charm and headed back down the stuffy hallway and the scary stairs into the sweltering heat of Manhattan.

While I walked up 207th toward Broadway to catch the bus home, I pulled out my phone and called Yolanda.

Without preamble, Yolanda said, "Abe? That you?"

I chuckled. Because we first met in the ER, Yolanda thought of me more as Abe Goldblume, M.D. than as Bram Gold, Courser. Mostly because I was the only doctor who took her seriously when she said it was a skinny, gaunt man who bit off Carlos's leg, not a big scary bear.

"Yeah, it's me. Got a couple questions for you. First off, how happy are you with Patel's?"

"Totally happy. Kawtha is great. Her prices are reasonable, and she's got this great installment plan for the really expensive stuff in case you can't afford it."

"And a rewards program."

"Don't all the magick shops have that?"

"Not Ahondjon." I sighed. It was looking more and more like I was going to need to make a switch. There was just one last question to ask. "How badly do her charms smell?"

"Huh?"

"Most of the magickal charms I get from Ahondjon are pretty stinky."

"I ain't never had any kinda problem like that with Kawtha."

That sealed it. I was definitely going to have to do a trial run with Patel's. "All right, thanks."

"What's the other question? And make it fast, my next client'll be here any sec."

"You got a gig?"

"No, a cross-fit client."

Belatedly I remembered that Yolanda had a day job as a trainer at Pinehurst Cross-Fit near her apartment in Washington Heights. "Right. Well, you still have Magellan, right?" Yolanda had named her dragon after the one from *Eureeka's Castle*.

"My kids'd disown me if I got rid of him. 'Sides, he's a sweetie. And he's good in a fight sometimes, too. Almost as good as Analia, except that Analia don't breathe fire."

"I heard she turned eighteen?"

"Yup."

I shook my head. "Wasn't she just eleven last week?"

"No, she was *born* last week, she was eleven on Sunday."

We both laughed. "Yeah. Damn. Anyhow, I got some questions about dragons that you might know the answers to."

"*Hell*, no, all I know about dragons is what Magellan likes to eat. You wanna talk to the expert in my house, and that's Kamilah. You got my landline at home?"

"I don't, no. You have a landline?"

"Carlos is home most of the time, and it's better to give that number to the schools and stuff for the kids. This way, if nobody answers, it all goes to the same voicemail, y'know?"

"Makes sense. Can you text me the number?"

"Sure, I'll do it when we're done. Anyhow, Kamilah's the one who knows all that nonsense. From the moment I got licensed, she's been gobbling up everything she can in books, online, you name it. Saved my ass a buncha times, believe me. She can tell you everything you want to know."

"I thought she was only six or seven."

"Nice try — she just turned sixteen."

"Next thing you'll tell me is that Eddie isn't an infant anymore."

"He's nine."

"Oy."

"Yeah, I know. I can't believe it either, and I *live* with 'em. Anyhow, Kamilah can actually keep track of all this craziness way better than I can."

I chuckled. "So Analia kicks ass and Kamilah knows lore. What do they need you for?"

"Food and shelter. They stop workin' for me, I stop feedin' 'em, simple as that. Why you think we *had* kids?"

I had gotten to the bus stop at this point, and watched as an M100 stopped, disgorged passengers, and even picked two up. That was not the bus I needed. I wasn't sure why anybody was taking it, that bus's terminus was only a few blocks north of here. Then again, it *was* air-conditioned, so it was probably worth paying the fare for a few blocks of cool.

Yolanda then said, "Actually, that reminds me'a somethin'. I was talkin' with Miriam the other day."

That surprised me, as Miriam was the Wardein of the Bronx, and Yolanda lived in Manhattan, which had its own wardein. "Why Miriam?"

"'Cause if I call van Owen, I might have to *talk* to him, and no thank you."

I couldn't really blame her for that. Damien van Owen had been Wardein of Manhattan since roughly the Mezozoic. And his attitudes were about that old, too. I've lost track of the number of times he's bitched and moaned about how stupid it was for them to let women be Coursers. A lot of the women Coursers in Manhattan — and a few of the guys, too — tended to talk to Miriam or Aaron Katz out on Long Island or Annette Annichiarico in New Jersey about magickal stuff to avoid having to deal with van Owen any more than necessary.

"Anyhow," she went on, "Miriam was tellin' me that you were due to take on an apprentice, and Analia's eighteen now, so she's eligible. She wants to become licensed on her own, and as scared as I am of my baby girl goin' out by herself, I also know I ain't never gonna hear the end of it if I don't let her apprentice with *somebody*. So whaddaya say?"

I didn't say anything at first.

Today, I'd been in an actual good mood, which I hadn't really realized until just now, when three sentences from Yolanda absolutely destroyed it. It had started with seeing Jackson — something about talking with that old codger made me feel better — and then the surprising joy of shopping at Patel's. I'd spent the last several hours not thinking about Rebekah or my parents, and it was glorious.

Finding out that Miriam was playing work yenta on me completely ruined it.

"Abe? You there?"

I had to take a couple deep breaths. It wasn't Yolanda's fault. She wanted someone to take her daughter as an apprentice. It made sense that she'd be talking to a wardein about it.

Which was why I didn't yell at her. She didn't deserve my temper, which was pretty short these days.

No, I'd save that for Miriam.

Finally, after a deep breath, I said, "Yeah, I'm here. I don't know what Miriam was talking about. I'm really not interested in taking on an apprentice right present."

"Oh, okay." She sounded really disappointed.

"Look, I'm sorry — talk to me again in a couple months, I've just got a lot on my plate right now."

"Really? Miriam said you hadn't been working much."

"Her info's out of date," I said through clenched teeth. A Bx7 bus was at the light a block away and would be at my stop in a few seconds. "I got two new clients today, in fact."

"Nice. I'm lucky I get one a week. All right, I'll tell Analia we gotta keep lookin'."

Now I felt like a complete schmuck. "I can call Kamilah any time?"

"Yeah, it's summer, so she spends all day on her computer anyhow. She thinks researchin' is fun, and I ain't about to talk her out of it. I'm just scared'a when she figures out that dating's a thing she could be doing, at which point, I'm gonna have to lock her in her room or somethin'."

I somehow managed to dredge up a chortle. My bus was now pulling into the stop. "I gotta go, Yolanda — thanks for the skinny on Patel's, and I'll give Kamilah a call later."

"Seeya later, Abe."

I ended the call and got on the bus. As I took a seat, my phone beeped with a text message: Yolanda sending me her landline number. I saved it in her contact info.

I waited until the bus got me to my stop before I called Miriam. I didn't want to be one of those crazy people who scream into their phones on a crowded bus. And I had a feeling there was gonna be some screaming.

As I walked toward my house from the bus stop, I waited for her to pick up.

Which she didn't do. "This is Miriam Zerelli. Please leave a message." When she first became the wardein after the accident, she'd identified herself as the wardein in the greeting, but that just confused spammers and wrong numbers and such. Plus, of course, there was that lovely group of concerned parents, the Mommies and Daddies of Godliness or whatever the hell they called themselves, who started harassing her. That stopped when their chief financial officer fled to a non-extradition country with all their funds and the organization fizzled out.

After the beep, I said, "Mimi, it's Bram. *Please* stop telling people I'm looking for an apprentice. I'm really really not, and I'm nowhere near the point where it's required, and the absolute last thing I want to do is have some kid following me around like an idiot for six months."

As I ended the call, I changed course to the Jewish deli and ordered a pastrami on rye and a black cherry soda to go, as I was suddenly starving. Yeah, I know, I had leftovers in the fridge, but sometimes you just need a pastrami on rye, y'know?

First, I stopped at home long enough to wolf down the sandwich, gulp down the soda, and snuggle Mittens before feeding him. Even with the drag effect of Miriam being annoying, it had actually been a decent day, and — especially after the consumption of a pastrami on rye — I felt together enough to use my car.

So I went downstairs to my Corolla, which was parked in the driveway. One of the reasons why I bought this house in particular was that it had a garage and a big enough driveway to fit the car, allowing me to use the garage entirely for storage. It was the holy grail of New York City living: off-street parking *and* on-site storage, both of which came with the house, so I didn't have to pay extra for them!

Just as I beeped the car unlocked, my phone rang. I pulled out to see that it was Aunt Esther. "Impeccable timing," I said without preamble. "I was just about to drive up to the synagogue."

"You said 'later in the afternoon,' Bram. It's getting into early evening."

"The sun's still up, it's afternoon," I said as I climbed into the car and started it up, tossing the bag with the Gans charm onto the passenger seat.

"The sun sets at eight-thirty, that's evening."

"I'll be there in five minutes." I ended the call before she could rebuke me. She was gonna do it in person shortly anyhow, so why go through it twice?

As I pulled out of the driveway, I realized I hadn't called Kamilah. I made a mental note to do so when I was done with Aunt Esther.

Chapter 6

My aunt was the rabbi at the Fieldston Congregation, which was a Reform synagogue on Independence Avenue, a few blocks north of Esther and Eli's apartment. (Eli had joked that he retired so he'd finally have an easier commute than his wife.) It was the go-to place for all the more liberal observant Jews in the northwest Bronx, as well as some folks who came down from Yonkers and up from northern Manhattan. There were, however, plenty of other temples in the area, including Conservative and Orthodox, so no matter what flavor of Judaism you practiced, if you lived in my neighborhood, you were set on the Sabbath.

The temple had a tiny parallelogram-shaped parking lot around the back. I found that there was only one spot available all the way in the back corner, between a Ford Focus and the synagogue's Dumpster. It took a few tries to aim my generally-easy-to-maneuver Corolla into it.

What was hilarious about this was that the Orthodox temple up on Henry Hudson Parkway and 250th had a huge parking lot. Most of the time it was empty, though, since Orthodox Jews didn't operate machinery of any kind on the Sabbath, and they all walked to temple. Meanwhile, Esther always had to start services late to give folks a chance to find a parking space after the measly seven spots in the lot were taken. And even then, people often walked in after it started.

Esther was standing by the entrance to the dining hall in the back, hands on hips, glaring over her glasses as I turned the car off and grabbed the charm. "About to leave, all these people are. Good thing I had some food handy, or they would've left an hour ago."

"Sorry," I muttered as I squeezed between my car and Focus. "The day kinda got away from me."

"Gee, if only you had some manner of portable telephonic device that would allow you to communicate with other people from a distance…"

As I approached her, I said, "Look, I said I was sorry, all right? Can you show me where you think the golem was?" I pulled the charm out of the bag. It looked like a snow globe, only the globe itself was opaque, and would glow a particular color in the presence of certain bits of Kabbalistic magick. The base had little Stars of David all around it.

"Can't you wait to do that? These people've been waiting…"

Esther trailed off when she noticed that the charm was already glowing orange.

Blowing out a breath, I put the Gans charm back in the bag. "They don't have to wait anymore. There's definitely golem clay around here somewhere."

"That, I could've told you from what everyone saw."

We walked toward the door to the dining hall in the back of the building. "Maybe, but this is harder proof. Eyewitnesses aren't always reliable."

"I *know* these people, Bram. In fact, *you* know some of them, even though you keep refusing to come to services."

"*Please* don't start with that, Aunt Esther? *Please*?"

Amazingly, despite my incredibly snotty tone, she looked contrite, holding up both hands before pushing her glasses back up. "You're right, I'm sorry. You're here to do a job, let's do it."

"Thank you."

There were eight people sitting at one of the big fake-wood round tables that were dotted throughout the big wood-paneled room like the spots on a Twister board. On the far end of the room was a counter with shutters closed over it—when they were open, you could see the big kitchen. There was also a door to that kitchen to the side of the counter, which was halfway open. The food Esther mentioned probably came from back there.

Said food had since been devoured, as the eight people at the table had empty paper plates and half-empty plastic water glasses in front of them.

"Everybody," Esther said as we approached the table, "this is Bram Gold—he's Mordechai and Rachael Goldblume's son. He's a Courser, which means he knows how to deal with the golem."

"I should hope to shout," said one of the five people at the table I recognized: Hiram Rothstein, who was both my second cousin—he was Esther and my father's first cousin—and also the synagogue's bookkeeper.

"Good to see you, Hiram. And Joseph, Robin, Ellie, it's been a while."

"I'm sorry we're seeing each other again like this," Robin said. I first met Joseph Weinberg and Robin Rosen at their wedding back when I was in grade school—they were patients of my parents—and I'd seen them a few times since. They were both lawyers, though not the official temple lawyers. I honestly couldn't tell you now what flavor of law they practiced, though I did remember that they were both different types of lawyers, and one of them did criminal law. Given that she actually had some charisma, unlike her husband, I was hoping that Robin was the criminal lawyer.

As for Elka Stolovitzky, she was the synagogue's Cantor, and also sang at pretty much every Jewish wedding I'd been to for the last ten years. And, for that matter, at one non-denominational wedding, as she crooned for my fellow Coursers Pete Guthrie and Yewhala Chatwal when they got married a few years back.

The fifth person I recognized was, of course, my client: Joshua Roth.

Esther pointed at the other three, elderly women who all had the same nose, color eyes, and cheekbones. "That's Sarah, Carol, and Eliana Guttman—they're Rabbi Guttman's daughters."

I nodded. Rabbi Guttman had been Esther's predecessor as the head of the synagogue. He died at the ripe old age of ninety-eight right before I graduated high school.

"Okay," I said, "I still haven't gotten the actual story here. There've been break-ins?"

"Living under a rock, or something?" Hiram asked.

Esther said quickly, "His cousin, my niece Rebekah? She went missing a few months back, so Bram's been a little distraught."

"So maybe someone else we should be hiring?"

Loved this reminder of why Hiram went into bookkeeping instead of, say, diplomacy. "I'll be fine, assuming someone can actually tell me what happened."

Robin spoke up. "We've been vandalized. Someone broke into the temple a couple times and knocked over some things and stole some items. We all were getting together to talk about the arrangements for the summer camp's final day, and several of us saw something strange."

I recalled vaguely that the temple ran the Guttman International Summer Camp in honor of the late rabbi, where Jewish kids from all over the world would get to spend a summer in New York City, see the sights, and generally have a good time. The final day was a big blowout picnic party, usually held in a park a few blocks down the road.

At least that was what I thought they were talking about. Not wanting to provoke Hiram's wrath again, I didn't profess any ignorance.

Then Robin looked at her husband, and Joseph picked it up. "I didn't know what it was, at first, and neither did any of the rest of us, but Joshua realized right away that it was the golem."

"What were you doing there?" I asked kinda snidely.

Joshua blinked. "I'm a volunteer for camp, I was here for the meeting, same as everyone else."

One of the Guttman sisters—I honestly couldn't remember which was which even though I was just introduced to them—said in a proud voice, "He's the leader of our counselors."

I shuddered at the nauseating thought of this nudnick being responsible for a bunch of people who supervised kids. Although what was really nauseating was how proud the Guttman sister sounded, like she was telling me about her son the doctor.

"We only caught a glimpse of the thing," one of the other Guttman sisters said, "but it looked like a pile of mud—and it was moving! I thought it was some kid who'd been rolling around in dirt or something."

"Then we went to go inside, and the padlock was broken," Hiram said, "so we knew something was wrong. And we walked into an incredible mess!"

The third Guttman sister added, "We came in here first, and the tables were all flipped, the chairs were all *over* the place…"

Robin said, "The worst was when we went into the sanctuary. The bimah was knocked over, and the money had all been taken from the tzedakah box. Amazingly, nobody took the Torah scroll."

Esther said, "That was the first time." She looked at Joshua.

He squirmed in his chair, then said, "Well, I knew what it was right away. It looked *exactly* the same as it did twelve years ago. Everyone else was worried about what happened to the synagogue, but I was just *really* scared to death that someone else had resurrected the thing." Joshua was now visually distressed. "I was *really* freaked out, so much so that, by the time the police were done, we decided to postpone the meeting and go home, I left my phone behind. So I came back here the next day to get it, and I saw the damn thing again—this time it was lurking outside the temple. It ran off before I could get close, but it may've been chasing the thieves."

"You saw the thieves?" I asked.

"No, but they broke the new padlock and trashed the sanctuary *again*, and this time the yad was missing. It's silver, it's probably worth something."

The yad was the pointer that was used by the rabbis when they read the Torah.

Hiram added, "The Torah scroll's worth a pretty penny, too. Matter of fact, that's worth more than everything else in the synagogue combined."

This much I remembered from when I was a kid and had my bar mitzvah here. "That's the scroll that was rescued from Austria before World War II, right?"

"We didn't get it until after the war," Esther said. "It was smuggled out of Vienna in 1942."

I nodded. "But they didn't take it?"

Robin said, "I'm not surprised. It's not the kind of thing you can take to a pawn shop. These are probably just kids looking for stuff to steal to sell for drugs or something. An old scroll, even one as valuable as this one, is too hard to sell off. That's also why this probably isn't the usual anti-Semitic hate crime."

"Of *course* it's a hate crime!" Hiram snapped. "What else could it possibly be?"

"A robbery," Robin said calmly. "The temple wasn't desecrated as such. They just took stuff with obvious street value."

"You got a funny way of thinking what the word *desecrated* means," Hiram muttered.

Robin sighed. "I just mean there were no swastikas, no graffiti, nothing like that. And the physical harm was mostly to the door, they didn't try to destroy anything sacred."

As much to get the conversation back on track as anything, I asked Esther, "And the cops don't have any leads?"

Esther shook her head. "Nothing useful, just a whole lotta fingerprints. But people come in and out all the time. These were smash-and-grabs, all three of them."

I shot her a look, and so did everyone else. For her part, Esther looked stricken.

"I meant—um, both times."

My aunt, I loved her, but she was a rotten liar. "Try again, Aunt Esther."

"Rabbi," Joseph said slowly, "are you telling me there was a *third* break-in?"

"Sort of." Esther pushed her glasses up her nose and started pacing around the dining room. "What I'm telling you, really, is that there was a *first* break-in, or at least an attempted one. The night of the meeting and the next day, those were the second and third. The first time was a week ago. They tried to break in, but they couldn't get past the lock."

"Did you report it?" Robin asked.

"Report what? They didn't do anything!" Esther flailed her arms.

"But you reported the second time, obviously," I said.

Esther nodded. "They came and took statements and did their forensics thing and all that."

"And have no leads."

"Like I said." Esther sighed.

"Did you tell anyone else about the lock?"

"A few," Esther said. "Some of the kids at the camp, some other people who were walking by at the time, and I complained about it."

"That's why I really think the—the creature is here to try to protect the temple," Joshua said. "I think somebody's trying to do what I did twelve years ago and keep it safe."

"Doing a crappy job," Hiram muttered.

"So did I." Joshua visibly shuddered, and for a nanosecond I almost felt sorry for him. "It's really hard to control. It's a lot of work just to activate it, and you have to *constantly* be on it."

"Zombies are the same way," I said blankly.

Everyone looked at me.

"What're you talking about, zombies are real?" Joseph asked.

"I—" I sighed. "Never mind, this isn't the time to get into what popular culture gets wrong. The point is, we need to find the golem. If it's been created to protect the local synagogues, we need to see if any of the others have been hit. Or, for that matter, if any of the other rabbis know about who might've animated it."

"I've already asked around, nobody knows anything," Esther said. She pushed her glasses up her nose. "No break-ins, no golems. Only one I haven't heard back from is Rabbi Kessel. Left him three messages, too."

"Figures." He was the rabbi for the imaginatively named Orthodox Synagogue of Riverdale. He and Aunt Esther never got along, so his not returning her call wasn't exactly a surprise. "All right, I'll go talk to the schmuck after I'm done here." I pulled the Gans charm out. "I'm gonna see if there's any residue left. Golems usually leave a big mess, so I'm gonna try to find some clay that got left behind."

The people at the table all looked at each other. "We cleaned pretty thoroughly in here," one of the Guttman sisters said.

"You didn't save anything?" I asked, incredulous.

Esther spoke before any of the Guttmans could. "I realize you haven't set foot in here since you were a teenager, Bram, but this is a *synagogue*. People, y'know, *worship* here."

"Yes, I *know* that, Esther, but you could've saved *something*. How'm I supposed to do my job if you won't even help me out by saving evidence?"

"Hey," Joseph said, "take it easy, Bram."

"Um," Joshua started slowly, "both times I saw the thing, it was outside. There might be some clay out there?"

Dammit, I really didn't want to be grateful to him. Then again, he *was* the client. "Yeah, okay." I looked at the table. "You all can go home. If I need anything else, I'll call you." I walked back toward the door, muttering, "Not that that's likely."

I went back out into the awful heat from the nice, air-conditioned dining hall, which reminded me why I didn't need to think happy thoughts about Joshua, because it was his stupid idea for me to come out here instead of staying inside where it was nice and cool.

Esther followed me out. "You want to explain what the hell's wrong with you?"

I really didn't want to deal with her right now. "Will you just let me do my job, Esther? Please?"

"You're doing this job for *me*, Bram, and —"

"No, actually, I'm doing it for that little twerp in there. *He's* my client. So kindly leave me the hell alone and let me do the job *he* hired me to do."

She stood there staring at me over her plastic frames, hands on hips, a look that never failed to scare the crap out of me when I was a kid, and which completely unmoved me right now. Between having to be in the same room as Joshua Roth, Miriam making shidduck with me and the Rodriguez family, and the fact that these idiots cleaned up all the clay residue without saving some had pretty much worn me down to the nub.

As I pulled the Gans charm back out, she said, "At some point in the near future, you're going to realize what a spectacular ass you're being. Until then, I think I'm just gonna keep my distance."

She walked back inside. *Good riddance*, I thought.

The Gans charm led me to a couple of small bits of clay, which I put in the bag with the charm. It wasn't much — just a few little bits the size of pebbles — but it might just be enough.

I knew two magick users in the area who knew their Kabbalistic magick, but one was on vacation.

So I called Deet Galanter.

"You've reached the voicemail of Carnac the Magnificent. I already know what you're going to say, so don't bother leaving a message." That was followed by a beep.

I always liked Deet, even if he did like stupid old jokes by dead talk show hosts. "It's Bram Gold. I need to track down a golem, and I've got a few bits of its clay. Can you help me out?" I left him my number, even though he already had it.

While I still needed to talk to Kamilah, first I wanted to get talking to Rabbi Kessel. Mostly to just get it over with. Besides, I was in the neighborhood, outside, not yet home with my air conditioner.

I squeezed between cars and managed to get the driver's-side door open just enough to squirm inside. Took me about a minute and a half to back-and-forth enough to get out of the dinky parking lot. It was only a couple minutes drive to the Orthodox Synagogue of Riverdale and its huge, nearly empty parking lot. There were only two cars in there — three, once I pulled in — a Lexus and a BMW. The former had a license plate that said, I kid you not, "RBBI KSL," so I knew that Himself was there.

The BMW must have belonged to the Cantor, because I went inside the sanctuary to see only two people: Kessel in one of the chairs and a tall, skinny man singing his heart out next to the bimah.

Kessel turned to look at me as I entered from the back. I was shivering, as the AC was up on high. Probably needed it really high for when the place was crowded with people, but I didn't get why it was like that now on a Thursday.

He turned back to look toward the front and said, "Take five for a minute, please, Michael?"

The Cantor nodded and wandered off through a door in the rear of the sanctuary.

I politely refrained from pointing out that "take five" means "take five minutes," so adding "for a minute" to it was nonsense. Mind you, it took a significant effort of will not to say it.

Standing up to face me, Kessel asked, "Can I help you?" The rabbi was really short, wearing a white shawl covered in Stars of David. He had steel-gray hair under his deep blue yarmulke, and underneath the shawl, he wore a tailored maroon shirt with Star-of-David cufflinks, and beige slacks that had creases so sharp you could cut vegetables with them.

"Hi, my name's Bram Gold—I'm looking into some of the—"

"I know who you are, Mr. Gold. I understand that Mrs. Liebman hired you because of some talk of a golem?"

"One of her congregants, actually, and it's *Rabbi Lieberman*."

Waving a hand that was decorated with a bright gold pinky ring, Kessel said, "Yes, of course. What does this fanciful notion have to do with us?"

"Well, the Fieldston Congregation has been vandalized a few times. Rabbi Lieberman—" I didn't think referring to her as my aunt Esther was a good idea, plus I wanted to reemphasize her title and how to pronounce her name. "—called all the local temples, but you're the only one who didn't get back to her."

"I'm under no obligation to keep Mrs. Lieberman informed as to the status of my building."

"I think it kinda matters to everyone if synagogues are being vandalized, don't you?"

"'Synagogues' haven't been vandalized, Mr. Gold, *a* synagogue has been vandalized, if you can even call it that."

"They stole money from the tzedakah box and stole the yad and knocked over the bimah. What else do you call it if not vandalism?"

"Very funny, Mr. Gold," the rabbi said, though I wasn't trying to be humorous, "but I meant if you can even call that country club on Independence Avenue a synagogue."

"That 'country club,' Rabbi, includes a very many good people among its congregants, including, when they were alive, my parents. They're dead now because of a golem run amuck, and that 'fanciful notion' appears to be back, based on several eye-witness accounts, including the daughters of Rabbi Guttman."

Kessel shrunk back a bit, though whether it was from my snotty tone—and the fact that I had half a foot on him—or because I invoked Rabbi Guttman, who had been a good friend of his, I couldn't say. It always drove Esther crazy that Kessel had been close with Guttman but regularly condemned Esther, especially given that Esther had pretty much the exact same views as Guttman.

Guttman, however, had one thing Esther didn't: a penis. And Kessel's brand of Judaism didn't allow women to be ordained.

"Then there's this," I added, pulling the Gans charm out. The globe started to glow a soft blue, which meant that whatever Kabbalistic magick there might be here was minor and harmless. Probably some simple protection spells on the Torah scroll or some such.

To his credit, Kessel recognized it right away. "You found evidence of a golem?"

I nodded. "On the grounds outside the synagogue, right where the people said they saw the thing. And it was after the second and third time someone tried to break in."

"Golems are to protect us, not commit crimes against us."

"Yeah, I *know* that, Rabbi." Normally I'd apologize for my tone, but I wasn't in the mood to be nice even before this schmuck started dissing my aunt. "Working theory is that someone created the golem after the first attempted break-in to try to protect the place."

"Didn't do such a nice job, if things were stolen."

"Golems are notoriously hard to control."

Kessel nodded. "Not just that, Mr. Gold, they are notoriously hard to create. It takes a special man to be able to do such, a man of devotion, a man of intellect, and a man of reason."

"The kid who created the golem that killed my parents twelve years ago was only maybe two of those things." I shook my head. "Look, it doesn't matter. The charm isn't glowing orange, so no golem here. And you say you haven't been vandalized?"

"Absolutely not."

I hesitated. "If I call my good friend Detective Lydia Toscano of the 50th Precinct, she won't tell me that there's a police report of you guys being broken into in the last week?"

"Are you calling me a liar, Mr. Gold?"

"Not if you answer my question with a 'yes'."

Kessel let out a breath through his nose that made him look and sound like a bull about to charge. "Yes, if you call the 50th Precinct, they will not find any police reports from this synagogue any time in the last two *years*."

"All righty, then. Thanks for your help."

I turned and left without shaking his hand or doing anything else, y'know, nice. Esther wasn't my favorite person in the world right present, but nothing called for that attitude.

Without even thinking about it, I drove the Corolla, not back to my house on Johnson Avenue, but to Katie's place on Greystone. I needed to see someone I *liked*...

Chapter 7

PLAN A FAILED WHEN CANDI, SOAKING WET, CAME TO THE DOOR TO inform me that she was in the midst of giving Katie her bath, and then Katie was going to sleep, and maybe I could come back tomorrow?

It was the first time Candi *didn't* complain that I didn't have a set of keys. And my own feeling that I shouldn't have a set pretty well intensified.

I agreed to come back around ten the next morning, for which Candi thanked me.

Tired, grumpy, and frustrated, I drove the few blocks home. I left the bag with the charm in the passenger seat of the car, since I was likely to be driving to wherever I might need it next, and if I brought it upstairs, there was a better-than-even chance that I'd forget it when I went out again.

I went inside, and kinda just stared at the door to what had been Rebekah's apartment for a few seconds. For a brief moment, I contemplated actually opening the door.

That passed pretty quickly, though. Instead, I went upstairs to change into a different T-shirt and shorts, then went one more flight up to work out.

Usually, when I'm feeling out of sorts, a good sweat helps me get through it. Today was not a usual day. I was still grumpy when I was done, only now I was covered in even more sweat than I had been walking around in the swampy morass that New York had become this summer.

I went back downstairs to shower, and when I was done, I noticed two voicemails on my phone.

"Hey, Bram, this is Robin. Rabbi Lieberman mentioned that the apartment in your building is available. I know it's for an awful reason,

I'm so sorry about Rebekah, but our daughter Dolev is looking for a one-bedroom. She was living with a roommate, but the roommate moved out and she can't afford the place on her own and she doesn't want to live with someone anymore, and— Well, I totally understand if you want to keep the light on for your cousin, but Dolev could really use a place. Let us know, please? Thanks!"

I erased the message. Sometimes Esther really lived up to the Jewish mother stereotype.

Although, I had to admit, if I had to rent to someone, renting to someone I knew would be good. Last time I saw Dolev, the oldest of Robin and Joseph's three kids, she was just starting high school, so the notion of her living on her own was kinda weird, but thinking about it, that had been when I was an undergrad, so she'd be in her twenties now. Which meant Saul and Hannah had to be teenagers, at least, by now.

"Uh, this is a message for Doctor Goldblume? My name is Kamilah Rodriguez. My mother is Yolanda Rodriguez? She said you'd be calling me to ask about dragons, but I haven't heard from you. I hope everything's okay."

I had completely forgotten about Kamilah. And I did need some good background on dragons.

Once I dried off and put on a bathrobe, I called back, plopping down on the big blue chair in the living room.

A deep male voice said, "Hello?"

"Carlos? It's Bra— Uh, it's Abe Goldblume."

"Oh, hey, Doc. Good to hear from you. Yolanda said you'd be calling."

"Yeah, sorry I didn't call sooner, but it's been a day. How's the prosthetic holding up?"

"Just got a new one last week, actually. The last one kinda died."

I blinked. They made those prosthetic legs to last. "How'd it die?"

"Magellan was going after a cockroach. He missed."

At that, I laughed, and I had to admit that it felt good to do that for the first time in ages.

Carlos continued: "They were gonna need to replace mine, anyhow. One of the bolts was coming loose."

"That's not good." As I said that, Mittens hopped up into my lap. I absently stroked his thick gray fur.

"Actually, Ellery said it was great, because apparently I stress test the prosthetics. See, I actually go out and walk around and stuff. Most of their clients just stay home all the time."

"Good for you."

"Thanks, Doc. Hey, somebody's gotta do the shopping. I guess you want to talk to Kamilah?"

"Yes, please."

"I'll put her on."

There was a pause, and then the same voice I'd heard on my voicemail said, "Is this Doctor Goldblume?"

"Yes, it is, but you can call me Bram. This is Kamilah?"

"Uh huh. How come your voicemail said your name was Gold?"

"Bram Gold is the name I use as a Courser."

"Then why do mamí and papi call you by the other name?"

"I met them in the ER when your father, um—"

"Oh!" She said that word loud enough that I had to pull the phone away from my ear. It was also enough to startle Mittens, who gripped my legs and then jumped off and ran to the hallway. This served as a painful reminder that my adorable Maine Coon was due to have his claws clipped.

I got up, winced, and headed toward the bathroom to put some antiseptic on the newly formed cuts on my thighs while Kamilah kept talking.

"You were the doctor who saved papi's life in the ER, right?"

"Uh, not exactly. I was just the attending in the ER. I did call the surgeon down—she's the one who saved your father's life. However, I *am* the one who told your mother about the wendigo."

"Oh, okay. So mamí told me you wanted to know about dragons?"

"Specifically about what type of dragon I might be dealing with." I filled her in on what Jackson told me and what I saw at his house.

"Can you send me a pic of the scale?"

"Sure. Can I text it to you, or—"

"I can't get pics on my phone." That was said in a long-suffering tone that struck me as Kamilah losing an argument with her parents when it came to what features were okay on her phone. "But if you have mamí's email address, I can see it there."

I decided not to comment on the fact that her parents didn't trust her enough to let her do pictures on her phone, but let her access her mother's email account. Then again, the email I had for Yolanda was probably solely for Courser use, and if Kamilah really was her primary research person, she needed to be able to get at that.

Either way, I used my phone to take a picture of the scale and then emailed it.

"Got it," Kamilah said a few minutes later. By this time, I had gone back to the chair and was sitting cross-legged, mostly to discourage Mittens. For some reason, he never sat on my lap when I crossed my legs, and I really didn't want to get clawed anymore tonight.

I said to Kamilah, "The client told me that the dragon itself was a brighter red, but it's normal for body parts of animals to lose their lustre when removed from the body."

"Does it breathe fire?"

"Not that he's seen, but he's also mostly seen it when it rains, so I'm not sure that's meaningful."

"The ones that breathe fire can do it in *any* weather, be*lieve* me," Kamilah said fervently. I suspected that Magellan had proved that theory rather handily. "But if it looks more like a snake, then it's prob'ly not a European one, like Magellan, or a Japanese or a Chinese one. They all usually got legs and wings and stuff. But also? Chinese dragons are associated with rain, so it could be that — you sure about no legs?"

"The client seemed pretty sure, yeah."

"Okay, so not Chinese. But it could be Greek, or Indian, or Korean, or Egyptian."

"Which one of those is likely to show up in the Bronx?" I asked with a grin.

"Any of them? Lotsa immigrants here. Most of the creatures here came from somewhere else. I mean, except for the Indigenous ones."

"All right, let's say it's most likely Greek, Indian, Korean, or Egyptian." All this talk of ethnicities was making me think of food. Then again, I'm Jewish, talking about drywall makes me think of food. I got up and headed to the kitchen. "Which of those come in red?"

"Any of them *could*? The Korean ones are *most* likely to be red, but the only dragons that *don't* come in red are the Greek ones — they're all green or brown."

"Gotcha." I pulled out one of Esther's Tupperwares, opened it and sniffed. Still seemed good. "Now how do I stop one? I'm assuming dragonsbane's out of the question, since none of the three remaining places are in Europe." That really hurt, as the dragonsbane was, as

Ahondjon had said, pretty expensive, and I just blew a bunch of cash on it that I couldn't even bill back to the client now.

"No, and you really shouldn't use it even if it did work. These dragons are mostly nice."

"Mostly?" I put the leftover chicken in the microwave.

"Well, okay, the Indian ones aren't nice or nasty, they just kind of, um, *are*? They're like animals, y'know?"

"All instinct?"

"Right!" Kamilah took a breath. "And the Korean and Egyptian ones are really nice. They, y'know, protect things and stuff. I dunno how you could get rid of any of them, or fight any of them. I know for *sure* that dragonsbane won't work, but... Can I do some more looking and call you back?"

"Absolutely. This was a huge help, Kamilah, thank you."

"It's okay. What?" That last was said away from the phone. "Okay. Mamí said she wants to talk to you."

"Okay."

Yolanda came on a second later. "Hey, Abe. Listen, I want to apologize about before."

"Not your fault," I said quickly. "You were just going on what Miriam told you, and honestly? I'm flattered that you'd think of me."

"You should be—ain't just anybody I trust with my baby girl. Still, I shouldn'ta pushed."

"No, you're fine. I'm just not in the best headspace right now after what happened with my cousin."

"What happened with your cousin?"

I sighed. Why did I open that can of worms? Or rip open that wound, however you wanted to look at it…

"Long story," I said quickly. "But it's what I really meant before about having a lot on my plate. Listen, thank Kamilah again for me, please?"

"You bet. And hey, look, I know it's rough talkin' about this stuff. I'm lucky, I got Carlos and the kids. So, y'know, if you need to talk to somebody?"

"Give you a call?"

"Oh *hell*, no, I mean you absolutely should give *Carlos* a call. He *loves* hearing about all this nonsense we go through."

I chuckled as the microwave beeped. "Thanks, Yolanda. I may do that. Talk to you later."

"Bye."

After putting the phone in the pocket of my robe, I fetched both the Tupperware from the microwave and a bottle of water from the fridge, and sat down at my computer. I hadn't checked my email or the various Courser bulletin boards all day. We were sometimes slow to adopt new technologies, but the joys of the Internet were something we dove right into. Having said that, we stuck with pretty basic ways of communicating: email and an encrypted bulletin board on a private server. Big social media sites were a little too public, and what we did was better off in the shadows.

Yolanda offering up her husband as a sacrificial shoulder to cry on was kind, but I didn't think I was gonna take her up on it. While it was true, I didn't have any family in the house—especially since Rebekah got herself exiled—I had Miriam, I had Esther, I had Hugues. I mean, okay, I was pissed at Miriam and I was pissed at Esther, and Hugues wasn't usually much help, to be honest, but...

Hell, maybe I *would* call Carlos

For now, though, I wolfed down Eli's yummy leftover chicken as I caught up on my email, most of which was junk.

One of them, however, was from Deet Galanter, with the subject line that just said, "Voicemail."

"Hey, Bram. Best I can do is confirm that the clay belongs to a golem but I'm willing to bet credits to navy beans that you already did that because you're not an idiot and you know how to buy a Gans charm or a Rosenthal amulet."

I snorted at that. Rosenthal amulets lasted longer—charms had a shelf life—but were also way more expensive.

"If you can give me a few days I can track down a tracking spell. See what I did there? LMK. But just reply to this e-mail, okay? I'm at my in-laws', and I'm replying this way because I can pretend to listen to Sam's uncle while composing an e-mail on my phone. Not so much when I'm talking on the phone. If I get a call, he'll just tell me to ignore it and then give me his theory on how the government's monitoring our cell phones and giving us polyps. Yes, really. I love my wife, and I even love her family, it's just uncle Moishe that I want to beat until he bleeds. I'm still bitter that she wouldn't let me get him a tin-foil hat for his birthday.

"Anyhow, e-mail me back. Thanks!!

"Best,

"Deet G."

I shook my head and chuckled. Glad to see I wasn't the only person ready to strangle family members today.

Hitting "reply," I composed a quick response: "Absolutely need the tracking spell. It's for Esther's synagogue. Some crazy person animated a golem after some break-ins, so while the cops go after the thieves, I have to go after the golem."

I went through the rest of my email, and then started on the bulletin board, and while I did so, got three chat requests.

I ignored the one from Charlie Kalani. That Hawai'ian Courser seemed to spend all his time online chatting with anyone stupid enough to accept his chat request, and I stopped being *that* stupid a few years ago.

The second was from Aric Smale in Michigan, who wanted to know if I'd seen Steve Najjar lately — I said I hadn't. Steve had just moved here from Detroit a year ago and had started coming to our Sunday night drink-ups at the Kingfisher's Tail. That's where a bunch of local Coursers got together to get drunk and gossip. But I hadn't been back to the bar on a Sunday night since we had our Irish wake for John McAnally, the Courser whose throat Katie had ripped out when Rebekah tried to free Malsum.

I didn't get into that with Aric, I just said I hadn't seen Steve.

The third chat request was from Deet, surprisingly enough, so I accepted.

The following text was already in the chat window when I went in: "Uncle Moishe is now talking about UFOs. The word 'Roswell' has yet to escape his lips, though I'm guessing it's only a matter of time."

With a small smile, I typed a reply. "Actually, Roswell didn't become part of UFO lore until the 1970s."

"Oh, I'm fully aware of that, belive me. People got used to looking up at the skies b/c they were scared of being bombed during ww2 like London was, and after the war they still kept reporting stuff they found."

"Okay," I typed as this was more detail than I really needed.

"*believe"

I laughed. I hadn't even noticed the typo.

Deet kept going, and I figured this was his way of not killing his uncle. "Some kook found old reports of people seeing weird stuff in the sky in Roswell in 47, the army said it was a weather balloon, and said kook figured it was a coverup, because it was after Nixon, and everyone decided the government was lying."

"Right," I typed for lack of anything better to say. I figured he'd get around to the point eventually.

"Anyway, that's not why I sent the chat request."

"Oh good."

"I wanted to talk to you about the golem. Ha ha ha," That last part must have been when he read my sarcastic reply. "What's the big deal if someone animated it if it's trying to protect the synagogue?"

I took a deep breath and gathered my thoughts before composing my reply. And by "gathered my thoughts," I really meant, "finish off Eli's chicken."

Then: "For starters, it's doing a crappy job of protecting the synagogue. For another, Esther doesn't know who did it or for sure why. Neither do any of the other local rabbis. That's not the sort of thing that should be going on without adult supervision, you know?"

"I've met some of the rabbis you're talking about, and I'm not sure 'adult' I sthe right word, but whatever."

"Fair point."

"*is the"

"I knew what you meant, I speak fluent autocorrect."

"That wasn't auto-correct, wise guy, that was my stupid fingers struggling to compose text on the tiny touchscreen on my phone."

"I don't know, Deet, I think you're doing fine."

"Says the guy probably typing this on his keyboard like a sensible person."

"Not my fault you're at your in-laws."

"No, it's Sam's fault. But she's perfect in every way, so I put up with it."

"She's reading over your shoulder, isn't she?"

"I have no idea what your talking about."

"Uh huh."

"*you're"

I got up to put the Tupperware in the sink, running some water into it to let it soak before I put it in the dishwasher later. "Later" would probably be "in another day or two," since I didn't fill the dishwasher until the dishes took up the *entire* sink, and I wasn't there yet. The one thing about not eating dinner at home five days a week was that it cut down on the dirty dishes.

I got back to the computer to this from Deet: "All right well the tracking spell is one I'd have to get from Ari."

My recollection was that Ari was Deet's mentor. My other recollection was that he'd retired. "Isn't he in Orlando on a boat?"

"Orlando is landlocked."

I laughed. "Whatever, in Florida on a boat."

"He does have a boat and when it's not sailing across the ocean blue it's in Boca Raton."

"I was close."

"Yes," and I could hear Deet's sardonic tones even though it was just black text on a white screen, "because Orlando and Boca are only 200 miles away from each other. That's practically next door."

"Whatever, it's all in Florida."

"Right and you live in Baltimore, yes?"

I sighed. He wasn't going to let this go, so I played along. "Absolutely, right by the Inner Harbor. You should come visit."

"Nah every time I visit charm city I get crabby."

I groaned so loudly at that pun, Mittens was startled and came over from where he'd plopped down on the blue chair to see what was up.

As I scritched him with one hand, I typed with the other: "arrrrrrrrrrrgh."

"Thank you thank you I'm here all weekend. Don't forget to tip your waiters otherwise they'll never fall down."

I stopped scritching the cat so I could type two-handed again. "ANYHOW..."

He typed, "*laughs*" Our chat program was pretty no-frills, so no cartoon smileys or graphically created emojis or anything like that. Just text.

"So you'll get in touch with Ari?" I asked.

"The problem is right now he really is sailing the ocean blue. He said he was going to the Bahamas. He doesn't check his messages on anything like a regular basis. I left one anyhow. But who knows when he'll get back to me."

I sighed. "Is there anyone else you can ask?"

There was no reply for quite some time, and I figured he was waylaid by his uncle for something.

Then my phone rang, scaring me out of ten years of life.

Pulling it out of my robe's pocket, I saw that it was Deet.

"Hey, I'm in the car, we're heading home. Sam's driving."

Distantly, I heard Deet's wife's voice. "Hi, Bram!"

"Please say hi to your lovely wife from me," I said.

Deet said, "Bram says he hates your living guts. Also that you're a terrible driver."

Sam, who was used to her husband, said, "It's good to hear from him, too."

"Anyhow, to answer your question, no there isn't anybody else I can ask. Nobody knows more about golems than Ari, you know why?"

"Because he's a genius?"

Snorting, Deet said, "Oh lordy, no, he's a crazy old nutjob with the brains of a pea."

"And he trained you, which explains a lot," I said with a smirk that I was sorry Deet couldn't see over the phone.

"Exactly. Hey, *you* called *me*, remember? Not my fault you have bad judgment."

"I have great judgment, but Teitelbaum's on vacation."

"Ha!" Deet's voice then got distant. "Hey, Sam, remember how I was saying I've been getting more calls? Turns out Teitelbaum's on vacation."

"That would explain why anybody would call you, yeah," Sam said dryly.

"So anyway," Deet said back to me, "Ari knows more about golems than anyone else because he's the only one who gives a damn. You know how many golems there've been in the last fifty years?"

"I really hope that's a rhetorical question, because—"

"Three. And that includes the one you're chasing now *and* the one from—uh, from a while back."

I winced. "It's okay, Deet, you can say, 'the one that killed your parents.' I'm a big boy."

"That's what *she* said!" he yelled in as loud and obnoxious a voice as possible.

Unable to help myself, I burst out laughing. "You're a crazy man, you know that?"

"Of course *I* know that, what's amazing is that it's taken *you* this long to figure it out. In any case, Ari's the only one who's got any kind of juice about this kind of thing. He's the one Hugues called back when the last one showed up."

"All right, thanks, Deet. Keep me posted?"

"Nah, I'm gonna totally keep you in the dark."

"Knew I could count on you. Love to Sam."

To his wife, he said, "Bram says he *still* hates your living guts. But he's changed his mind about you being a bad driver, only because we've made it this far without dying."

"Next time, you walk home," Sam said.

"Good, I can get my steps in." Back to me: "Take care, Bram."

"You too, Deet."

I ended the call and then leaned back in my chair and smiled. It was always good to hear from Deet.

However, I was also exhausted. Between the lousy sleep the previous night, my workout, dealing with two cases at once, being pissed at two of my favorite people, and frustration at not being able to see Katie, I was already tired. Conversing with Deet was always a high-energy prospect, and it drained what little reserves I had left.

Shutting down the computer, I gave Mittens one of the mac-and-cheese cat treats he loved, and went to bed.

Chapter 8

AFTER ANOTHER CRAPPY NIGHT'S SLEEP, I WOKE UP TO THUNDER AND lightning and the patter of rain on the window.

I wanted to sleep for another hour, but the rat-a-tat of the rain combined with thunder meant that wasn't going to happen. So I shambled to the kitchen to start the coffeemaker, then took a shower.

When I got out, there was a text message waiting for me from Candi: "Katie's sitting up and watching one of the baking shows if you want to come over."

That woke me right up, and I hadn't even poured my coffee yet. Not getting to see her was the rancid cherry on top of the shit sundae that far too much of yesterday was.

However, typing my response was interrupted by an incoming call. It was Jackson.

"Mr. Gold, it's Bart Jackson. The dragon's back!"

Of *course* it was. He'd said it showed up a lot when it rained.

I still had no idea how to deal with the thing yet, but I *had* told him to call me when it came back.

"Okay," I said, "I'll be right there."

"Thank you, Mr. Gold. Right now, it's kinda slinkin' 'round the back yard."

"All right, I should be there in about fifteen minutes."

I poured coffee into a travel mug and put the lid on it, then threw some clothes on: another black T-shirt, the same pair of jeans. I grabbed my phone, erased the text I'd started to Candi and replaced it with: "Have to see a client, but will try to stop by after."

I actually remembered to check the weather report on my phone for a change. It was still over ninety degrees out, with the humidity, obviously, at one hundred percent, what with the rain. The good news was that the rain was supposed to stop inside the hour. The bad news was that today's low was eighty-eight.

I put on a light waterproof jacket that Miriam got me after the twelfth time I complained about how long it took my denim jacket to dry out after I wore it in the rain, and my wide-brimmed outback hat. The jacket would probably be too warm, but at least it would keep my torso and arms dry.

Summer rainstorms were always a crapshoot in New York City. Sometimes it served to cool things down. Sometimes it just made the humidity even more unbearable.

As soon as I stepped outside the front door to the house, I realized, to my chagrin and total lack of shock, that it was the latter. I was sweltering in the jacket and hat just from walking the few feet from the front door to the driver's side of the car, as well as the several minutes it took for the air conditioning to kick in.

Rain always made people's driving get a billion times worse, and I lost track of the number of lumbering buses, sedans going too slow, SUVs going too fast, and double- and triple-parked cars I had to deal with on the way over. Plus I sipped my coffee at the same time that I drove over a pothole on Kingsbridge Road, which resulted in hot black coffee on my chin and chest. Fun times.

Jackson was standing on the front porch when I got to Briggs Avenue. There weren't any parking spots, so I just put the car in front of a hydrant three doors down from Jackson's house. It was a risk, but I didn't want to waste time trying to find a legal spot.

I put my phone in camera mode—if nothing else, I wanted to get a good picture of the dragon to show Kamilah—and then got out and ran through the rain down to Jackson's place.

"Thanks for coming out in this mess, Mr. Gold," Jackson said as I hopped up onto the covered porch.

"That's what I'm here for." I tried to sound friendly and helpful, but my own voice sounded bitter and pissed to me. Mostly because I was bitter and pissed. I wanted to see Katie, not deal with a dragon.

But Jackson was paying me. In fact, he'd already paid me. This was what I did for a living, so I needed to damn well do it.

I went through the house to the sliding back door to the yard.

At first, I didn't see anything.

Sliding open the door, I saw some movement under the privet. I pulled out my phone and aimed the camera at the hedge.

A giant red serpent slinked out. I took several pictures.

The head looked like several dragons I'd seen: the eyes were very wide, as was the mouth, which was full of sharp teeth; the snout was rectangular, and there were horns over each eye, and feathered brows that looked like a massive mustache extending a few feet in either direction from under each nostril.

But underneath that head was the body of a red serpent.

Some dragons, I knew, were at least somewhat sapient—I seemed to recall that Magellan, as an example, responded to words humans spoke to him—so I tried the direct approach.

Holding up both hands, I said, "Easy. I just want to make sure you're not here to harm anyone."

The dragon slithered into the main part of the yard. At the end of its body was a flared, feathered protrusion that seemed to be made of the same material as the mustache, but wider and flatter, making it look almost like a lotus flower got stuck on its tail.

"If you don't want to hurt anyone, that's fine, I just—"

I couldn't finish my sentence because that tail whipped around and knocked me on my ass.

I fell against the window that was next to the sliding glass door. I did, at least, have the wherewithal to thrust my hands down to help break my fall, and it didn't feel like I broke anything. The back of my head and my butt both were sore, but I could live with that.

Struggling to get to my feet, I tried to figure out how I would deal with this when the dragon turned and slithered back and out of sight.

Once I got up, I ran out into the still-pouring rain and thrust aside the privet hedge bushes.

There was a hole under the hedge that was already filling in with mud that the dragon had displaced. It must have burrowed into the ground.

Jackson was standing in the doorway to the kitchen. "You okay, Mr. Gold?"

Getting to my feet, I felt a shooting pain in my left knee. I must have twisted it at some point. I limped back to join him at the back door, saying, "I've been better."

"I'm so sorry, Mr. Gold, I had no idea it would do that. It never did that to me, just sat there in the yard."

"Did you ever approach it like I did?"

"Once. It just stared at me."

"That could mean it knows that this is your house and viewed me as an intruder. Or maybe it realized that I was more of a physical threat than you are, no offense."

Jackson snorted. "I'm eighty years old with a shiny new hip that my body ain't used to havin' yet, Mr. Gold. None taken."

"The good news is," I said as we slowly moved into the house, Jackson sliding the door shut, "I got several good pictures. This'll help me identify it and have a better idea how to deal with it."

"All right, Mr. Gold, you're the pro."

Yeah, I really felt like one helluva pro right now. "Listen, do you have anywhere you can stay for a bit? I'm worried that I got its back up, and it may attack you next."

Shaking his head, Jackson said, "Nah. My wife died twenty years ago—cancer."

"I'm sorry."

"Thank you. I got three kids, but one's in California with her family, one's in Oregon with his family, and one's in Australia all by his lonesome, if you can believe that. I only hear from 'em once every couple months. Ain't really got any friends these days. Most of 'em were really Mahalia's friends—that's my wife—and we lost touch after she passed. And, truth to tell, I ain't been goin' to church much since she passed, neither. Only company I've got is the old Kindle I picked up at a yard sale last year and my tee vee."

I winced, both from how alone Jackson was, and from how much my knee hurt. Suddenly, my being pissed at Miriam and Esther didn't seem so smart. And at least I *had* them.

"All right, Mr. Jackson, I'm gonna go see if I can figure out what kind of dragon this is. I'll call you later, all right? And if it comes back—"

He nodded. "I'll call you, absolutely, Mr. Gold."

"Meantime, stay in the house. Don't open the back door for any reason, okay?"

Jackson nodded.

"And hey," I added with a game attempt at a smile, "I've dug around your back yard twice—you can call me Bram."

With a smile, he said, "That's very neighborly of you, Mr. Go— uh, Bram. My friends call me Bart, and anyone willing to dig around in *that* back yard is definitely a friend, even if I am payin' him."

"Thanks." I opened the front door, hoping there wasn't a soaked parking ticket on my Corolla.

"Hey Bram?"

I turned around to face him, wincing again from the knee.

"As a friend—get that knee looked at?"

I decided not to get into the fact that I was an MD and could examine myself, and just said, "You bet. Talk to you soon, Bart."

Miraculously, there was no ticket on the car, but whatever relief I felt from that was eliminated by the shooting pain in my knee as I got into the driver's seat.

Felt like a sprain. If it wasn't still pouring, and if I wasn't out in public, I'd have grabbed the first-aid kid out of the trunk and wrapped the knee. I had a good knee brace at home and would put that on after I iced it.

There was a text from Candi telling me that Katie was asleep, so I missed my window to visit her.

Happy joy.

Before I texted her back, I emailed the pictures of the dragon that I took to Yolanda's email address with the subject line, "Dragon pics for Kamilah."

Then I texted Candi: "It's fine, I hurt my knee. Gotta go home and take care of it. Come by tomorrow?"

Candi typed back, "What you do to your knee?"

"Feels like a sprain," I texted in response.

"Ice it, put a brace on it, elevate it, and GET SOME REST."

"You remember the part about me being an MD, right?"

"Ain't met a doctor yet who knew how to treat himself."

I chuckled. "Fair point. Gotta drive home. See you tomorrow?" I put the phone down after sending that last text so I could start the car and drive home. Thank goodness it was the left knee, since the left leg doesn't really do anything when you're driving.

Got home fifteen minutes later in time for the rain to have stopped. Small favors.

Grimacing as my knee shot pain all over the top of my shin and the bottom of my thigh, I limped up the stairs. First I went into the bathroom and popped three ibuprofen. After that, I pulled an ice pack out of the freezer, took my pants off and dropped them on the kitchen table, and collapsed into the blue chair. I put my left leg up on the chair's arm and then put the ice pack on my left knee.

Mittens wandered down the hall from the bedroom and gave me a look and a butt wiggle that both indicated a desire to jump in my lap.

I leaned forward a bit, pointed at him, and said, "No!" in as loud a voice as I could manage.

Mittens gave me a look for several seconds, then padded over to the couch and started grooming himself in a peevish manner.

It occurred to me that I didn't actually check his food or water bowls when I came in, and I for damn sure wasn't getting up again any time soon. The stupid cat weighed upwards of twenty pounds; he could afford to miss a meal. And I just had to hope he didn't eat my face while I slept.

And then I heard a buzzing noise from the kitchen, at which point I remembered that my phone was in my pants. Which were in the kitchen.

I looked over at the couch. "I don't suppose you want to get my phone for me, Mitt?"

Mittens ignored me in favor of making sure his butt was squeaky clean.

Nobody editorializes quite like a cat.

With a sigh, I hauled myself up and half-limped, half-hopped to the kitchen.

Upon seeing this, Mittens immediately went to his food bowl. "Mrow?"

After grabbing my phone from my pants pocket, I stood entirely on my right foot and dumped some food into his bowl. Then I hopped back to the blue chair and fell back into it.

There was a text from Candi. "See you tomorrow IF your knee is better. It's not better, keep your ass home with the leg elevated."

I started to type something snotty, erased it, then just typed, "Yes, ma'am." One thing I have learned in my years as a physician, most of them working emergency, is that you respect the nurses. Even when they're telling you things you already know.

I also checked my email, and there was a reply from Yolanda's address.

"I think I know what this is ok to call? -Kamilah."

It was easier to just answer that question by calling, so I found Yolanda's landline on my recent numbers and hit it.

Carlos answered. "Hey, Doc."

Obviously their landline had caller ID, and now Carlos recognized the number from yesterday. "Hey, Carlos. Your daughter apparently has something for me?"

"Yeah, prob'ly. She's in the kitchen putting some lunch together, hang on."

That reminded me that I hadn't actually eaten anything today. Having that thought suddenly made me hungry. In particular, I had a fervent desire for protein. The only leftovers I had in the fridge were rice, roasted veggies, and sauteed asparagus. No way in hell I was cooking anything myself on a bum knee.

Luckily there were half a dozen restaurants right up the street from me, and several more on Riverdale Avenue a few blocks away, and most of them delivered. It was just a question of what I wanted to eat.

And whether or not I was willing to get up again and buzz the delivery person in.

However, that decision was easy enough to postpone, as Kamilah came on the phone.

"Hi, Bram!"

"Hey, Kamilah. You got the pictures, obviously."

"Uh huh, and I think what you got is an imugi."

That was an unfamiliar word. "Is that a type of dragon?" I knew the question was a stupid one as soon as I asked it.

Luckily, Kamilah was polite enough not to say so. "Kind of? It's Korean, for one thing, and it's kind of a dragon-in-training."

The dragon's place of origin made sense — there was a decent-sized community of Korean-Americans in Jackson's neighborhood — but the rest of it, not so much.

Kamilah continued: "I should've guessed it was an imugi from the way you talked about it before. They're serpents that eventually get to be dragons. Nobody's really sure how they become dragons — some legends are they become a real dragon after a thousand years. Some others are that they gotta capture a shooting star."

"Are they harmful?"

"Mostly they're supposed to protect crops, and sometimes be a good-luck charm."

I wondered if maybe this imugi knocked me on my ass because it thought I was going after the back yard.

"Will they protect anyone, or just Koreans?" This was a legitimate question. There were a lot of supernatural beings who were *incredibly* fussy about who they would interact with.

"Usually it's just their own people. Most of the ones we get here in America are with Korean people who come here. Honestly, most of them are *in* Korea. The only ones I could find someone talking about here were in Los Angeles in their Koreatown."

"Okay. Anything else?"

"Well, they're usually nice? So I don't know how to stop them, since usually people don't want to. But if it attacked you—I don't know, Bram, I'm really sorry."

Poor kid sounded heartbroken. "No, no, you're fine. This is really helpful—now at least I've got a starting point for figuring this all out. I owe you one, okay?"

"Oh yeah?" I could *hear* the kid's nasty smile from here, and I was already regretting telling a teenager I owed her something. "Well, mamí said you didn't want to Analia to be your apprentice."

I winced. "It's not that, exactly—I don't want *anyone* to be my apprentice."

"Don't you have to have one some time?"

"Some time, yes. Not now. Trust me, if I was gonna take on an apprentice, Analia would be at the top of my list."

"Well, if you owe me one, then I think you should let Analia be your apprentice now."

"Uh huh." I sighed. "Look, I'll think about it, okay?"

"Okay, but if you say no, then you still owe me one."

"Fine. Talk to you later."

Chapter 9

I RETRIEVED MY LAPTOP FROM THE COUCH — JUST BARELY IN ARM'S REACH, thank goodness — and settled in to do some research. I spent the better part of an hour bopping around to several different web sites that provided information about real estate and home ownership, specifically of the houses in Bart's immediate vicinity. That gave me a few potentially useful e-mail addresses, and I sent messages to all of them.

And then my stomach started growling. I still needed to figure out what to do for food.

I took the ice pack off my knee. It didn't hurt as much — the ibuprofen had finally kicked in — and I needed to take the cold off it for a bit in any case.

It was also Friday, which meant tonight should've been when Miriam and I went to the burger place.

But I hadn't actually *spoken* to Miriam directly since before I'd left that snotty-ass message with her after I talked to Yolanda. She hadn't called, emailed, or texted me, and I couldn't really bring myself to blame her because, well, it was a *really* snotty-ass message.

And completely unwarranted. She was just trying to help me out. I'd been isolating like crazy since Rebekah, which was half of why she and Esther were insisting on feeding me five days a week (the other half being that I wasn't eating much unless I was with one of them). Having someone else to care about probably would help with that.

Thinking about that type of support reminded me of what Bart told me: that he didn't really have anyone. Even though I was an only child whose parents died when I was eighteen, I still had immediate family in Esther, Eli, Isaac, and Judy, I had a massive extended family, and I had found family in the Zerellis, my fellow Coursers (well, *some* of my fellow Coursers), some of the local magick users like Deet and José Velez, and a big chunk of my parents' patients. If I had a dragon menacing me in my house, I had a huge range of choices of places to stay until it was safe.

Bart had to stay in a home he could barely move around in, and could only go to the second floor of with the help of an electronic device.

I needed to be a little more grateful for what I had, was where my mind was going with this.

So I called Miriam.

Once again, I got voicemail, which meant either she was busy, or she saw it was me and didn't want to talk to me. After the beep, I said, "Hey, Mimi. So I managed to twist my knee while losing a fight with an imugi. Pretty sure I just sprained it, but I'm elevating it and icing it right now. I'm also starving and wondering how you would feel about us doing a lunch delivery from the burger place instead of going there for dinner tonight. We could eat it in your kitchen, and I could give you a groveling apology in person. Let me know."

One and a half minutes later, Miriam called me.

"It better be a massively groveling apology," she said without preamble.

"It will be, though in deference to my sprained knee, would it be okay if I dispensed with the getting-down-on-my-knees part?"

"I'll think about it. More seriously, though, you okay to walk over here?"

"No, but I can drive."

There was a brief silence. "It's less than a mile, and you're gonna waste gas and spit carbon monoxide into the air?"

"Medically speaking, it's the best thing for my knee. And I'm *really* hungry, and I *really* need to do this apology in person."

"I'll definitely agree with you on that last part. I want to glower angrily at you, and I need you here for that."

"Well, we could do a video chat," I said with a grin.

"The glower is not as effective on a computer screen."

"True."

We figured out what we were going to order, Miriam put it through on the burger place's web site, and we ended the call.

Now I had to get out of the chair.

All told, the hardest part wasn't getting out of the chair, or putting the knee brace I kept under the bathroom sink onto the bad knee, or putting a fresh pair of pants on over the brace, or even the less-than-a-mile drive a few blocks to Miriam's place on Seward Place.

No, the worst part was going down the one flight of stairs. Total agony, which pretty much undid all the work the ibuprofen was doing to kill the pain.

I drove with a white-hot knife slicing into my kneecap, turning onto Seward Place and driving between the two ten-foot stone posts with the ornate pattern engraved in each. Most people thought it was an architectural feature, but those patterns were wards that kept unwanted people out. Even though I'd already told her I was driving over and that I was going to apologize, I breathed a sigh of relief when the Corolla made it through those wards into the driveway — which these days was empty, as Miriam had no use for a car. The accident totaled Mike's Escalade, and she sold her Jetta after she got out of the hospital.

The house itself hadn't changed hardly at all in the last dozen years. In fact, the only major difference between the view I had now climbing out of my Corolla and the view I had twelve years ago when Miriam told me what she could about Joshua Roth's fate was the front patio, which had been refinished and fitted with a ramp.

Inside, the giant house was a little bit messier than it had been when Mike was the wardein, but the mess was in piles instead of strewn all about, with plenty of clear pathways so Miriam could navigate in the wheelchair. Like Bart, Miriam had a chairlift installed so she could get to the second floor, though she rarely went up there since the accident, and Miriam had also had all the interior doors either removed or changed to swinging doors.

She also had had central air conditioning put in, mostly because she wanted to be able to deal with all the AC in the house from one remote control rather than go from window to window to turn on and off the various window units that Mike had had throughout the house. That AC was working nicely, instantly evaporating the sweat that was beading on my forehead just from the short walk from my car to the front door.

Miriam was in the kitchen putting various condiment bottles next to the place settings and the pitcher of ice water she'd already put out. Her hair had gone prematurely gray in her twenties, but she'd still kept it waist-length, until the accident. She'd cut her hair to shoulder-length after that. Over the years since, her once-perfect skin had gotten a bit blotchy, which in my medical opinion was due to job-related stress.

But she also loved her job, and was damn good at it, so imperfect skin was probably a small price to pay.

She looked up from her wheelchair as I limped in. "You look like shit."

I let out a bark of laughter that sounded like a burst pipe. "Thanks. Look, Mimi, I'm sorry. That phone message was out of line, and—"

Holding up a hand, she said, "Apology accepted."

"Oh, come on, I've barely started groveling!"

She wheeled herself closer to me. "It's fine. You *were* out of line, but so was I—I had no business volunteering you to Yolanda like that, at least not without talking to you first."

"Well, I mean, it's not a terrible idea. Analia's a good kid, and I do need to take an apprentice one of these years, I just—"

"Food's here," Miriam said. The delivery guy must have just walked through the wards. Her phone, which was on the kitchen table, buzzed, and she grabbed it. "Yup, text message from the delivery service."

Then the doorbell rang. "I'll get it."

"Hang on." Miriam reached into the pouch she kept on the side of the wheelchair and pulled out a ten-dollar bill. "Tip."

I took the bill and limped through the foyer to the front door, opening it to a blast of humidity. I took the food from the delivery guy and gave him the ten, at which point he smiled broadly and said, "Thanks so much! Have a fantastic day!"

"You, too!"

I closed the door and limped back into the nice, cool house, putting the big bag full of burgers and fries on the table. "My cheeks hurt," I muttered.

"That's 'cause you're smiling, boychik."

I winced. "Mimi, what'd I tell you about trying to bring the Yiddish?"

"Same thing I tell you about calling me 'Mimi'."

I shrugged. "Fair enough. And have I really not been smiling that much?"

Miriam pulled the two burgers out of the bag, and unwrapped the one marked "CB," which had her double cheeseburger with lettuce, tomatoes, and bacon. "I think the better question is, have you smiled, like, at all the past four months?"

"Fine, whatever." I unwrapped my own double hamburger with bacon, onions, pickles, ketchup, and relish. Miriam had removed the top bun and was now squirting a bunch of mayonnaise onto her burger. "You do know that they'll put mayo on the burger if you ask, right?"

"Three problems with that," she said as she finished applying liberal doses of mayo to her burger and replacing the top bun. "One, their mayo sucks. Two, they never put enough on."

"If their mayo sucks, why is it bad that they don't put enough on?"

"Hush, you. And three, the time between when it's made and when it finally makes it to my front door is long enough that the mayo soaks into everything. It's a condiment—it's supposed to supplement the burger, not take it over. I want a burger with a hint of mayo, not mayo with a hint of burger."

Looking at the rather impressive quantity of mayonnaise that was now seeping out the sides of her burger, I said, "Your definition of 'hint' is way different from mine."

"Yeah, yeah, yeah." She pulled out the big paper cup filled with fries, dumped a bunch of them onto the plate next to her burger, and then squirted mustard out all over them, followed by a drizzle of malt vinegar.

I dumped the remaining fries onto my plate, squeezed out a pool of ketchup to dip the fries in on the side of the plate, and then poured water for both of us.

"Thank you," she said as I handed her the glass of water, and then she took a bite of her burger. Bits of mayo squirted out the sides as she made nommy noises.

Shaking my head and chuckling, I sat down across from her. "Oooooh."

Miriam sighed. "You sound like an old man."

"Only because of the flamethrower being applied to my left knee right now." I grabbed a fry and dipped it in the ketchup. Much as I wanted the protein, I hated cold fries, so I always ate them first.

I felt my phone buzz in my pocket, so I took it out to make sure it wasn't something important. There was a text message waiting.

"Everything okay?" Miriam asked.

"Yup. Park's reminding me about my shift tomorrow night."

Miriam raised an eyebrow. "Didn't you swear to me last time you worked a Saturday night shift that you'd never put yourself through that again?"

I nodded. Saturday nights were always the busiest time in the ER. "Swore to you, yes. Swore to Park, not so much. Also he rarely considers my needs when plugging me into the schedule." Dr. Cho Park, my supervisor at Montefiore, barely tolerated my existence as it was, and the only reason why he did so was because he could plug me in pretty much anywhere to fill a need, since I was only there two shifts a week.

"Hopefully your knee will be up for it."

"Yeah." I sighed. "Especially since I can't call out for a Saturday night without incurring the wrath, not just of Park, but everyone else working that shift, unless it's for something way more serious than a sprained knee." I dipped another fry in ketchup and popped in my mouth before saying, "And that means I need to take it easy tomorrow."

"Maybe go visit Katie? That'll just be sitting at her side and reading *Frankenstein* to her, right?"

"We'll see. Candi made it abundantly clear that I wasn't allowed to come over unless my knee was in better shape."

Miriam raised an eyebrow as she chewed on her burger. "You told Candi about your knee?"

"Yeah."

"*That* was stupid."

"Yeah, but if I didn't, and I showed up with a limp, I'd get a much harder time."

"Fair enough."

"Besides, I'm not sure those visits to Katie are really doing any good. I mean, even if she can hear me, I'm fairly certain that she's pissed at me."

"Oh, will you *stop* that?"

I flinched. Miriam didn't usually snap at me like that.

She went on: "For crying out loud, Bram, you didn't shoot her, Bernie did. And he did it because Katie was possessed by a pissed-off wolf god and had already killed John."

"Yeah, I *know* that, Miriam, I was *there*. And I was the one who stopped Bernie from shooting her the first time, which is why she had *plenty* of time to kill John."

"You were trying to keep her safe. It didn't work. Shit happens in this job, Bram, you *know* that. The entire borough was being beaten up by Malsum trying to break loose, and every dog and werewolf around was acting against their will. You made a decision to try to protect an innocent life, and it didn't work. Yes, it's terrible, but you can't let it define the rest of your life."

"Easy for you to say," I muttered.

"What was that?"

"It wasn't your fault that this whole thing happened! *I* was the one who gave Rebekah the apartment, I was the one who gave her access to all my weird-ass books, I was the one who didn't even *notice* that she'd been teaching herself magick behind my back, and I totally missed that she was killing off immortals and wiping out binding spells and nearly causing the world to end. The whole damn thing was my own stupid fault!"

"Bram—"

But I was on a roll. "And you want me to take on an apprentice? Bad enough I said yes when Katie asked me out, since it made me be a colossal idiot in the field when she was possessed, but what about Rebekah? What was it in her learning the magickal ropes and deciding to murder three people to free a vengeful wolf god that made you think me bringing *another* young woman into this crazy-ass world of ours would be a *good* idea? Ow!"

It was only after I felt the shooting pain in my knee that I realized that I'd stood up and had tried and failed to pace. More gingerly, I sat back down and, for lack of anything better to do, finally took a bite of my burger. The savory taste of the bacon and the spices in the meat combined with the coolness of the ketchup, the roughness of the relish, and the harshness of the onion to distract me from how miserable I was.

"You finished?" Miriam asked as I chewed.

I nodded.

"Good, because you're an idiot."

"Miriam," I said with a full mouth.

"Shut up, you had your rant, now it's my turn. You've been wandering around under a cloud for four months now, and I was willing to give you a pass for a while, but enough is enough. This is *not* your fault."

"So whose fault *is* it, if not mine?"

"Rebekah's."

That brought me up short. I nearly choked on my burger.

"She isn't your daughter, Bram. She's an adult by every measurable metric, who is responsible for her own choices and her own decisions. Yes, you provided her with the reading material, but *she's* the one who chose to use it to commit horrible acts. I don't see how you could've been a better role model for her—you're a kind, compassionate, considerate person who does your job well. There's no way she got being a murderer from you."

"She didn't get it from Isaac and Judy, either."

"Who knows where she got it from? That's not the point—the point is, it's *not your damn fault*. So, for the love of all the living, will you *please* stop blaming yourself? If Rebekah's life got screwed up, it's *Rebekah's* doing, and she's already paying the price for that. It's about time you stopped paying a price yourself and get back on your damn horse." She accentuated her point by shoving the rest of her cheeseburger into her mouth, which, I gotta say, diluted the impact of her message a bit.

"Miriam—" I started, but she kept going, even though her mouth was full of burger.

"And another thing, what makes you think you'd be *bringing* Analia Rodriguez into anything? She's hip-deep in the game already. She goes with Yolanda on a lot of her cases, and she's held her own. You really think that you *not* taking her as an apprentice is gonna keep her safer somehow?"

"Well—"

"She's already *in* our world, Bram. Yolanda is scared to death right now, because her little girl is eighteen and wants to do the same stupid-ass thing she's doing, and Yolanda won't always be there to protect her. You're the one who told Yolanda about our world."

"That was so she'd know what nearly killed Carlos." I had no idea why I sounded so defensive when I said that.

"I know that, and it was the right thing to do. Yolanda chose the life, same way you did after your parents were killed. And Analia and Kamilah are part of it, too. But Yolanda knows and trusts you more than any other Courser. That's why I said you'd be open to it when she asked me if you were available."

That got my attention. "Hang on, she asked for me?"

Miriam nodded as she grabbed a fry. "By name."

"She didn't tell me that." I took another bite of the burger. After I chewed and swallowed, I finally said, "Look, I'll think about it, okay? I still don't think I'm in the best mental shape to handle an apprentice right present, y'know?"

"I think having someone else to focus on will *put* you in the right state—but," she added quickly before I could respond to that, "it's your choice. No rush yet, just think about it."

"I will. And I'll give Yolanda a call later."

"Good plan. Meantime, try to take it easy, okay?"

I nodded and took another bite of my burger.

Miriam then asked, "Are you sure that was an imugi that knocked you down?"

I swallowed my burger and said, "Kamilah was sure when I showed her a picture."

"Okay." Miriam shook her head. "They're just not usually violent, so I'm not sure why it would attack you like that. Is your client Korean American?"

"No, African American."

"That's even weirder."

"Well, I'm digging into the local—"

I was interrupted by my phone buzzing. I picked it up and saw that Aunt Esther was calling.

Answering the call, I said, "Yeah, Esther, what—"

"The Spuyten Duyvil Temple got hit."

"Oy."

"Oy is right. The cops are there now, and guess who caught the case?"

"Lyd?"

"Yup. So get your tuchas over there, see if it's the same people who hit us, and see if there's any evidence of the golem."

"Yeah, okay. I'll keep you posted." I hesitated. "Why are *you* calling me about this? You're not my client, Roth is."

"I wasn't sure you'd answer the phone if he called."

I rolled my eyes. "Fine, I'll get right over there."

"Call me when you're done."

"I will." Ending the call, I then said to Miriam, "Good thing I brought the car over. Another synagogue's been hit—the one down near Henry Hudson Park. And the good news is, Lyd caught the case."

Besides being the detective who handled my parents' death investigation, Detective Lydia Toscano of the 50th Precinct was one of the few NYPD cops who knew all about our world, and she mostly tried to keep the rest of the NYPD out of it.

I wolfed down the remainder of my burger, and awkwardly got to my feet.

"Let me get you some aspirin," Miriam said.

"Already took three 'vitamin I' less than an hour ago," I said, using the joke name for ibuprofen that we often used around the ER. "I'll be fine."

She gave me a look that indicated that she thought I was full of it, but what choice did I have? I had a case…

"Be careful, okay, Bram?"

"Aren't I always?" I said with a cheeky grin.

"Almost never."

I shrugged. "Fair point. I'll try my best, at least."

I arrived at the Spuyten Duyvil Temple to see a small crowd gathered in the tiny parking lot in front of the building. At the far-right side of the building was a walkway to the entrance, and that entire walkway was surrounded by yellow crime-scene tape.

Four sedans were parked haphazardly in the tiny lot, not actually in the marked spaces: two blue-and-whites from the 50th Precinct, a Chevrolet with NYPD tags, and an SUV labelled as being from the NYPD Crime Scene Unit. I shoved my Corolla on the far end of the lot in the left-most of the parking spaces. Grabbing the bag with the Gans charm and putting it over my shoulder, I left my pleasantly air-conditioned vehicle and again stepped out into the swampy air of summer in the Bronx.

The good news was that my knee felt almost normal, which meant that the ibuprofen and the brace were doing their work.

Two uniformed officers were standing guard in the walkway that led from the sidewalk to the front entrance, both wearing gold "50" pins on their collars. I didn't recognize either, but one was a broad-shouldered man named Alvarez, according to his nameplate, the other a thin but absurdly tall Irish-looking man whose nameplate I couldn't see.

As I approached, a tall, skinny man in a suit broke off from a conversation and walked toward me. He had a silk yarmulke monogrammed with the initials "DH" right in the middle of the bald spot in his crown. Surrounding that bald spot was short, thin brown hair, and he also sported a salt-and-pepper goatée. He was wearing a sweat-stained polo shirt and khakis.

"Excuse me, are you Mr. Gold?"

"Um, yeah," I said.

He offered his hand. "I'm Rabbi Honigsberg. Rabbi Lieberman called and said you'd be coming by."

I returned the handshake, which was sweaty and clammy, but I couldn't really blame him for that given the weather. "Pleased to meet you, Rabbi."

"Likewise. Terrible thing, this, just terrible—and not just because we're all being forced to take a shvitz out here instead of being in the nice cool temple. Rabbi Lieberman tells me that someone is trying to protect us with a golem?"

"That's the working theory, yeah."

He shook his head. "Bad magick, that. The golem is a creature of destruction, and only to be used in dire straits."

"You don't think vandalizing a place of worship counts as dire straits?" I asked.

"Eh." Honigsberg shrugged. "Nobody's been hurt. Probably boys being stupid. Boys are always being stupid. You don't use a shotgun to kill a fly, and you don't use a golem to stop a vandal." He took a handkerchief out of the front pocket of his khakis and dabbed his forehead. "Also, as far as I can find, none of the local scholars are aware of this use of kabbalistic magick, and that is very very bad."

"Very very bad is usually when I get called in," I said with a small smile. "I'm gonna see if Detective Toscano will let me in."

"I can help with that. See that officer there?" He pointed at Alvarez. "He's family. Married my niece. Not a bad kid for a Catholic."

That surprised me. Spuyten Duyvil was a Reform Orthodox temple, and they usually frowned on marrying outside the Chosen People. But I decided it would be impolitic to bring that up, especially since we were about to ask the gentile in question for a favor.

Honigsberg turned toward the walkway. "Juan!"

Alvarez looked over, sighed, and said, "Look, Tio, I told you, as soon as—"

Waving an arm in front of his face, Honigsberg said, "Eh. Not me, my friend here. This is Mr. Bram Gold, and he needs to speak with Detective Toscano."

"I can't bother the detective with—" Alvarez started, but the rabbi cut him off.

"Just tell her he's here, will you please?"

I jumped in before this turned into a family fight. "Officer Alvarez, it's okay. Detective Toscano's an old friend, and I'm here on official business — I've been retained to investigate things regarding the break-ins at the Fieldston Congregation. I just need to see if there are any similarities."

Alvarez frowned at me. I'd gotten good over the past few years at phrasing things in such a way that made me sound like a lawyer or a private investigator without actually calling myself that. As long as nobody asked for credentials, I was good.

But then Alvarez said, "Wait, you were at the Palmer crime scene a few months back, right?"

I nodded. Ben Palmer was one of the immortals Rebekah had been responsible for killing. Palmer had spent his long life gathering lots of money and becoming a wealthy philanthropist. When he was killed, Toscano had caught the case, and it still remained open (since the murderer was currently in the Nagashima Dimension).

"You know the detective never closed that case. Kinda put her in the doghouse with the sergeant."

I winced. "Yeah. That was the same thing, me looking into something similar, but it turned out to be a dead end." That was my first real lie of the conversation.

"Well, I don't know that she's gonna want you 'round here. You're bad luck." Alvarez was now standing with his arms folded.

I sighed. "Look, Officer, just tell her that I'm here. If she wants to see me, she'll let you know. If she wants me to keep my tuchas behind the yellow tape, I'll keep my tuchas behind the yellow tape, okay?"

At first, it looked like Alvarez was going to say no, but then he looked over at Honigsberg, and he seemed to crumble.

I felt his pain. I'd collapsed similarly under Esther's gaze many a time.

"Fine, I'll ask her."

As Alvarez went over to talk to the taller officer, Honigsberg smiled at me. "He's a good nephew."

I decided to go for broke. "He must be if you're all right with your niece being married to him."

"Eh. Two other nieces, I got — one married a Southern Baptist and the other married a Buddhist, and they both converted for their husbands. Elissa, at least, is still Jewish. Of course, my brother and sister-in-law, they're beside themselves. The way I see it, you take what you can get."

"Can't argue with that."

"So this Courser business," Honigsberg said, "you can actually make a living at it?"

"You *can*." Many of us had side gigs, like my doctor work and Yolanda's cross-fit work, but there were plenty who did it full-time. "Depends on how good you are at it, and how much of a client base you build up." I grinned. "You know, like any freelance contractor."

Alvarez was talking into the radio pinned to his chest now. He was too far away for me to hear.

Then he walked back over to us and lifted the yellow tape. "She wants to see you inside," he said.

I ducked under the tape. Honigsberg tried to do likewise, but Alvarez held up a hand and lowered the tape. "No, Tio, just Mr. Gold."

"Eh. Can't blame a rabbi for trying."

Alvarez gave him a look that said, *yes, I can*, but he wasn't suicidal enough to say it out loud.

Lyd was waiting for me in the small vestibule between the two sets of glass doors that led into the synagogue. She was in her late forties, short, with a round face, a body that gave the impression of being oval-shaped under the formless pantsuits she tended to wear on the job. Her steel-gray hair was kept short, though I noticed it had grown out a bit since I last saw her — which was, in fact, the Palmer crime scene.

"So," she said, pulling a pack of cigarettes out of her pocket, "you *are* alive."

"You had doubts?"

She shrugged. "Let's take a walk, Brammy."

I had really been hoping to be taken into the nice, air-conditioned synagogue, but it looked like that wasn't going to happen.

Lyd led me out the door and in the other direction down Independence, away from Honigsberg and his gaggle of congregants. She lit up her cigarette and puffed away at it.

I waited patiently for her to start the conversation, since I was the one asking her for a favor.

We walked a bit, and when we passed the front of a small, red-brick house, she finally asked, "What happened to your knee?"

I didn't think I was walking with much of a limp, but not a lot got by Lyd. "I sprained it fighting a dragon."

"What happened to the dragon?"

"It ran away."

Lyd puffed on her cigarette. "So I ain't heard shit from you in months. I mean, the least you coulda done was tell me who actually killed Palmer, so at least I'd know the case was closed in my head."

I winced, and wiped away the sweat that was beading on my forehead. "I'm sorry, Lyd, I—" I swallowed, almost choking on my own words. "It was—it was Rebekah."

"Wait, what?"

"My cousin, Rebekah, she—"

"Hang on." She stopped walking and puffed on her cigarette. "I saw a missing-persons report on her. You're telling me—" She shook her head. "First of all, you're telling me your fucking *cousin* did this? The one who couldn't match her socks?"

"The very same," I said quietly.

"So she did this? And then she ran away? You ain't caught her?"

"What? Oh, no, not at all, I—" Again I choked on my own words. "No, the missing-persons report was for Isaac and Judy. We had to tell them *something* when we—"

As I struggled to explain it, Lyd held up a hand. "Stop. I don't need the specifics, and based on the look on your face right now that says that you'd rather die than explain this to me, you don't *want* to give me the specifics. You're telling me she did it, she killed Palmer?"

"And Warren Mather, and Anne DeLancey."

Lyd nodded. "And she got punished for it?"

"*Oh* yeah."

"That's all I need to know." She started walking again, and I kept pace with her. We crossed the street and headed back toward the synagogue on the other side. "Christ, no wonder I haven't heard from you. That's gotta be rough."

"You have no idea."

"Oh, I got some idea, believe you me." She shuddered, and I wondered what past trauma I just reminded her of.

I didn't ask, though. Instead, I said, "So look—"

"Yeah, the synagogues. We got blood this time. If their DNA's in the system, great. If not, at least we got something to test a potential perp against. So what am I missing that's got you here?"

"Your CSU guys find any kind of weird clay or mud in the synagogue?"

"Hell if I know, I stay outta those guys' way. They find somethin', they'll tell me."

I unshouldered the bag and pulled out the Gans charm. "I need to activate this near the crime scene. It'll let me know if the golem that tried to stop these guys from going after Esther's synagogue tried it here, too. Hell, it's probably the golem that cut the bad guys and gave you that blood sample."

"So golems are real, too."

"Yeah. In fact, it was pretty much a golem that got me into this business."

"It was?"

I nodded. "Killed Mom and Dad."

Lyd frowned. "Wait, I thought your parents died in an accident."

"That was the official story, but the ceiling didn't fall in from bad maintenance, it fell in from a golem smashing through it."

"Jesus fucking Christ. Y'know, one'a these days, I'm gonna find out that there's a mythical creature that really *is* mythical, and I'm gonna have a heart attack from the shock. Just please, fucking tell me unicorns are fake."

Phantom pain in my ribs from my last encounter with such a creature twinged me when she said that. "Sorry."

"Fuck. Well, my niece'll be happy, anyhow."

"She probably won't be after meeting one," I said with a rueful look. "They are far from nice."

I felt my phone buzz in my pocket, but I ignored it. That was what voicemail was for, and Lyd was actually being nice to me, and I didn't want to screw that up.

Indicating the charm with her head, she asked, "So what's that thing do?"

"It's a Gans charm. It'll detect if there's any kind of Kabbalistic magick at work here."

"All right, gimme the thing, I'll bring it in. And before you say anything, no fuckin' way I'm lettin' you in there. I had my ass handed to me for lettin' you into Palmer's place, and Sarge still thinks it's because you stuck your oversized nose into my crime scene that the case is still open."

For about half a second, I thought about arguing, then decided there was no point. My choices were either to give Lyd my expensive charm and trust her to tell me the truth as to whether or not it glowed orange, or to not know if the golem was present at this bit of vandalism.

I'd been trusting Lyd for almost as long as I'd been a Courser, and both Mike and Miriam Zerelli had been trusting her longer than that.

"Okay. Be careful—it's expensive." I handed her the charm. "Though I almost said no for that remark about my schnozz."

Lyd snorted and started walking faster. "Let's get back, it's a billion fucking degrees out here."

I smirked. "It ain't the heat, it's the humidity."

"No, it's the fucking heat *and* the fucking humidity, and they can both go to hell." She finished her cigarette, dropped it on the sidewalk, stepped on it, then continued at her brisker pace.

"Isn't littering a crime, Detective?"

"Kiss my ass, Brammy."

When we got back to the synagogue, she went inside, and I hung back on the far side of the crime-scene tape, pulling my phone out of my pocket. Sure enough, there was a missed call from Deet Galanter, as well as a text message from the same number that read, "Call me back."

I found Deet's number in my phone's recent calls and tapped it. He answered on the second ring. "Joe's Pizza, Joe's not here."

"Sorry, I'll only talk to Joe. He's the only one who gets the pizza right."

"We're Jewish, Bram what the hell do we know from pizza?"

"My best friend's Italian."

"Yeah, but all the pizza places in town are run by Eastern Europeans."

I chuckled. "What's up, Deet?"

"Well, I've got good news and I've got bad news. The bad news is, I've got no word yet from Ari. I've left four messages now, each one more urgent than the last, and on the last one, I didn't even say anything funny, so he knows it's serious."

"Wow. That must've been, like, physically painful for you."

"Oh, it was, believe me."

I gazed over at the synagogue. "Well, I hope he gets back to you soon, 'cause another synagogue was hit."

"Oh, crap. Which one?"

"Spuyten Duyvil Temple."

Deet made a gagging sound. "Remember yesterday when I was talking about the local rabbis? Honigsberg's who I was mostly thinking about. He still wear a monogrammed yarmulke?"

"Yup."

"What a putz. Still, that sucks, generally."

I sighed. "So what's the good news?"

"I may have another line on the spell we need. There's a guy in Pittsburgh named Avram Steinmetz who's supposed to be an expert on golems, but I'm having a hard time tracking him down. He used to be a rabbi, but he got into a fight with another rabbi and disappeared. No one seems to know where. I had a couple leads, but nothing yet."

"Should I be concerned that all the experts on golems tend to go off the grid?"

"Probably, yeah."

As I was talking, Lyd came back out through the door just long enough to hand the Gans charm to Alvarez and point at me. The officer then carried the charm over — not really keeping a particularly tight grip on it, which made me incredibly nervous — stepping under the tape to approach me.

"Hold on a sec, Deet." I lowered the phone and gave Alvarez an expectant look.

He thrust the charm in my face. "Detective Toscano says it turned orange. Said you'd know what that means?"

I nodded, unshouldered my bag, and held it open for the officer to place it inside. He did so, and then walked off without another word.

Guess he thought I was still a bad-luck charm for closing the case.

Thing was, this time I wasn't looking for the guys who did it, I was looking for the guy who created the thing that made them bleed. With luck, this *wouldn't* mean another open case under Lyd's name.

I put the phone back to my ear. "Just got confirmation that the golem was here at Spuyten Duyvil, too."

"Happy joy. I'll keep leaving messages for Ari and keep trying to find Rabbi Steinmetz."

"Thanks, Deet."

"You know you're getting billed for the time I spend trying to find Steinmetz, right?"

"No problem."

Deet hesitated. "You agreed to that *way* too quickly."

"Let's just say I have *no* problem tacking that onto this particular client's expense sheet."

"Gotcha. Talk to you later."

"Bye."

I had to pass the gaggle of congregants on my way back to the Corolla in any case, so I exchanged quick pleasantries with Honigsberg, then got in the car and headed back home.

As soon as I got upstairs and scritched Mittens, I called Esther.

"I'm glad you called," she said before I could even start to fill her in on what I just found out. "Turns out the Rothstein Hebrew Center got hit two days ago, too. They never filed a police report, and Al Rothstein only told me because his wife smacked him in the head until he did."

I barked a laugh. I'd only met Rabbi Rothstein, who was the fourth generation of rabbis in his family that had run that particular temple since the Great Depression, once. But he had a tendency to ignore any problems and hope they went away. Luckily, his wife was a good rebbetzen; Hope Rothstein had made smacking Al on the head until he did something right her life's work.

Esther continued. "So that's three synagogues that have been hit. More to the point, that's three synagogues in the association that have been hit."

I frowned. "What association?"

"Right, I forgot, you don't actually *come* to services..."

That prompted a loud sigh from me.

"Don't sigh at me, bubbele, if you can't even be bothered to go to the temple *where your aunt is the rabbi*, then I don't know what to do with you."

"Why start knowing that now?" Mittens was glowering at me, so I went to get some food and refill his water dish while I talked. "What association, he asks again?"

"The Heightsdale Temple Association. It's a bunch of synagogues in Washington Heights, Inwood, Spuyten Duyvil, and Riverdale. We do community outreach and networking and events and such. You should swing by Rothstein with the Gans charm to be sure, but it looks like these putzes are making the rounds of all the Heightsdale members."

"I'm guessing Kessel's not part of this kaffeeklatsch?"

"An organization with him in it, I would *not* be part of." I could actually *hear* Esther peering at me over her glasses as she said that.

"Which may explain why Kessel didn't get hit." I put Mittens's food bowl down, and the little freser shoved his face in it immediately. "As it happens, I *did* swing by Spuyten Duyvil with the charm, and the golem was there—and Lyd told me the perps left blood this time, so the golem might be getting better at the protect-the-temple thing."

"That's good. But we still don't know who animated it, and I'm getting worried that we're gonna get some innocent bystanders hurt."

I shuddered. "Yeah."

"Plus," Esther said, "what if that blood was someone who wasn't involved?"

"I think Rabbi Honigsberg would've mentioned it if it was one of his people who got hurt."

"Fair point. Anyhow, I think we need to stake out the other six Heightsdale synagogues. There are two more in Riverdale, one in Inwood, and three in Washington Heights, and I want to have a Courser on each one."

"You think Roth can afford five more Coursers?" I tried not to make that question snotty. I'm pretty sure I failed.

"We only need four—two of the ones in Washington Heights are around the corner from each other. Anyhow, the association has a war chest for stuff like this." She hesitated. "Well, not *exactly* like this, but you know what I mean. I'll get the other rabbis on board with helping Josh pay for it. Any recommendations for who to hire besides Hugues?"

Without even hesitating, I said, "Yolanda Rodriguez for one of the ones in Washington Heights." If anybody deserved to have the work thrown at her, it was Yolanda, especially the way I'd been screwing around with her wanting Analia to apprentice with me. Besides, she *lived* in the Heights.

I also wasn't surprised that the first person she thought of was Hugues—after all, he was who she hired twelve years ago, too.

"Beyond that, you can't go wrong with Dahlia Rhys-Markham, Sal Antonelli, Eddie Mohapatra, Yewhala Chatwal and Pete Guthrie, Saladin Cruz, Kaela Provencher, or Abby Cornwell. No, wait, Antonelli's down in Florida visiting his mother, so you won't get him, but the others are all good people."

"Gotcha. I'll see who's available after services."

Geez, I forgot it was Friday. "Okay. I'll fill Miriam in, and she may have some other Courser recommendations."

"Sounds good." Esther hesitated, then: "You okay, Bram?"

"Yeah, why?"

"You actually sound like yourself."

I let out a half-laugh, half-sigh. "Yeah, I had a good talk with Miriam before you called about Spuyten Duyvil."

"About damn time. I gotta go, we'll talk later."

Chapter 11

THE ONE THING WE DIDN'T NEED TO WORRY ABOUT WAS A SYNAGOGUE being hit on a Friday night. Every break-in that had happened occurred when no one was in the temple in question, and all of them were pretty crowded for Shabbat services, obviously.

Saturday morning was a different story, though.

According to the text Esther sent me late Friday night right before I was about to go to bed, they'd hired Abby to cover the temple in Inwood, and Hugues and Yewhala to do the other two in Riverdale. (Yewhala was by himself, as Pete was on another gig. The husband-and-husband team only sometimes worked together, as they made more money if they worked separately.) That left Yolanda with the appropriately named Audubon Congregation on 179th Street near Audubon Avenue, and me with the two that were near Bennett Park over on Fort Washington Avenue and 185th Street.

Washington Heights in the northern part of Manhattan earned the second word in that place name, as the neighborhood was hilly as hell. Bennett Park itself was on the highest point in all of Manhattan. The park—named after James Gordon Bennett, the publisher of the *New York Herald*, who owned the land in the nineteenth century—had a playground and benches and a big grassy area.

The nice thing about it being so high is that you got a great view of the buildings on Fort Washington on the east side of the park. In fact, you have to go down a flight of stairs to get to the street from the park on that side.

One of the synagogues I was checking out was down that staircase and across the street on Fort Washington: the Hudson Heights Jewish Center, a big boxy gray building right next to the entrance to the A train station. I'd come up out of that entrance when I got here. It was just easier to take the bus to the subway down here rather than waste forty-five minutes trying to find a parking spot that wasn't even guaranteed to be anywhere near where I needed to be.

The other synagogue was the Burstein Shul around the corner on 185th, a smaller Art Deco building.

I took a seat on one of the wooden benches near the playground, plunking a duffel bag next to me, which contained the Gans charm and a bottle of water, as well as a few other items both magickal and otherwise that wouldn't do a damn bit of good against a golem, but which always lived in that duffel. It was easier to just have anything I might need in the bag instead of unpacking and repacking the thing every time.

Well, easier on my brain, anyhow, so I wouldn't have to worry about forgetting stuff. Easier on my shoulder, not so much, as the damn thing got heavy. Luckily, I already had some ibuprofen running through my system, as I'd taken three this morning before coming down here to get rid of the pain that was still in my now-swollen left knee. I had the brace around that knee again, too.

The good news was that there was a break in the weather. It was only in the high eighties temperature-wise, instead of the low nineties, and it was *much* less humid. This meant I wasn't *completely* drenched in sweat just from the act of coming up the stairs from the subway and then up more stairs to the park while carrying a heavy-ass duffel.

From this vantage point, I could see both buildings clearly. I pulled the water bottle out of the duffel and gulped some down. Just the walk here from the subway had me parched.

"Fancy seein' you here, Doc."

I looked up to see a familiar face. It was, however, on an unfamiliar body, as the last time I saw that face, it was on a person who was several inches shorter. "Analia?"

Yolanda's oldest daughter walked up to me and grinned. She was wearing a T-shirt that had some anime character or other on it, purple leggings, and bright red sneakers. Her dark hair was cut short—last time I saw her as a pre-teen, her hair was down to her waist. One of her hands was clenched into a fist.

"What brings you here?"

Analia grinned. "Heard a rumor that there was a golem that might hit one of these two places. Figured I'd check 'em out." She held up her hand and unclenched her fist to reveal several tiny pellets of clay.

Very familiar-looking tiny pellets of clay.

"Where'd you find those?"

Jerking a thumb toward Fort Washington, she said, "Across the street by the A train entrance."

I yanked the Gans charm out of the duffel, and tried not to think about how I totally missed that when I came out of that same entrance ten minutes ago.

The charm rather obligingly turned orange. "We have a winner."

"That means it's been here recently, right?"

With a sigh, I said, "Not necessarily. It could've been here weeks ago."

Analia gave me a look. "Seriously? With all the people that walk around here? Plus, it rained the other day. Trust me, it ain't the same gunk on the street now that was there a week ago."

I regarded her with a certain respect, as those were all excellent points. I was thinking about how there had still been residue near Esther's synagogue, but that'd been buried in the grass in an area that hadn't been cared for in a bit, and which didn't get a lot of foot traffic. It was all before the rain, too.

Taking a seat next to me, Analia said, "Anyhow, I figured I'd come up and give you a hand."

"Trying to audition for the apprenticeship?" I asked with a smirk.

Analia let out a long breath. "A'ight, here it is—I wanna be a Courser like mamí. I mean, I'm pretty much there anyhow, y'know? I'm always goin' with her on jobs, and I'm eighteen now, so I should be makin' my own money. And you are *literally* the only Courser mamí will trust to apprentice me, if you can b'lieve that."

I didn't, actually. I knew I was her first choice; I didn't realize I was also her only one. "Really? There are lots of other Coursers who are, frankly, better at this than I am."

"Yeah, but mamí don't know any of 'em that well—except for Tio Frank. I mean, yeah, she goes out drinking with some of y'all, but..."

Frank wasn't actually Analia's uncle, but rather Frank Paulino, the Courser Yolanda apprenticed with. He had trained about a dozen other Coursers in New York, including Abby, Yewhala, and Pete. In fact, he was the one who introduced Pete and Yewhala, and was best man at their wedding.

But he retired after Yolanda was licensed, so he wasn't an option to train Analia.

By way of stalling as much as anything, I asked, "I'm guessing you just graduated high school, right?"

She winced at that. "Not yet?"

I raised an eyebrow. "What does that mean?"

"I flunked physics. Sucks, 'cause I got A's in everything else. I'm takin' it again in summer school right now so I can get my diploma."

"What about college?"

She shook her head. "Nah. I wanna be a Courser."

I chuckled. "The two aren't mutually exclusive. Plus, you really need a fallback."

"What for?"

"You might get hurt. Look at your dad."

Analia stared at me as if it had never occurred to her that she might get badly injured on the job. This despite the fact that the dangers of the job were in front of her face every day in her father's missing leg.

Then again, I was her age when I decided that I only wanted to be a Courser.

I leaned back on the bench. "Lemme tell you a little story, Analia…"

I GAVE ANALIA A QUICK PRÉCIS OF HOW MY PARENTS GOT KILLED, AND that Hugues Baptiste was the Courser they'd hired to find out who'd animated the golem.

I got to the part where I'd left off with Katie: Miriam reassuring me that Joshua Roth had received a just punishment for his crime.

The front door to the Zerelli house opened, and Miriam and I turned to see Wardein Mike Zerelli walking out onto the porch. "Bram? What can I do for you? Is everything okay?"

"Uh, yeah, Mr. Zerelli, I just wanted to ask you something — do you know if Mr. Baptiste has taken on an apprentice yet?"

"He hasn't, no." Mike then smiled ruefully. "Funny you should ask that, I was just sending him his fee for the job, and part of what I put in the message accompanying that payment was a reminder that he *still* hasn't taken on an apprentice. If he doesn't get one soon, I may have to sanction him." Mike frowned, then. "Why do you ask?"

"You've been teaching me all kinds of stuff, Mr. Zerelli, and I really appreciate it. But I think my next step is to become a Courser."

"I thought your next step was med school," Miriam said.

Shaking my head, I said, "Someone else is gonna be where I am right now. I wanna be able to do for them what Mr. Baptiste did for me."

It was still early summer, and I spent the entirety of the rest of the season trying and failing to convince Hugues to make me his apprentice. I even had a great argument: It would get Mike off his back — a win-win! But he wouldn't go for it...

At one point in late August, about a week before I was supposed to go back to Harvard, Hugues talked to Aunt Esther, and after that, he invited me over to dinner with his wife and his then-nine-year-old daughter.

After a really yummy dinner — Hugues's wife Roseline made a fabulous beef tassot with black mushroom rice — the two of us went out onto the tiny patio of Hugues's tenth-floor apartment in Co-op City. A planned community built in the 1960s on the grounds of the old Freedomland U.S.A. theme park after the latter went bankrupt, Co-op City was made up of a mess of gray high-rise apartment buildings of similar designs in five sections. It probably looked futuristic when it opened in the late twentieth century and looked incredibly retro and monotone now.

"Look, child," Hugues said to me, "your parents, they wanted you to go to medical school, okay?"

"Well, yeah. But that was when they were alive, and I was gonna go into the family business and join their practice and eventually take it over so they could retire and take 'round-the-world cruises. But they're not gonna do that and I'm not gonna do that." I sighed and then told him what I told Mike: "If someone else goes through what I went through — and what the family of that poor woman on Palisade Avenue went through — then I wanted to be able to *do* something about it."

"Yeah, but what about what your parents wanted?"

"What do you mean?"

"They be payin' for it, and they want you to be a doctor, okay? So here's what we'll be doin'. You return to school, achieve your MD, become an actual doctor person, and then we shall speak about my training you. That's what is best, okay?"

"I WASN'T AT ALL OKAY WITH THAT," I TOLD ANALIA, "BUT I ALSO DIDN'T have a choice. The alternative was Hugues refusing me all together, and besides, this plan was Aunt Esther's."

"She's the rabbi, right?"

I nodded. "My beloved aunt *probably* figured that by the time I got back into the swing of things at Harvard, my righteous anger would've burned out, and I'd be back to being dedicated to becoming a doctor, and I'd forget all about this Courser stuff."

Analia laughed. "Well, *that* didn't happen."

"Yes and no. Hugues was right, it was what my parents wanted. So I spent the next six years at Harvard, got my MD, and then I became Hugues's apprentice."

"And now you're a Courser *and* a doctor," Analia said, nodding.

"Right. My fellow Coursers are pretty grateful for my medical skills when they get hurt in ways that are *really* hard to explain to your average Urgent Care or ER doctor." I smiled. "And sometimes you're the only one who believes a guy who says a wendigo bit his leg off."

"Right." Analia blew out a breath. "Well, look, I'm goin' for my adult black belt in the fall, and after that, *Kaicho* said he was gonna have me teachin' more, and *that'll* pay. So I'll be a'ight."

Before I could point out that that probably wasn't going to make her enough money to get her own place—it was barely gonna be enough to pay for her phone service and maybe food—I noticed something. Turning, I saw movement next to the Burstein Shul. I stood up.

And then I sat back down when I realized that it was just a large dog on a long lead. The dog was sniffing the sidewalk and the human holding the lead was now coming into view. They were both walking down 185th from Pinehurst Avenue to Fort Washington.

I sat back down. "False alarm."

"How *do* you beat a golem, anyhow?"

"It's actually both really easy and incredibly difficult. For starters, you can't beat it with any kind of weapon outside an RPG or a thermonuclear device."

She grinned. "I'm guessin' you ain't got one'a those in the bag?"

"No, plus the whole point of this exercise is to avoid collateral damage. Besides which, blowing up parks is generally frowned upon, especially ones full of kids."

"I dunno," she said, glancing back at the playground, "some'a them kids are *really* annoying…" She was still grinning, though, so I was *pretty* sure she was kidding.

"Anyhow, if you see the golem, you'll notice that it has three letters in Hebrew inscribed in its forehead. That word is emét, which means *truth*. To stop the golem, you erase the first of those three letters, at which point it says mét, which means—"

"A lie?"

I pointed at her and smiled. "Good guess, but no. It means *death*, and that'll make the golem disintegrate."

"You're right, that does sound easy."

"Yeah, but the trick is to get close enough to be able to do that. Considering that the golem is usually somewhere between seven and eight feet tall, and is superstrong and often violent, getting anywhere near its head is something of a challenge."

Waving her left hand back and forth, Analia asked, "Waitasec— seven and eight feet tall?"

"Yeah."

"Then why'd you think that dog was it a minute ago?"

Shrugging, I said, "I saw movement. Better to be safe and check it out than dismiss it before you know for sure. Besides, I said they're *usually* seven-to-eight feet tall. They're not always, and right now, the only person who's even seen this thing is the world's least reliable source."

"Who's that?"

I hesitated. "My client."

"Why'd you take the job if he ain't reliable?"

"The client is Joshua Roth."

Analia's eyes went wide. "The same dude that did the golem thing last time?"

I nodded.

"Damn. That's messed up."

"Tell me about it." My phone buzzed with a text message. It probably wasn't Bart, as he didn't strike me as the texting type, but it could've been somebody else important.

"Hang on," I said as I took the phone out of my pocket. Sure enough, it was a text message from Lyd.

"Got synagogues thief. Tried to unload at pawn shop on Bailey Ave. Local Jewish kid, believe it or not."

"They caught the bad guy," I told Analia as I was typing a reply to Lyd: "Good to know, but sorry that it's a Jewish kid. Sheesh."

"That's great," Analia said.

I shook my head. "Not entirely. It's not the neo-Nazi-type we were expecting—it's a Jewish kid. Might even be one of the congregants."

Lyd's text reply: "Yeah, I know. We got him at the 50."

I looked at Analia. "Okay, well, as nice as this is, it doesn't give us the golem, just who the golem's been going after. And based on what you found across the street, it's probably still around here somewhere."

I heard a loud crack of shattering glass and looked over at 185th to see that one of the second-floor windows in the shul had been broken from the inside, tiny shards cascading down onto the sidewalk. Miraculously, no one was right under it at the time. One woman was jogging down the sidewalk toward it, but she just crossed the street when she saw the broken glass without breaking stride.

I love this town…

There had to be someone inside doing that damage. Even if it wasn't the golem, we were being paid to protect the Heightsdale Association synagogues…

"Let's go," I said, getting to my feet.

With a bright smile, Analia got up, too. "You said 'let's'? I can help?"

I hadn't really thought it through, I just started thinking of this operation as a "we" thing kind of by default.

"Well," I said in reply, "if nothing else, you've got *way* better martial arts training than I do. And our odds are better to get near the thing's head if there's two of us to split the thing's focus."

"Great."

I started to move off, but Analia hesitated. "What about your bag?"

It was an understandable question. Nobody with a brain in their head would leave an unattended bag alone in a public park like this, both for the owner's fear of it being stolen and for everyone else's fear that it might have been left behind on purpose with something like a bomb in it.

I was about ten feet away at this point, while she was still standing in front of the bench. "See those characters sewn into the flap?"

She peered down at it. "Yeah."

"Now come over here."

She walked over to join me, and then took a look at the bench. "Where'd it go?"

I could still see it, of course, but the runes were set to not affect me. "If I'm near the bag, it's visible to everyone, but if I move three yards away from it, I'm the only one that can perceive it in any way. Nobody else can touch it or pick it up or even sit on it by mistake. I bought that after I dropped my old bag in Soundview Park chasing a cuco. Ran halfway across the park before I subdued the thing, and meanwhile, someone called the bomb squad about the abandoned bag."

"What's a cuco?"

"Ask your sister," I said with a chuckle. "Let's go."

There was no direct access from the park to 185th—the joys of all the hills and uneven ground—so we ran down the stairs to Fort Washington, and then around the corner.

The synagogue had three ornate doors in the front of the building, and all three were locked. "How the hell did it get in?" I asked as I yanked futilely on each of the doors.

"There's an entrance around the side," Analia said.

I shot her a look.

She shot me one right back. "I live six blocks away—I know my neighborhood, okay?"

"Okay." There was an alleyway between the shul and the huge apartment building next to it. Like every alley in town, it had a gate, but this one was unlocked with a busted handle, probably courtesy of our golem.

We both went in, walked down a narrow cracked cement walkway, past a Dumpster, to find two brown metal doors. One was closed and had a padlock on it. The other was ajar, about a quarter-way open inward, and had a large dent in its center.

Pointing at the partly open door, I said, "I'm gonna go out on a limb and say this is the entry point."

As I moved toward it, Analia right behind me, I was startled by the sound of rending metal.

Whirling to the left, I saw the other being ripped apart, which wasn't something you saw every day with a thick metal door designed by people who live in a big city and want to keep uninvited people from entering.

The door then flew across the alleyway and clattered against the brick wall of the apartment building.

A large—at least seven feet tall—featureless rusty-orange human body shape lumbered into the alley through the doorway.

"Featureless" wasn't entirely accurate: there were two recessed circles that passed for eyes, a horizontal slit that was sort of a mouth, and the Hebrew characters אמת etched in its forehead.

All we had to do was get close enough to erase the א. No problem.

"I'll go left," I said, "you go right. We'll see who he goes after—the other one tries to erase the character on the right."

Analia kept her eye on the golem, but cried out, "*What*? You said the *first* character!"

I closed my eyes and sighed and tried not to make a comment about gentiles. "In Hebrew, words go from right to left."

"For real? Like in Japanese?"

"Yeah."

"O-okay."

The golem chose that moment to lunge at Analia. She shifted left to get out of its way—easy enough to do even for someone untrained, as the big guy was kinda slow—but then she tried to palm-heel the thing in the head.

It made a kind of squelching noise, but was unaffected otherwise.

"Ew," Analia muttered as she backed up and then ran down the alley.

I dashed in the other direction, trying to see who it'd go after.

For a second, it didn't move, so I tried to get closer to it.

That got its attention. It turned and moved toward me even as I was slowly moving toward it.

Analia took advantage of it turning its back on her to do an impressive low sweep. She got down in a crouch with her left leg while her right leg was completely straight and swung around in an arc to take out the golem's legs.

At least, that was the theory. Her right ankle collided with the golem's leg with a yucky squelching sound, but the golem didn't lose its footing.

It did distract the thing, though, and it turned to see who had kicked it.

I was only a couple feet in front of the thing now, so I tried to take advantage of that to jump up and try to erase the character from the golem's head.

Naturally, my left knee chose that moment to buckle and send fiery streams of pain all up and down my leg.

Screaming in pain and collapsing to the uneven ground got the golem's attention away from Analia, and it turned and lifted its giant hands in an apparent attempt to pound me very hard on the head.

Given what it did to a metal door, I didn't like my chances. I tried to roll away, but my leg wouldn't cooperate, and I wound up curling into a ball on the pavement.

"Doc!" Analia cried out and leapt forward. She dove sideways, her left arm raised to protect her head and intercept the golem's fists.

I heard bones snap as she collapsed on top of me.

She rolled onto her back, crying out in pain also. I struggled to straighten up and defend myself.

But the golem was now wandering down the other end of the alley, which had a small wall. The golem climbed over the wall and continued onward out of sight. There was probably another alley on the other side, between the buildings on Fort Washington and the ones on the parallel street. For all I knew, it extended all the way to the next block up.

The pain in my knee was starting to subside—it was only incredibly painful now, not starbursts-in-the-eyes painful—and I was able to crawl over to where Analia was laying, tears streaking down her cheeks.

"Fuck, this *hurts*," she said in a ragged, sob-wracked voice. "Don't tell mamí I said, 'fuck,' okay? She'll kill me."

I checked out her arm, touching it gingerly, resulting in a wail of pain. "Yeah," I said, "pretty sure that's broken."

I tried to get to my feet and collapsed again. The knee was *not* going to be of use to me right now.

And the golem was gone, with neither of us in any shape to chase after it.

I pulled out my phone and called 911. While I waited for the ambulance—which was probably gonna come from the Allen Hospital up in Inwood right at the top of Manhattan island—I texted the bad news to Esther that we lost the golem, and also let the other Coursers on the job know where the golem was.

Then I texted Yolanda directly and let her know that Analia was hurt.

The response was not what I expected: "What the FUCK is she doing with YOU?"

I heard the sirens as I typed in my reply: "She came to Bennett Park to help me keep an eye on the temples here. You didn't send her?"

"Hell no I didn't send her!"

Oh boy…

Chapter 14

THE AMBULANCE THAT APPEARED ON 185TH BY THE MOUTH OF THE ALLEY was indeed from New York-Presbyterian's Allen Hospital, so I let Yolanda know where we were being taken. When the EMTs got into the alley, I identified myself as Doctor Abe Goldblume and told them about Analia's arm and my knee.

Nobody had asked me how Analia's arm got broken, or what we were doing behind a synagogue's alley, yet, but those questions would be forthcoming. I was already putting the cover story together as they looked over Analia. When they tried to get her up, they discovered that she had also injured her right ankle. The pain of trying to stand on it overwhelmed her, and she cried out and went into shock.

I hopped into the back of the ambulance with one EMT and the shocky Analia and got up to Allen in less than fifteen minutes. My bag was still back in Bennett Park, but I couldn't ask the EMTs to get it, as they couldn't perceive it, but neither could anyone else. It'd be safe until I had a chance to head back down there to fetch it.

Assuming I remembered, anyhow.

We were lucky in that the ER was at a slow point, which doesn't always happen. They took Analia right away, and I filled out her paperwork as best I could.

I was sitting in the waiting room, trying hard not to think about the last time I was in here, which was to visit Katie before she was discharged. Yolanda came storming in, which proved to be a great distraction from thinking about Katie, as my fellow Courser looked like she wanted to, as they say, choke a bitch.

She looked around, saw me, and came and sat down next to me. "She better not be dead, 'cause I'm gonna kill her."

"I'm sorry, Yolanda, I—"

She held up a hand. "Not your fault, Abe. My baby girl got a mind of her own. And yeah, I *know* she's eighteen now, but *damn*."

I looked around to make sure nobody was paying any attention to us, then said in a lower tone of voice, "What about Audubon?"

"That's why it took so long to get here—had to find someone to take over. Lucky for me, Frank was free."

"I thought he retired."

"He did, but he helps me out sometimes when I need an extra pair of hands. Shoulda asked him to sit on my damn daughter."

Holding up both hands almost defensively, I said, "I honestly thought you sent her up to Bennett Park to help me out."

"Hell, no. I didn't even tell her you was there, so I don't know how—" Then she closed her eyes and sighed. "But I told Kamilah. Great, now I gotta kill *both* my daughters."

"For what it's worth, she did really well—and, uh, she kinda saved my life."

"Kinda?"

"Okay, definitely. The golem was about to pound me on the head, and I was in agony from my knee."

"What happened to your knee?"

I sighed. "Twisted it chasing a dragon—or, rather, according to the other daughter you plan to murder, an imugi."

"Nah, I ain't gonna murder Kamilah. Much." She sighed. "And honestly? I normally woulda probably been fine with Analia helpin' you out today. But she's got a physics test Monday mornin', and I *know* she ain't studied for it yet. She already failed this class once, and I really don't want her goin' around without even a high school diploma."

"I get that."

"Doctor Goldblume?"

I looked up to see the same physician assistant who'd come out before to fill me in on Analia's progress. She was a short, slight woman with straight dark hair tied in a ponytail. Her name badge read BALASUBMRAMANIAN, and she insisted that we just call her "Becky," not entirely without reason.

"Oh, hi, Becky. Um, this is Yolanda Rodriguez, she's Analia's mother."

Becky brightened. "Oh, I'm glad you could make it. Analia's doing very well. She has several bone fractures in her left arm and right leg, and also two strained ligaments in her right ankle. You can go back and see her in a bit."

"I'm guessin' I can't bring any weapons back there?"

Eyes widening, Becky stammered. "Um, I don't think—"

"I'm kidding. Mostly."

"I hope so." Shuddering, she turned to me. "You can come back now, Doctor Goldblume."

Becky took me to a small enclosure and gave me a once-over: the usual checking of blood pressure and heart rate and temperature and such. She gave me privacy to remove my pants and put on a hospital gown, and then she properly examined my knee.

"How's the pain?" she asked.

"It's calmed down a lot—down to a dull throb."

She nodded. "All right, but I still think you should get an MRI."

"Let me guess, it'll be a few hours before it's available?"

Chuckling, she said, "It's almost like you work in an ER."

"Almost, yeah," I said with a wry grin. "Look, I've got a ton of stuff to do today, and it doesn't hurt *that* much, and I'm doing an overnight shift tonight at Montefiore. If it acts up again, I'm already set to be in a really-o-truly-o hospital for eight hours tonight. I mostly just wanted to make sure Analia was okay."

"I think that's acceptable. Let me go get your paperwork so you can sign out—you can put your pants back on, too."

I smiled gratefully. "*Thank* you, Becky. You're a lifesaver."

"I bet you say that to all the PA's."

"Nah, just the good ones."

She chuckled and left. I took off the gown and climbed back into my pants. I also checked my phone. There were three texts. One was from Yolanda saying she'd gone back to visit with Analia. One was from Abby Cornwell, saying there was no sign of the golem on Isham Street, about eight blocks south of where I was, and also where the synagogue she was guarding was located.

The third was from Robin Rosen, probably wondering why I hadn't gotten back to her about renting my downstairs apartment to Dolev.

"Bram, may I call please? It's important."

Okay, maybe it wasn't about her daughter's living situation. I texted back for her to give me a bit, as I suspected that any conversation I was going to have with her would not be ideally had while sitting in the middle of an emergency room.

I filled out the paperwork, then headed out. While walking, I texted Yolanda that I was leaving. Outside, there was a long stretch of sidewalk alongside the hospital on Broadway, and I found a spot against the fence to lean on. I texted Robin that now was a good time.

The phone rang with the generic ringtone, and I slid my finger across the screen, then put it to my ear. "Hey Robin."

"Bram, I'm sorry to bother you, but can you come over to our place?"

"Um, I guess so? You still in the same building on Arlington?"

"Building? Bram, we bought a house on Delafield when Hannah was born."

Shows what I know. "Right, sorry. What's this about?"

She hesitated. "Our son's been arrested."

My eyes widened. "What'd Saul do?"

"Well, apparently, he's the one who broke into the synagogues."

I almost dropped the phone. "Saul? He's only, like, twelve years old."

"Bram, he's seventeen."

I *really* need to start paying closer attention to my friends' kids' ages. "Oh."

"And we found some really weird stuff in his room. Can you come up here?"

This sounded more like a job for Miriam, but they called me. And the golem had been avoiding crowds, and the Burstein Shul was a crime scene now, so it and Hudson Heights were probably safe for the time being. And there were Coursers on all the other Heightsdale synagogues. So I could probably go do this.

"Yeah, okay," I said to Robin, "text me the address. I'll be up there soon as I can." If they were on Delafield Avenue, I just had to take the same bus that I would've taken home from here, only further north. And there was one coming up Broadway that was currently stopped at 218th Street.

"Thank you, Bram, we *really* appreciate it."

"No problem, Robin. See you guys soon." I ended the call and jogged across Broadway to the 219th Street stop. That was a mistake on two levels—one, if I'd just walked across, I'd still have made the bus, and two, the throbbing in my left knee went into overdrive.

By the time I got on the bus, I'd gotten the address, which was just a block away from the last stop on this bus line at 263rd Street and Riverdale Avenue. I took a seat in the back—while the bus was moderately full, it wasn't as densely packed on a Saturday afternoon as it would be during the week.

It took the better part of half an hour for the bus to make its way over the perpetual congestion that was the Broadway Bridge and through Kingsbridge and up the hill to Riverdale before finally arriving at my stop, which was all the way up by the College of Mount Saint Vincent at the north-western-most border of the Bronx. I spent that time texting Esther and Miriam and filling them in (and getting both their approval for doing this rather than continuing to keep an eye on two synagogues that probably weren't going to be targeted now). I also got updates from Abby, Yewhala, and Hugues, all of whom said there was no sign of the golem at all—not even residue like what Analia found. Both Yewhala and Abby had Rosenthal amulets, so they knew whereof they spoke. As for Hugues—well, my erstwhile mentor had more experience with golems than most, so I trusted his judgment even though he didn't have the same gadgets as the rest of us. Truthfully, Hugues had never been big on charms and amulets and talismans and the like—my use of them came out of growing up around the Zerellis—but he always got the job done.

I also texted Deet Galanter in the hopes that he'd tracked down either Ari or Steinmetz, but he hadn't.

My left knee buckled a bit when I got up to get off the bus at the last stop, but I straightened pretty quickly. I was definitely gonna need to have this looked at when I went to work tonight…

I walked down 263rd one block to Delafield Avenue. Robin and Joseph had a big two-story house near the corner, back about three car lengths from the street, with an immaculate privet hedge in front. I walked up the driveway to the steps that led to the front door and rang the bell, trying to pretend that my knee wasn't now throbbing.

Joseph answered the door. He was barefoot, wearing a plain blue T-shirt and denim shorts. He looked like someone had run over his puppy, which is probably what most parents would look like if their son was arrested for vandalizing holy places that are sacred to your friends and family.

"Thanks for coming, Bram."

He let me into their house with its central air, which was still welcome even on a low-humidity day like this. I'd spent the morning and early afternoon either outside or in a crowded ER or on a crowded bus, so a place that was actually cool and not full of people was a welcome relief.

I walked in to see a staircase right in front of me, with a hallway to the left side of it. That hallway had a set of French doors that were currently closed, and which probably led to their living room, and I could see that the far end of it opened up into what looked like a dining room.

A Keeshond came running down the hallway from the dining room and barked at me.

Joseph held up a hand. "Easy, Nachas."

I knelt down and let the pooch smell my hand. He sniffed it thoroughly, licked it twice, then turned and ran back into the dining room.

Joseph said, "Believe it or not, that means he likes you. Ignoring you is his primary expression of kindness. If he didn't like you, he'd be barking a lot more."

I stood upright a little too fast. Wincing, I tried not to cry out in pain.

"You okay?" Joseph put a hand on my shoulder.

"Fine," I lied. "Just some knee issues. It'll be okay."

Joseph didn't look convinced—and my talking through clenched teeth wasn't all that convincing anyhow—but he just led me up the carpeted staircase to the second floor.

There was another hallway upstairs that went down the center of the house, with three doors on either side. "Hannah's at camp, thankfully, so they don't have to deal with this," Joseph said.

Two of the doors were small, and I figured they were a bathroom and linen closet. The four open doors would all be listed as bedrooms if the house was ever on the market.

One looked like it belonged to a teenager, with lots of stuffed animals on the single bed, with a really nice painting of a dragon fighting a unicorn over it. The wall opposite the bed was decorated with posters of bands and anime characters I didn't recognize.

The next bedroom looked like two grownups were living in it as it had very few decorations, two dresser-drawers with jewelry boxes atop them, no stuffed animals, and a queen-sized bed. The third I was guessing had been Dolev's, then had been converted into a home office after she moved out, with two desks with computers on them, bookcases filled with law books, and a landline attached to the wall.

The fourth was where Robin was sitting. She too was barefoot, wearing a tank top and sweat shorts, and she sat on an unmade single bed. There was a giant bookcase on one wall that was filled with graphic novels and various other big paperbacks. The walls otherwise just had a large twelve-month calendar with writing scrawled on various dates, and a huge desk with a ton of stuff on it. This had to be Saul's room.

Robin stood up when I entered and pointed at the desk. "Hello, Bram. Will you please *look* at that?"

I did as she asked. I saw a jar half-filled with soil, a mostly empty bottle of spring water, a wad of orange clay, and a leatherbound book with words in Hebrew inscribed in gold on the cover. (My own Hebrew was rusty, as I hadn't practiced it much since my bar mitzvah.) There was also a silver pointer, and two sheets of paper with more words in I think Hebrew, but transliterated into the Roman alphabet.

"He created the golem, didn't he?" Robin asked.

I sighed and nodded my head. This was all the same stuff that Hugues found in Joshua Roth's room twelve years ago.

"I don't understand," Joseph said, "he was arrested for breaking into the synagogues."

"Yeah." This wasn't making any sense. We'd been assuming that whoever animated the golem was doing it to protect the synagogues and screwing it up the same way Roth did a dozen years ago.

Robin asked, "Could he possibly be using the golem to break into the temples? Is my son really that much of a little shit?"

"Robin," Joseph said chidingly.

"What?" Robin stared at her husband. "Bad enough he's doing Kabbalistic magick without any kind of consultation with the scholars, but using a golem *against* us? 'Little shit' is the *nicest* way I can describe him right now."

I pulled my phone out of my pocket. "I need to talk to the wardein."

Miriam answered on the first ring. "What's happening, Bram?"

"Well, it looks like Saul animated the golem and has been using it to rob the synagogues."

"Seriously?"

I nodded, then remembered I was on the phone. "Yup. I'm in Saul's bedroom looking at a desk covered in a golem animation kit."

"Grab everything, bring it here."

"Gotcha." I looked over at Joseph and Robin, who looked beyond stricken. "I gotta take all this stuff to Miriam."

"Please do," Joseph said calmly but urgently.

Much less calmly, Robin said, "I do *not* want this stuff in my house!"

"I don't blame you," I said dryly.

Miriam then said, "There should be something to track the golem—a spell or a charm."

"No charms or amulets," I said. I checked the desk drawers, but they just had typical teenager desk stuff: school supplies of various sorts, a passport, and a bunch of charging cables. None of it had anything to do with Kabbalistic magick.

"Send me a picture of what's on the desk," she said.

I pulled the phone from my ear, switched it to the camera, and took a picture of the desk, then texted it to her.

"Okay, got it," she said a few seconds later. "Let's see—dammit, the spell on the paper is just a transliteration of the animation spell."

"What about the book?" I asked.

"It's a biography of Rabbi Loew that was written in the eighteenth century. It's possible there's a tracking spell buried somewhere in there, and I'll dig around my copy of the book to see if it's there, but I doubt it."

I heard a phone ring. Joseph got up. "That's the office phone." He went out into the hallway, and a moment later I heard him say, "Joseph Weinberg. … What? … Um, okay. … Okay. … Okay. … You sure? Just her? … Wonderful. All right. Thank you, she'll be down there as soon as she can." He came back into Saul's bedroom, looking rather confused. "That was an officer at the 50th Precinct. Saul's invoked, and he wants you." He stared right at his wife.

"Not both of us?"

Joseph shook his head. "According to the officer, Saul said, 'I want my mom the shark. Dad only needs to come by if I need an accountant.'"

Okay, well, that confirmed that Robin was the criminal lawyer of the couple. Based on the accountant line, Joseph must have done tax or estate law or some such.

I still had Miriam on the line, and she said, "Bram, we need to find that golem. Can you go with Robin to talk to Saul?"

The volume on my phone was up loud enough that everyone in the room was able to hear everything she said anyhow, so I just looked at Robin expectantly.

Robin blinked. "I guess? I mean, I can bring you in as an associate or something."

"Good," Miriam said. "Your conversation will be privileged, so no one will be eavesdropping. We've *got* to find that golem before someone else gets hurt."

"Someone *else*?" Joseph asked.

I said quickly, "It attacked the Burstein Shul down on 185th. Me and another Courser tried to stop it and failed; she got hurt." Analia wasn't really a Courser, of course, but that was the easiest way to explain it.

"Oh my goodness." Robin shook her head. "I can't *believe* this is happening." She walked out toward the hallway. "I need to change into something more presentable."

I looked down at my jeans that were scuffed and stained from fighting the golem. "Yeah, me, too. I'm gonna take this stuff and get changed. Meet at the five-oh in half an hour?"

Robin nodded, and then continued to her bedroom.

Joseph found me a shopping bag and I put all the stuff on Saul's desk into it. He then walked me downstairs. Nachas was waiting for us at the bottom of the stairs, running around in circles.

"I think he wants to go out," Joseph said with a sigh. He was barefoot, but he slipped into a pair of moccasins and also grabbed a lead that was on a hook by the door.

"I'm sorry about this." Then I remembered the voicemail Robin had left for me about their daughter's need for a new place to live. "And hey, I might be able to help Dolev out. When this mishegoss is all over, let's talk about it, okay?"

Breathing a sigh of relief, Joseph said, "Thank you. Dolev's been all beside herself."

We both left the house. Nachas led Joseph down Delafield toward 261st, while I went up to 263rd to catch the bus home. I checked my phone, and getting a car service would take seven minutes to arrive and another ten minutes to get to my house. There was a bus at 263rd waiting for me and I got on it. It'd get me home sooner than the car service would, and it was cheaper besides.

Of course, I could've charged the car service to Roth. Maybe I would anyhow…

WHEN I GOT ON THE BUS, I TOOK A SEAT BY THE BACK DOOR AND PULLED out my phone. I hadn't checked my email since just before I left the house to head to Bennett Park—I probably should've while I was sitting in the waiting room of the Allen Hospital ER, but I was too busy being in pain and worrying about Analia.

To my great glee, one of the emails was a reply from Jimin Choi, one of the people I'd e-mailed during my real-estate research of the houses around Bart Jackson's place. Best of all, Choi provided me with even more information than I was hoping for. This would be useful for Bart, though whether or not it was good news or bad news would really be up to him.

Still, at least one of my cases was progressing nicely.

The bus dropped me off across the street from the café where Katie and I had our one and only date. To my disappointment, I realized that there was no way I was gonna get to sit with her today. Mind you, that had always been a possibility—there was every chance that I would've spent the entire day sitting in Bennett Park—but it still hurt that I'd miss yet another day to be with her.

First, I went to Miriam's place and dropped off the shopping bag full of golem stuff. As I put the bag on the sofa in her living room, she asked, "You okay?"

"I'm fine," I lied.

Which she, of course, saw right through. "You're not fine, you're limping, and you look like you haven't eaten all day."

"I'm limping because my knee's still a mess, and I look like I haven't eaten all day because I haven't eaten all day."

She pointed at her kitchen. "There's a Tupperware in the fridge with some mac and cheese I made last night for the bitch session."

I smirked. Once a month, a bunch of the local magick-users got together at Miriam's place to complain about things. I was half-convinced that they mostly complained about what pains in the ass Coursers are, but Miriam was too polite to say that out loud to me. The reason I was only half-convinced of that was because Miriam wasn't usually *that* polite, at least not to me, as we'd been best friends for far too long.

I took the Tupperware home with me. As I went inside my building, I stared at the door to Rebekah's old apartment.

Yeah, I needed to let Dolev move in there. It was time to move the hell on.

I just had to actually go inside and clean the place out.

I told Joseph we'd talk about it when this was all over, and that was when I would think about cleaning the apartment out. Right now, I had places to be.

Going upstairs, I was greeted by a Maine Coon who was obviously *starving to death*, so I refilled Mittens's food and water bowls after putting the Tupperware in the microwave.

Then I went into the bedroom to see what I had by way of nice clothes to wear as a lawyer's associate.

I didn't own any ties anymore—all the ones I had when I was younger were long gone—but it was the middle of summer, so I figured I could get away with a button-down shirt and khakis. I found a not-too-wrinkled blue shirt and light green pants and changed into them.

Footwear was a bigger issue. I used to have a pair of nice shoes, but they got eaten by a Massacooramaan. Last winter, the Sookdeo family in Wakefield hired me to be at their daughter's wedding in case the monster in question decided to crash the party. Since Massacooramaans are creatures of water, and the wedding was on City Island, it was a significant risk. Sure enough, the giant hairy creature—imagine Bigfoot, but with smelly wet fur—showed up at the reception. I was able to get rid of it, but not until the hairball ate my shoes. I hadn't gotten around to replacing them, mostly because this was the first time since then that I had had occasion to dress formally.

I did find a pair of boots in the back of my closet, which were all dusty, but a damp paper towel took care of that.

There was no way I was driving down to the five-oh—parking near police precincts is damn near impossible—so I ordered a car service on my phone while I wolfed down the mac and cheese.

By the time the car dropped me at the precinct, I'd gotten a text from Robin saying she was on her way, which meant I didn't have to worry about being late, at least. So I stood like an idiot on the corner of Kingsbridge Avenue and 236th Street waiting for her.

Ten minutes later, I finally saw her walking down Kingsbridge toward me. She was barely recognizable as the same person I had seen in her son's bedroom. She'd changed into a beige suit with a white blouse, a pearl necklace, and high heels. Her hair was loose, and she had put on a bit of makeup—just some eyeliner and a light amount of lipstick.

As she came up to me, she said, "Sorry I took so long, I couldn't find a place to park."

I kindly refrained from telling her how and why I took a car service down, and instead followed her through the double glass doors wedged into the corner of the big boxy building. We walked up the four metal-rimmed stairs and then through the creaky wooden doors to the reception area, moving past about half a dozen plaques for those officers who fell in the line of duty.

Facing the large white wall with the five-oh's insignia painted on it was the main desk, behind which sat a balding white guy with a thick mustache and sergeant's stripes on his sleeve.

As soon as we'd walked through the glass doors, Robin's entire affect had changed. Her pace had gone from a casual stroll to a determined stride, her heels clacking sharply on the linoleum floor. Her face had completely hardened, and when the sergeant looked up at her, she spoke about half an octave lower than she normally did.

"Robin Rosen, attorney for Saul Weinberg. This is my associate, Mr. Gold. I'm here to talk to my client."

The sergeant, whose nameplate read O'REILLY, pointed at a wooden bench down the corridor from the desk. "You and your flunky have a seat, Ms. Rosen. We'll let you know when your client's up from holding."

Robin put her hands on her hips. "He's not in an interview room?"

Sergeant O'Reilly rolled his eyes. "Not yet. We ain't gonna have some asshole takin' up valuable interview room space while we wait for his lawyer to deign to show up. Believe it or not, there's other stuff goin' on here today. Have a seat."

"I need to see my client's arrest report while I wait."

O'Reilly kept pointing at the bench. "Fine. Have a seat."

The bench in question had three people sitting on it, none of whom looked happy. Then again, if they were on a waiting room bench in a police precinct, it was unlikely that they were there for a joyous reason.

Robin declined to sit; instead she stood next to the bench, arms folded, and glared at the sergeant. Amazingly, he didn't turn into a pillar of salt under her withering gaze, but it wasn't for lack of trying on that gaze's part.

Me, I sat, as the alternative was putting more strain on my knee. I pulled out my phone and saw a text from Deet: "Still nothing from Steinmetz. I just tried calling Ari and his voicemail is full, so that's completely not encouraging. I'll keep at it, though."

Two of the other three people on the bench were fetched to be brought back into the bullpen by uniformed officers, while a third got up when someone came out. They hugged and left in silence. At some point, an officer came in and went to O'Reilly's desk with a file folder. The sergeant pointed at Robin—still glowering at the desk—and the officer handed the folder to her. From that point on, she read through its contents, sparing O'Reilly from her pitiless stare.

Two other people came in, talked to the sergeant, and then joined me on the bench. No eye contact was made at any point.

Some time later, Robin came over to me, but still didn't sit down. "You're not gonna believe this. Not only did they catch my idiot son trying to pawn the yad from our synagogue, but they also found his prints at Spuyten Duyvil, so even if the pawn shop hadn't called it in, they'd have gone after him anyhow."

I frowned. "They have his prints on file?"

She nodded. "We had a break-in a few months back—client of mine who was pissed that I didn't get him off sent some bozos to vandalize the house. They took all our prints for reference samples, and the case is still open."

Finally, O'Reilly took a phone call, then said, "Ms. Rosen, you guys are up. Someone'll take you back in a minute."

"About time," Robin said, closing the folder.

A uniformed officer—thankfully, not one I knew, as it would've been really embarrassing if one of them saw me pretending to be some kind of legal representative when they already thought of me as a quasi-private investigator—came out and led us back to an interview room.

Unlocking the door, the officer silently held it open, then closed and locked it behind us.

Sitting behind the tiny table was Saul Weinberg, who shared his father's wide nose and mousy brown hair, but had his mother's penetrating hazel eyes. He also looked surprisingly bored as he sat in an interview room handcuffed to the table, which was not the look I was expecting from someone so young who'd been arrested.

"So," he said without preamble, "you gettin' me off this bullshit charge or what?" He sounded exactly like a teenager—which was, to be fair, the case—who had done something minor and was waiting to get chewed out by his mother before going back to playing with his phone or whatever—which was very very much *not* the case.

"How, exactly, am I supposed to do that, Saul?"

Waving his non-handcuffed hand around, Saul said, "I dunno. Do that lawyer thing you do."

"You were trying to pawn an item stolen from our synagogue."

He shrugged. "They don't know how I got that."

"They also have your fingerprints at the Spuyten Duyvil Temple, which you've never set foot in, as far as I know. And your prints are all over our yad, and you haven't done a Torah reading since your bar mitzvah. That's, at the very least, probable cause to check your DNA, and I've got no grounds to object. I'm going to go out on a limb and say that your dumb ass was too stupid to clean up the blood you left behind at Spuyten Duyvil."

I held in a chuckle. Robin had been in lawyer mode right up to that last sentence, when she reverted to being Saul's mother rather than Saul's attorney.

"Oh come on, you've gotten assholes off on way worse than this," Saul said.

"Due to lack of evidence, Saul, not because I have any kind of superpowers."

Saul rolled his eyes. "Well, that's some bullshit."

Looking to the ceiling in supplication, Robin said, "How can someone who animated a golem be so stupid?"

"I dunno," I muttered, remembering Roth, "seems to be a prerequisite."

Apparently noticing me for the first time, Saul stared at me in much the same way that you stare at a fly that has died of drowning in your soup. "Who's *this* asshole?"

Robin glared at her son. "Of all the people in this room, kiddo, you're the last one who should be casting aspersions on others."

"Fine, who's this *guy*?"

I chuckled. "Among other things, I'm the one who confiscated the little golem assembly pieces on your desk."

"Hey!" Saul made as if to get up, then belatedly remembered that he was handcuffed to the table and sat violently back down with a thud on the plastic chair. "You ain't got no right to do that!"

"Actually, I do, since I confiscated it on behalf of the Wardein of the Bronx."

"What the fuck is a war-deen?"

I sighed. "Only the person in charge of regulating magickal activity in the region of her responsibility. In other words, someone you should be familiar with if you're gonna go around wielding Kabbalistic magick."

Robin was shaking her head. "What the hell were you *thinking*, Saul?"

"I was thinkin' I could use the help of somebody big and strong who'd do what I said. Pretty damn good accomplice, y'know?"

In a tighter voice, Robin said, "You're referring to the golem as your 'accomplice,' and you're wondering why I'm having trouble with the concept of just getting you off?"

"And," I added, "it isn't just the NYPD you got problems with. 'Cause once they're done with you, the wardein's gonna wanna have words with you, just like she did the last schmuck who thought animating a golem was a great idea. If you want that conversation to go well, you'll help me out right now."

Robin turned to look at me with confusion. "What happened to the last schmuck?"

"Well, unlike your son here, he was actually repentant and sorry for what he did, so he just had his memories messed with so he couldn't re-create the golem."

Now Robin regarded Saul with a look of fury. "And if he's not repentant?"

"That usually runs to things like exile to another dimension."

Saul chuckled. "Shyeah, right. Don't give me that bullshit."

"You really think that people can just go around and animate golems without consequences?" I asked. "You think you're the only one who tried something like this? The only one in your lifetime? You don't think it's regulated? You don't think there's consequences for abusing this kinda power?"

"Go fuck yourself."

Robin said, "Listen to me, you stupid jackass, I can do absolutely *nothing* to help you until you stop acting like an abusive jerk and start acting like someone who wants to help himself get out of trouble."

"I thought getting you to be my mouthpiece would do that," Saul said, sulking.

"Fine." She turned to look at me. "What can my client do to help himself here?"

I was looking at Saul as I answered. "Tell me how to track the golem."

"Why would I do that?"

"Well, two reasons. One, the golem was last seen wandering around Washington Heights, and it could hurt someone without you nearby to control it. Two, it'll make it more likely that the wardein won't go hard on you."

Saul leaned forward, sneering at me. "I think you're makin' this war-deen shit up, and I could give a fuck what the golem does, long as it keeps trashin' those Heightsdale fuckers."

"So you *were* specifically going after the synagogues in the association," I said.

"Why?" Robin asked. "The association does good work!"

Saul stared at his mother like she was insane. "Seriously? The bastards wouldn't let me come back as a camp counselor after that first year! It was total bullshit!"

I blinked. I had to admit, I was kinda hoping for something a bit less — stupid? Petty? "Seriously? You animated a devastatingly powerful creature because you didn't get your old summer job back?"

Robin put her hands palms-down on the table, and based on the look on her face, she did that to keep herself from hauling off and belting her kid. "You didn't get that job back because three kids got hurt on your watch that first year!"

"That wasn't my fault!"

Clearly, this wasn't going anywhere useful for me. I shook my head and got up from my chair.

Robin whirled to look up at me. "Bram?"

"There's nothing I can do here. You're on your own, kid."

I turned to leave.

It was Rebekah all over again. No compassion, no guilt, no remorse at what he'd done. Hell, it was worse than Rebekah — she did what she did because she thought she had been righting an ancient wrong. She'd gone about it in the worst possible way, but it at least started out from a good place.

So had Roth, if it came to that. He'd been trying to use the golem for what it was supposed to have been created for: to protect Jews.

This little pischer? He was bitchy because he didn't get rehired to do a job he sucked at. He was worse than Rebekah, worse than Roth.

And I hadn't thought either was possible.

I was done here. I knocked on the door to the interview room so the officer could unlock it and let me out. I silently strode past him and through the bullpen back to the front door, using my phone to summon another car to take me home as I did so. I had just enough time to go home and change before hopping in my car and driving back to Bennett Park to retrieve my duffel bag, finally, and then head over to Montefiore for my shift. At some point in there I texted Miriam to bring her up to speed.

My ER shift was as crazed as usual on a Saturday night. I barely had time to think, which was good as far as thinking went. Those fleetingly rare occasions when I did have that time resulted in annoyingly dark thoughts. About Rebekah, about Saul, about Roth, about myself, and about Katie.

And there was still a golem running loose.

It was bad as far as my health went, as there just wasn't time to do an MRI on my balky knee. There wasn't even really time to do an X-ray. However, Doctor Ahuja took a quick look at it during one of those few breaks in the action, and she was fairly certain I just strained my ACL. By the time my shift ended at four a.m., she'd written me a prescription for the heavy-duty ibuprofen.

After signing out and saying goodbye to the nurses at four, I looked at my phone and found several text messages that had been left during my shift.

Two were from Robin, the first telling me that she was accompanying Saul to his arraignment, the second saying that he was released under her care and had been charged with theft, criminal trespass, breaking-and-entering, and possession of stolen goods. I was actually really impressed that they released him without bail, but it was his first offense, he was a juvenile, and his lawyer was also a) his Mom and b) a respected criminal attorney who was trusted by the judiciary and the DA's office. Part of me wondered what the over/under was on how long they'd let the little twerp continue to live under their roof, but that was a question for another day…

Between those two texts was one from Miriam, replying to my text filling her in, and also assuring me that she'd deal with Saul in due course, which didn't bode well for the young Mr. Weinberg.

There were also a series of texts in the chain that Esther had started with me, Yolanda, Hugues, Abby, and Yewhala, with all of them reporting that there was no sign of the golem—in Yolanda's case, passing on a message from Frank, who hated texting.

And, finally, one was from Deet Galanter: "Finally got in touch with Steinmetz. Have I got a divination spell for you!"

Chapter 16

ONE OF THE JOYS OF BEING A DOCTOR WHO WORKS IN A HOSPITAL IS THAT you have access to the hospital's pharmacy with a pharmacist on duty twenty-four hours a day. So even at four a.m. on a Sunday morning, I was able to fill Ahuja's scrip and take the good stuff right away. As I headed to my car, I texted Deet: "Thank you very much, call me when you see this, and if you haven't cast the spell yet, please CAST THE SPELL."

As soon as I got home, I collapsed on my bed, not even bothering to take my clothes off. Or feed the cat. Or grab my mail, which I had also neglected to do when I came home from the five-oh.

It felt like I'd only just gotten to sleep when the phone rang, but it was actually just after eight a.m., which meant I'd slept for three-and-a-half hours, apparently.

It was Deet. I slid my finger across the screen, put the phone to my ear, and said without preamble, "Please tell me you cast the spell."

"Cast what spell?"

"Deet…" I was *not* in the mood for this.

"I not only cast the spell, I cast it twice — once about an hour after I texted you, which was also an hour after Steinmetz got back to me, and again five minutes ago. Your golem has been hanging out in a section of Fort Tryon Park all night."

That park was just north of the Burstein Shul, so it hadn't gone far, at least. Last time I'd been in that park was four months ago when I had to hunt down and return a unicorn. As I'd indicated to Toscano, unicorns were not the fluffy fun creatures of joy and rainbows pop-culture would lead you to believe. That surly, violent beast had broken out of the fifteenth-century binding spell from the famous tapestry hanging in the Cloisters, a branch of the Metropolitan Museum of Art located at the highest point in the park.

"Thanks, Deet." Then I frowned. "Why an hour?"

"Took that long to find all the components in the toxic landfill I laughingly refer to as my storage unit. Which ain't cheap, by the by — the components, not the storage unit. I mean, the storage unit ain't cheap, either, but that's my problem, not yours. Your problem is that the vial of still water, the clay, and the rune-covered yad are all expensive as hell, plus I used the last two charges on my Loewe charm, so I gotta replace that, and I'm gonna have to bill you for *all* that."

"I told you, it's fine." I tried to sound convincing when I said that, though I was feeling a lot less cranky toward Roth than I had been. Either way, I needed that spell cast, so money was no object here. I mean, it *was* an object, but it was Roth's object, and maybe Esther's and the Heightsdale Association's, not mine.

"Okele-dokele. I'll cobble together an invoice and send it in a bit."

I winced. "Hang off on that, Deet. We haven't actually captured the stupid thing yet, and I wanna keep that spell in reserve in case I screw this up and we have to find it all over again."

"That's a reasonable point. I mean, this is *you*. You're pretty likely to screw this up at least once more."

I rolled my eyes. "Thanks for the vote of confidence. I gotta get myself together and go after this thing."

"I'll text you the map spot."

"Thanks, Deet. Love to Sam!"

After that call ended, I clambered out of bed and started the coffeemaker going. Then I changed into different clothes that I hadn't slept in: a long-sleeved Harvard shirt that was still as light as a T-shirt, mainly in deference to the fact that I was going after a creature made out of clay, and it had a shot at getting messy, as well as a fresh pair of jeans, and my heavy-tread boots. Given the weather, I would've rather a T-shirt and shorts and sandals, but, again, messy.

I washed my hands and face. A shower would have to wait — I didn't want to let the golem run around loose in the park any longer than necessary. Besides, I was likely to just need another shower when it was all said and done.

While I waited for the coffee to finish brewing, I called Esther and brought her up to speed.

"Based on my first encounter, I'm gonna need an extra set of hands—and feet—on this one. Can we keep Yolanda on the job so she can give me a hand? She's got a pet dragon, too."

"With you, what does she need, if she's got a dragon?"

I chuckled. "She probably doesn't, but this was my gig first, so…"

"It's fine. The compensation, we'll work out later."

"Great."

Deet had finally texted me a map with the location of the golem. It was in a clearing that was right near the entrance to the park on Broadway near Sherman Avenue.

I gulped down some coffee, and then called Yolanda.

Carlos's voice sounded on the other end. "Hey, Doc."

"Hiya, Carlos. Is your wife around?"

"She's just brushing her teeth after her shower. Oh, wait, here she is now." His voice got a bit distant as he moved the phone away from his mouth. "It's Abe Goldblume."

Then Yolanda came on the line. "Heya."

"Hiya. How's Analia doing?"

"She's home. She got a cast on her arm, a boot on her leg, and my foot up her ass. Can you believe that girl was tryin' to weasel outta the physics test 'cause'a this?"

I swallowed more coffee. "Well, she *does* have broken bones."

"I don't care if she's in a damn coma, she's takin' that test tomorrow!"

"Well, can I ease your troubled mind by offering you more work?"

Yolanda's tone immediately changed from pissed-off-Mom to happy-friend. "You can offer me work any damn time you want, Abe. Gonna need bail money for when I finally snap and kill my daughter. What's the gig?"

"Same gig, really. The golem's been located in Fort Tryon Park, and I could use some help subduing it. If you and Magellan could meet me at Broadway and Sherman in about twenty minutes?"

"It might be a little longer—it's Sunday, the buses don't run that often—but I'll get there fast as I can."

"Great! And wear something you don't mind getting messy—we're basically going after ambulatory mud here." I hesitated, then decided to go ahead and say it. "Look, I wanna say I'm sorry again about being such a putz about Analia being my apprentice. Once all her bones are healed up, we should talk about me taking her on."

"Assuming I ain't strangled her to death by then, sure."

I chuckled. "Okay, then. See you and the dragon soon!"

Mentioning Magellan reminded me that I owed Bart Jackson a phone call. I poured some more coffee into a travel mug and called Bart on my way downstairs.

Surprisingly, after four rings, I got the familiar voicemail message: "This is Bart. Either I can't come to the phone right now or I don't feel like talking on the phone right now. Say your piece after the beep, and I'll ring you back when I feel like it."

It was Sunday morning, so he could've been at church. He said he wasn't going to church much these days, but maybe today was one of those rare occasions.

Or maybe he was in the bathroom. Or just didn't feel like answering the phone.

After the beep, I said, "Bart, it's Bram Gold. I have some news. Call me back when you get a chance, please. And don't worry if you get voicemail, it'll just mean I'm too busy fighting a golem to answer my phone."

I ended the call just as I walked out my front door to a blast of hot, humid air. It felt like it was about ten degrees hotter than it had been yesterday. And here I was in a long-sleeved shirt and boots. Sigh.

I got into my Corolla, hoping the AC would kick in soon, wondering if Bart would think I was kidding about the golem.

Honestly, I kinda wish I was…

Getting there was pretty straightforward — Sunday morning was one of the few occasions when New York City was generally free of awful traffic — and I left a voicemail for Miriam filling her in as I drove. I wondered what *she* was doing on a Sunday morning. And I shuddered at the possibility of dealing with Saul Weinberg being one of them.

Parking was blessedly easy, as all the spots that had meters on them six days a week were free to park at on Sundays. I was able to slide between an SUV and a mini-Cooper on Broadway, just a block south of the entrance.

I got out of the car, beeped it locked, and walked up Broadway on the western side of the street, which had a short wall that separated the park from the sidewalk. To my immediate left on the other side of that wall was a big clearing. Past that was a big hill, and if I looked up, I could see the stone bell tower that sat atop the Cloisters.

As I arrived at the break in the wall that served as a park entrance near Sherman Avenue, I saw a bus pull into the stop on the eastern side of the street. Yolanda disembarked, a gigunda purse over her right shoulder. She was wearing a plain blue T-shirt that had a couple of stains on it and leggings that looked a bit worn.

She waved when she saw me, then jogged across the street to meet up with me.

Grinning, I said, "I sure hope there's a dragon in your purse."

"Yeah, I just gotta wake him up. He's gonna hate that. By the way, I used up all my transit karma—the bus was just pullin' in when I got to the stop. Next one ain't for another twenty minutes *at least*."

In retrospect, I should've offered to drive down the extra twenty blocks or so to pick her up at her place. But it worked out okay, so I just got down to business: "Our best bet is for all three of us to distract it from different directions and hope that you or I can stop it, which we do by—"

"Erasing the first character in the word written on its forehead, Analia told me. She also said it's the one on the right because it's written in some weird-ass language?"

Yolanda had been having a rough weekend, so I decided not to snidely point out that Hebrew existed *way* before English was a gleam in the Anglo-Saxons' eyes. Instead, I just said, "Yeah, the one on the right."

"Okay. I got me a Maccelli charm with one charge left. Kamilah said it prob'ly won't work, but it might, so I figure it's worth a shot."

Maccelli charms were designed to freeze animated corpses. Strictly speaking, golems weren't that, but as she noted, it was worth a shot.

Before I could say any of that out loud, I heard a loud scream from inside the park.

"Crap," I muttered and turned and ran between the two posts that flanked the park entrance.

Yolanda trailed behind me but caught up and then ran past me. As I struggled to keep up, I remembered the fact that before she was a cross-fit instructor, she was a gym teacher at Cardinal Marini High School. She was in *way* better shape than me, even if I hadn't had a bum knee.

Smoke was starting to puff out from her purse, and I had the feeling that the act of Yolanda running had woken Magellan up. If he was cranky about that, I really hoped he took it out on the golem and not me…

Fort Tryon Park was built on several big hills. This section was at the bottom of a couple of them: a big more-or-less rectangular grass clearing surrounded on two sides by hills, one by trees, and one by Broadway. There was a pathway that circumnavigated the clearing, and I saw the golem lumbering after a guy in a tank top, shorts, sneakers, and a sweatband on his head, who was screaming as he ran away from it.

Suddenly, a small green form burst forth from Yolanda's purse and flew into the air. That was Magellan. Unlike the imugi in Bart's back yard, Magellan was small enough to fit in Yolanda's (to be fair, very large) purse and also had four limbs and wings.

Oh, and he breathed fire.

Magellan, now airborne, flew alongside Yolanda, who pointed at the golem and said, "Go get 'im, Magellan!"

Making a weird braying noise, the dragon flew forward toward the large clay creature and exhaled a stream of fire at it.

That, at the very least, got the thing to stop menacing the jogger. Unfortunately, that's all it did, as the fire didn't seem to have any impact on the creature. Still, the golem stopped and turned to face Magellan. This allowed the jogger to get his bearings and then run like hell toward one of the paths up a steep hill.

He was gonna have a fun story to tell his colleagues at work. Or his family over dinner. Or to post to his social media. Or to tell his probably skeptical therapist.

Magellan dove in for another shot, but this time the golem backhanded the dragon, and he went flying toward one of the trees.

Yolanda didn't even break stride, running right up to the golem, then ducking under its attempt to do the same thing to her that it did to Magellan.

Well, if she wasn't gonna be worried about the little dragon, then I wasn't, either.

Sure enough, I heard a "mneh!" sound and Magellan was now flying back toward the golem. He didn't look hurt. He *did* look pissed.

I ran around to try to get behind the golem, figuring that if Magellan and Yolanda could distract it, I could jump up onto its back and erase the א from its forehead.

Once I got about ten feet away, I started running right toward it.

This was a decent plan, all things considered, but I failed to take a cheesed-off dragon into account. Magellan was now flitting about the golem's head, shooting flames right at its upper torso—including the very spot I wanted to jump onto.

I skidded to a stop and almost bumped into the golem's back.

The golem was flailing at Magellan, but it moved so slowly, and Magellan was now wise enough, that nothing landed.

I looked over at Yolanda, who was also keeping her distance lest her dragon burn her alive. "Maybe now with the charm?" I said.

Nodding, she opened her purse and dug around inside.

The golem then got a lucky shot in on the dragon, and Magellan went flying across toward one of the rocky outcroppings that was the side of a hill.

I was still behind it, so I took a deep breath and leapt toward the thing's back.

The plan was to wrap my arms around its throat and my legs around its chest. I'd hold on with my right arm and both legs and use my left hand to erase the א.

Like the plan to use Magellan to distract the golem, it was a good plan in theory that failed a bit in execution. In this case, my stupid knee—which had been fine right up until that nanosecond—decided to buckle, and instead of jumping up to the thing's neck, I only got about as high as his thoracic region.

Wrapping my arms around the golem's chest, I felt my right arm and both legs go squelch against the soft clay—but my left arm didn't. The left side of the golem's chest was hard as a rock.

That was the same part of the creature's chest that Magellan had breathed fire on.

Yolanda had finally liberated the Maccelli charm from her purse and was holding it out at the golem.

The golem, pretty much ignoring the schmuck clinging to its back, started stalking toward her, completely unaffected by the charm.

"Dammit!" Yolanda dropped the now-defunct charm onto the ground and turned and ran.

Magellan chose that moment to reappear and open his mouth to breathe lots of fire.

I was too low down on the creature's back to reach its forehead, and I wasn't doing any good just hanging there. Now I was in danger of being crispy fried. Luckily, Yolanda had led the golem off the paved path that circumnavigated the grass, so when I let go of the golem and fell on my ass, it was on soft dirt and grass instead of hard pavement.

From my position on my gluteus maximus, I noticed that the golem's left arm wasn't really moving all that much, either. It was using its right arm to block the dragon's fire from reaching its head as it continued to run toward the center of the clearing.

Apparently, dragon fire baked the clay enough to harden it.

Having no idea if the dragon could actually understand me or not, I cried out, "Magellan, go for its legs!"

The dragon ignored me. Yolanda turned around and was now jogging backward—she didn't have to go that fast, as the golem was lumbering slowly. "Magellan!"

At that, the little guy *did* respond, flying up above the golem's head and turning in midair to look at her.

She pointed at the golem's legs as she continued to jog backward.

The golem was gaining on her, and I really hoped that Magellan followed what she was suggesting.

Sure enough, the dragon swooped down and let out a *huge* plume of flame below the golem's waist.

For about two seconds, anyhow—after that, the fire started to sputter and die out, and Magellan began to cough.

However, the damage was done. The golem's legs had petrified. Its right arm pinwheeled, and the creature fell forward, crashing to the grass with a squelchy thud.

Clambering to my feet, ignoring the pain shooting through my left knee, I dashed to the fallen golem in a limping run.

It was trying to get up, but its left arm was as useless as its legs, so it had no leverage as it was just using its right arm.

Magellan had now landed at Yolanda's feet and was still coughing, smoke puffing out of his nostrils. Yolanda reached down to pick him up.

As the golem struggled to rise I moved to stand in front of it. It was looking up as it strained, giving me a perfect shot.

I reached down and dug my finger into its forehead right over the א and then shoved my finger downward, scraping out the outermost bit of clay, and removing that character.

Backing up, I whipped my right hand downward, causing the clay to scatter on the grass.

The golem's forehead now just had מת on it. Instead of *truth*, it said *death*.

A moment later, the golem stopped struggling to rise and fully collapsed to the ground. A moment after that, it started to disintegrate, the clay hardening (or continuing to harden for the parts Magellan had breathed on) and then crumbling to a large pile of rust-colored dust.

I leaned my head back, closed my eyes, and let out a long, relieved sigh.

Then I looked over at Yolanda, who now had a dragon draped around her neck, like a large scaly cat, head resting on her left shoulder, rear limbs dangling off her right shoulder.

"Glad *that's* over," she said.

"Yeah." I indicated Magellan with my head. "He okay?"

She nodded. "Just ran outta gas. Too much fire all at once. He'll take a nap, eat a few apples, and he'll be back to havin' his usual bad breath in a few hours."

There was golem dust on my right arm, most of the front of my shirt, and the front of my pants. After using my left hand to wipe the dust off my right arm, I pulled my phone out and dashed off a quick text to Esther that just said, "Golem is toast."

Yolanda stared down at the dust pile on the grass. "What do we do with that?"

I shrugged. "Nothing *to* do. It's harmless now."

"Shouldn't we—I dunno, clean it up or somethin'?"

"There's a perfectly good Parks Department that has people to keep the place clean, and besides I forgot to pack my broom and dustbin."

"I guess. Just don't sit right not to clean up our mess, y'know?"

"It's Saul Weinberg's mess, not ours, and we did the important part of cleaning it up, which is rendering it as a pile of nothing instead of a rampaging monster."

Yolanda grinned. "Yeah, okay, fine. I'm gonna get this little guy home to his basket."

"Want a ride? My car's parked down on Broadway."

"Beats waitin' forever for a Sunday bus. No way one comes as fast on the way back. And this way I don't gotta stuff Magellan back into my purse."

"Great." We both started walking back toward Broadway. Magellan at this point had fallen asleep on Yolanda's shoulders.

My phone buzzed, and I looked at it to see a text back from Esther: "About time."

I started yelling at the phone. "Seriously? I didn't even have a way of locating the stupid thing until midnight last night, and you're bitching about how long it took?"

Yolanda regarded me with concern. "Why you yellin' at your phone?"

"I'm yelling at my aunt."

"You get that she can't hear you 'less you actually *call* her, right?"

Chuckling, I said, "Hey, c'mon, I coulda been doing talk-to-text."

"Nah, phone makes a noise when you do that."

"Touché. And I'm yelling at the phone because it will do more good than actually yelling at Aunt Esther. I get it out of my system, and I don't have to listen to her rejoinder, probably given while staring at me over the top of her glasses."

We got to the sidewalk, and I decided to actually give Esther a call.

Without preamble, she said, "The golem's *really* taken care of?"

"It's an orange stain in the grass, courtesy the two best Coursers in New York and one most excellent dragon."

"Two best? Hired a third person to join you and Yolanda, did you?"

"Ha ha."

"The character on the *right* you remembered to erase, yes?"

"No, I totally forgot my entire three decades of being Jewish. *Yes*, I erased the character on the right." I rolled my eyes as I walked down the sidewalk. Next to me, Yolanda had her hand over her mouth to stifle a giggle.

"Good."

"Who should Yolanda and I send invoices to?"

Esther hesitated. She probably hadn't thought that far ahead, but the Heightsdale Association was now paying for at least part of this.

"Send 'em to me," she finally said. "I'll sort it all out."

"Great. Talk soon, Aunt Esther."

I ended the call just as we got to where my Corolla was parked.

As I beeped it unlocked, I said, "Thanks again for the help, Yolanda."

"Hey, I'm gettin' paid," she said with a grin as she opened the door and got in the passenger seat. "Hell, I oughtta be thankin' *you* for the work. If you ever show your ass up at the Kingfisher's Tail again, I'll buy you your first beer."

I sighed as I started the car up, looking forward to the blast of the AC.

I hadn't been back to the Kingfisher's Tail in months. I hadn't felt like I'd be welcome, or even if I was, that I'd be fit company.

But that was just stupid.

Being stupid had kinda been my thing the last few months. Time I changed that. "You're on," I said, pulling out of the parking spot and onto Broadway. "And hey, mind if I come up and see how Analia's doing?"

Yolanda winced. "Not now, okay?"

That surprised me. "Why not?"

"Besides the fact that you look like a really big cantaloupe?"

We'd come to a red light at 193rd, and I glanced down at my stained shirt and pants. "Fair point."

"Besides that, if we talk about Analia bein' your apprentice, it'll make her happy, and I ain't in *no* kinda mood to make her happy for a while."

The light turned green. "You had me at cantaloupe, but okay. Let me know when you're ready for us to sit down and talk about it."

"Absolutely."

A few minutes later, I hit another red light at Fairview Avenue. "It's probably for the best anyhow," I said. "I got a buncha stuff I have to do after this."

"Hope changin' clothes is the first thing."

I snorted. "Definitely. And after that, I gotta pick up some rice, some cabbage, and some Twinkies."

Yolanda turned and gave me the same look she'd given me when I was yelling at my phone. "Say *what*?"

I grinned. "My other client," was all I'd say in response.

Chapter 17

AFTER DROPPING YOLANDA AND THE SNOOZING MAGELLAN OFF AT THEIR place on 179th Street, I drove back home, stopping just long enough to put my shirt and pants in the hamper, wash off my face and chest, then change into a Bronx High School of Science T-shirt, denim shorts, and sandals. Oh, and feed Mittens, of course, who meowed indignantly at how neglected he'd been lately.

As I washed up, I noticed in the bathroom mirror that my hair was flying out in all directions and my beard now made my chin look like an overgrown privet hedge. I *really* needed a damn haircut…

Next step was to go to the supermarket up the street and get the rice, the cabbage, and the Twinkies.

My phone rang just as I finished paying for everything at the self-checkout. I pulled it out and saw that it was Bart. I cradled the phone between my ear and shoulder while I packed up my bag. "Hey, Bart."

"Sorry to call you back so late, Bram. Had trouble sleepin' last night, so I finally took a pill around two a.m., and I'm only just wakin' up now."

"No worries. Is it okay if I come over now and give you the news in person?"

"Absolutely. I'll put a pot'a coffee on for both of us."

"Sounds good."

I didn't bother going back upstairs. Mittens would survive. I just threw the bag of groceries into the back seat of the Corolla and drove over to Briggs Avenue.

The New York City highways were all designed to get people in and out of Manhattan from the suburbs, with absolutely no regard for the people of the outer boroughs, who were just there for commuters to drive past, at least as far as city planner Robert Moses—the architect of the aforesaid highway system—was concerned. Not that I was bitter about that at *all*…

But it meant that the only way to get from my place in Riverdale to Bart's in Jerome Park was either to navigate a mess of local streets or take a parkway north almost into Yonkers and then another parkway south. Luckily, on a Sunday afternoon, the traffic on Kingsbridge Road and Jerome Avenue wasn't *too* bad, so I went that way. Which was good, as I hated the idea of going up and around on the parkways…

There weren't any parking spots on Briggs itself, so I turned onto 199th, where there were also no spots, then left on Valentine Avenue.

Hilariously, I found a spot right in front of the house that was directly behind Bart's, which had a realtor's for-sale sign in front of it, a SOLD sticker diagonally across the front of the sign. I, of course, already knew that from the real-estate research I'd been doing, confirmed by the subsequent e-mail from Jimin Choi.

I walked down to 198th, over to Briggs, and back up to Bart's place, grocery bag over my shoulder.

He was sitting on one of the lawn chairs on the front porch. The plastic table had a metal carafe with the lid screwed on tight, an open metal pitcher with white stuff in it, a small white sugar bowl, and two mugs. The mug next to Bart, which had the "I ♥ NY" logo on it, contained a steaming light brown liquid. The other mug, which had two different New York Yankees logos on either side of the handle, was empty.

"Good to see you, Bram," Bart said. "Have a seat. 'Fore you ask, the AC went and died on me last night, so it ain't no better inside. S'why I couldn't sleep. Got a repairman comin' today." He shook his head and smiled. "Never thought I'd live to see the day a repairman'd come on a Sunday, that's for sure."

I sat down, putting the grocery bag at my feet, and poured some coffee out of the carafe into the Yankees mug. "Makes your life easier, certainly."

"Well, yeah, except for the part where they say they'll be here between one and six. Don't much matter to me none, I wasn't goin' noplace nohow, but for most folks? That's a long time to sit on your behind waitin' for someone."

"True." I took a sip of the coffee, which was perfectly serviceable, and then said, "So I've got news. You know that house right behind you on Valentine?"

"Yeah, nice old lady lived there—Mrs. Choi, I think's her name. Ain't seen her in a while, though."

"Well, you wouldn't have—Aera Choi died about six months back."

Bart winced. "Oh, may the Lord rest her soul."

"She and her husband Jae bought the house when they emigrated here from Korea in the 1980s. They also brought with them their infant son Jimin, and an imugi named Kyung-Soon. Jae, unfortunately, worked in the World Trade Center, and he died on 9/11. Jimin moved to Queens after he graduated college, and Aera lived alone in the house for the rest of her life." I smiled wryly. "Well, not *completely* alone, she still had Kyung-Soon. According to Jimin, the imugi's been in their family for seven generations."

"Lord, have mercy," Bart said. "So what's it doin' in *my* garden?"

"Not entirely sure. Jimin was surprised that his mother still *had* her. But based on what I've learned about imugi, they serve as protectors of crops and as good-luck charms." I refrained from saying that I learned about it from a sixteen-year-old. "My guess is that Kyung-Soon came to your yard because she needed a new place to protect. Or be a good-luck charm for."

Bart took a sip of his coffee. "What I think you're sayin' to me, Bram is—what *are* you sayin' to me?"

"I think that Kyung-Soon just wants a new place to live. And she'll protect your house and garden and maybe bring you good luck."

"But she attacked you."

"I was digging around trying to interfere with her—she probably saw me as a threat. Also, she probably wasn't entirely in her right mind, since nobody's fed her in ages."

"Lord, have mercy—I gotta feed her?"

"Well, you don't *have* to." I sighed. "Look, it's up to you. You can keep her, or you can ask me to get rid of her."

"What about her son—Jimin, you said his name was?"

I nodded.

"Don't he want her?"

"He really really doesn't." Jimin's email was incredibly emphatic on that particular subject. "But he did say that Kyung-Soon was always a good companion if you wanted company and left you alone if you didn't. You were telling me that you didn't have a lot of people in your life these days…"

"Yeah." He sipped some more coffee. "You said she ain't been fed?"

"Not since Aera died, no."

"So what's she eat?"

I grinned. "Funny you should ask." I picked the grocery bag up off the porch floor and placed it dramatically on the plastic table. Reaching into it, I pulled out each of the three items in succession. "She loves rice," I said, plunking down the bag of Jasmine rice I got, followed by the head of cabbage, "and cabbage, and also," I added, grabbing a white box, "Twinkies."

"Twinkies?" Bart asked, incredulous.

"That's what Jimin told me. He said you should cook the rice, but you don't have to bother cooking the cabbage."

"Or the Twinkies, I imagine."

Chuckling, I said, "Yeah, and keep her to one Twinkie a day, or she gets a little hyper."

Bart was now rubbing his chin. "As it happens, I keep rice in the house, but I appreciate you gettin' the cabbage. And the Twinkies, I guess." He took a longer gulp of his coffee, finishing what was in the mug. "Yeah, okay."

I frowned. "Yes" wasn't a good answer to an either/or question, so I prompted him: "Yeah, okay to what?"

"I'll keep her around. You said she'll leave me alone if I wanna be left alone, right?"

"That's what Jimin said, yeah."

"I could use some good luck, that's a fact." He reached down onto the floor of the porch and picked up his cane, then used it to brace himself to stand up. "C'mon, let's not let that poor thing starve anymore."

We went through the house to the kitchen, which was even hotter than it was outside. He washed the cabbage and then chopped it up with a large knife. While he did that, I opened the Twinkie box and pulled one out, undoing the plastic wrap around it.

He put the cabbage bits in a bowl and we both went through the sliding door to the back. As he put the bowl down near the privet hedge, I held out the Twinkie.

A few moments later, Kyung-Soon came slithering out from under the hedge. She went straight for the Twinkie in my hand and chomped down on it so fast she almost got my fingers with it.

Then she went for the bowl of cabbage, which she ate a bit more slowly.

"Huh." Bart just stared at her gobbling up the vegetable matter. "Will you look at that?"

"Now if anything goes wrong, call me right away, all right?"

"Absolutely. But you know what? Just lookin' at her chowin' down like that—kinda reminds me of a dog I had when I was a kid." He reached down to pat her on the head. "Good girl, Kyung-Soon."

I tensed—I wasn't sure touching her was such a hot idea—but the imugi just looked up for a second, made a cooing noise, and then went back to eating.

"Thanks very much, Bram. I 'preciate you helpin' me out, but mostly I 'preciate you bein' a good person. I know this is a job for you, but you went above and beyond that. Lotta folks woulda been all about gettin' ridda the monster and that's it. But you didn't do that. Heck, you brought her food! I know you said you're Jewish, but as far as I'm concerned, you'd make a damn fine Christian. And I mean a *real* Christian who does good works, not like those men in suits on the tee vee, or those priests that misbehave with boys, or nothin' like that. I mean you do what Jesus preached, and that's a rare thing in this day and age. So thank you."

I found myself utterly warmed by Bart's words, even though the notion of being a good Christian was one that I found pretty ridiculous, all things considered. But I got what he meant. "Thanks, Bart. I better get going and leave you to bond with your new friend. I'll send you an invoice for the rest of it." I hesitated. "I don't suppose you have an email address?"

"I do, but I'd truly rather you just sent one by regular mail. I gotta use apps and things on my phone with all my doctors and suchlike, but that's about as much technology as I wanna deal with aside from my Kindle."

I smiled. "No problem. I'll mail it to you—and you can mail me a check back."

Bart nodded. "Thank you very kindly, Bram."

I left him to it, walking back into the stuffy house and through it to the front.

As I walked down toward 198th, I wondered if the air-conditioner repair guy was going to see Kyung-Soon, and how he or she would react to her...

"So after I left Bart's, I called Miriam to let her know that all's well that ends well, and when I should come over for dinner, since Sunday night is when she usually cooks for me. Except there was some kind of crisis in the Curia. No idea what that was about, but it required several wardeins to get together and figure things out about matters *way* over my pay grade. Whenever something like this happens, Miriam usually just says she can't talk about it and either changes the subject, goes for some alcohol, or both. Either way, though, dinner was off."

I was telling all this to the catatonic Katie late Monday morning, sitting on the easy chair next to her bed, the copy of *Frankenstein* sitting on the chair's arm. Candi was taking advantage of my presence to get some sleep, as she'd been up half the night. Katie apparently kept being awakened by bad dreams over and over all night long. But she was calmer now, and Candi looked *exhausted* when I showed up at around ten-thirty Monday morning.

So I caught Katie up on everything that had happened since I was here last.

I had, at some point, run downstairs to pour myself a glass of water from the pitcher in the fridge, and I took a big gulp of it before continuing.

"Yolanda'd been bugging me about finally going to the Sunday night drink-up at the Kingfisher's Tail. I went home and took a quick nap. Then I changed into something a *little* bit nicer than a T-shirt and shorts and drove over to Woodlawn." I didn't usually take the car, because I often ended the evening too inebriated to operate a motor vehicle, but I hadn't planned on drinking *that* much my first night back in months. "I was nervous about going, but everything was fine. People were glad to see me, Yolanda bought me my first beer like she promised, and I got to hear all of the usual crazy-ass stories that everyone tells. My favorite was when we digressed off of Courser stories to little-kid stories. It was all Saladin Cruz's fault, he talked about something ridiculous his kid did at her seventh birthday party, and then Yolanda told some *really* embarrassing stories about all three of her kids, and then Hugues talked about the first time his daughter brought a boy home. It was pretty nice." I sighed. "Helped that Bernie wasn't there."

I gulped down the rest of my water. Bernie Iturralde was the one who shot Katie after she killed John, and generally he was an unpleasant person to be around.

Getting up from the chair, I said, "I'm gonna get some more water."

"Thir—thirsty…"

I nearly fell back down into the chair. That was Katie saying that. "What was that?"

She turned her head and was looking at me with a glassy, vacant expression. "Thirsty."

"I'll get you some water."

I ran out of the room and first went to Candi's bedroom to wake her up. She needed to run some checks on her, which I probably could've done, except for being too verklempt to remember, like, *any* of my medical training. Besides, this was Candi's actual job…

Candi was snoring, and she made a horrible snorting noise before opening her eyes. "What the hell?" she grumbled at me in a bleary voice.

"Katie spoke."

Suddenly, Candi was wide awake, and she sat up straight. In a totally non-bleary voice, she asked, "She what?"

"She spoke. Said she was thirsty. I'm gonna get her some water, but I thought you'd want—"

Throwing the covers off her, she pushed past me and exited the bedroom. I pointedly did not react to the fact that she was only wearing a tank top and panties.

I went downstairs and refilled my water glass and poured one for Katie.

By the time I got back upstairs, Katie was sitting up in the bed and Candi was checking her vitals. I handed Katie the water.

She grabbed it eagerly and gulped two-thirds of the glass down.

"That's better," she said, catching her breath after such a long gulp of water.

"How you feeling?" I asked hesitantly.

"I—I don't know." She looked at Candi. "How'm I feeling?"

"Heartrate's a bit up from usual, but nothing horrible," Candi said. "BP is fine, blood-oxygen levels are the same, temperature's good, lungs are still clear—it's pretty much the same as it was yesterday, except you're sitting up and talking now."

"Which is good." I hesitated again, then asked the question I had to ask. "What's the last thing you remember?"

Katie sipped more water, and then smiled. "You getting up and saying you're gonna get me water."

It took me a second to parse that. "You remember everything?"

She nodded. "Mostly—I think?"

"All right," I said, "let's go back a little further. How far back do you remember?"

"Being in a bed in a hospital." She frowned. "Then nothing, then before that, I was in the Tortoise and Hare after going for a run."

I let out a long breath. "So you don't remember being possessed?"

"I was possessed?"

"By Malsum, a wolf-god. Long story, which is just about the only story I *didn't* tell you the last four months."

Katie nodded. "I know, thank you, Bram. I just—I couldn't—" She gulped down the rest of her water. "I was awake and aware of everything. I remember the doctors and nurses at the hospital, I remember you and Miriam and Candi all taking care of me, but I couldn't—couldn't *do* anything. And I don't really know why?"

Reaching for her now-empty glass, I said, "Let me get you some more water."

"Thank you," she said breathily. "God, it's so—so *weird*."

I went downstairs and poured more water and wondered what this all meant. I was worried that Katie wouldn't forgive me for what happened, and now I found out that she didn't even know what happened.

I was probably gonna have to tell her. Hell, Candi probably would at some point if I didn't.

But not now. Now I just needed to enjoy her being awake.

I got upstairs with the water. In the interim, Candi had put on a silk bathrobe.

Katie gulped down some more of it. "This is gonna sound ridiculous, but—" She put the water down on the nightstand next to the lamp. "I'm exhausted, and I really want to sleep."

"You didn't get much sleep last night," Candi said.

In a hopeful voice, which filled me with glee, Katie asked, "Will you be back tomorrow?"

"I can be back after dinner tonight if you want."

"Make it tomorrow," Candi said in her fiercest nurse voice.

"Tomorrow, then," I said right away.

"Good," Katie said. "I wanna know what happens next in *Frankenstein*."

Indicating the book that was still on the arm of the chair, I said, "Well, you can just read it yourself now."

She looked away shyly. "I'd rather hear you read it."

That made my heart sing. "As you wish."

I turned to leave, saying, "See you both tomorrow," but then as I was crossing the threshold Katie spoke.

"Bram?"

I turned my head to look at her. "Yeah?"

"Clean out Rebekah's apartment."

She really had heard everything I said. While I hadn't discussed the specifics of Malsum's temporary freedom and possession of all the dogs and wolves in the Bronx, I had talked about Rebekah, and especially about my reluctance to even go into her old place, much less clean it out and re-rent it.

"I will," I said, and left.

I walked home with a spring in my step, barely even *noticing* the heat and humidity that blasted me in the face as soon as I left Katie's centrally-air-conditioned house. Stopping at the deli for a pastrami on rye, which I brought home, I munched down on it while I took care of all the paperwork. I did up invoices for both Josh Roth and Bart Jackson. I know Esther had said to bill her, but Roth was my *actual* client. While the Heightsdale Association had taken over the gig once it was clear they were being targeted, Roth was still the one who hired me and gave me a retainer. He could work out how to divide the payments with Esther.

That took a couple of hours—had to double check all the fees and expenses and such—then I emailed Josh his invoice, and printed out Bart's. I had envelopes, but no stamps, so I took a trip to the post office to buy a stamp and mail Bart his invoice from there.

By the time I got back home, I had a notification that I'd gotten an electronic payment from Josh Roth for the entire amount of my invoice.

Okay, then.

I called Esther.

"Everything all right, Bram?" she asked, sounding concerned.

"Actually, everything is fantastic, for a change. Katie's talking!"

"Mazel tov!"

I caught her up on what happened with Katie, and then I said, "And Roth already paid me. I emailed him the invoice less than an hour ago."

"Good for him."

"Mind if I ask a stupid question?"

"Why would I start minding that now after all these years?"

I sighed. I walked right into that. "What does Roth do for a living?"

"He's a lawyer. Won a big class-action suit a couple years back, so money, he's got plenty of. He probably won't even let the association pay our share."

"Huh."

"You still coming for dinner tonight?"

"Absolutely. I already missed eating with Miriam last night, I'm not gonna miss a home-cooked meal two straight nights."

"Is Miriam okay?"

"Yeah—wardein business, is all."

"Oh, you'll love this—Saul Weinberg ran away from home."

I choked a laugh. "To do what, join the circus?"

"According to Joseph, he couldn't deal with being in the house with his parents kvetching at him for giving them tsuris over this golem business, so he left. Robin, of course, called the cops, since he was released into *her* care, and they found him at his best friend's house and arrested him."

"He went to his best friend's house?" I asked incredulously.

"Yup."

"How is someone smart enough to animate a golem so stupid?"

"That question is on everyone's lips. So now he's gotta pay bail or stay in jail, and Robin and Joseph are tryin' to figure out what to do."

"My advice'd be to let him rot."

"Mine, too, but they also don't want him to suffer at other people's hands the way he would in Mott Haven." She chuckled. "They'd rather he suffered just at *their* hands."

"I'll give them a call later. See you around six?"

After ending the call with Esther, I scritched Mittens and thought about Joseph and Robin and their kids, and about Rebekah, and about Josh Roth, and about any number of other things.

First, I sent an email to Roth.

"Got the payment, thank you. Glad we were able to stop the thing before anyone was killed this time."

Wincing, I went back and erased that last sentence. "Glad we were able to stop the thing. I know I said I wasn't ready to hear your apology, and then you apologized anyhow, and I guess I just wanted to tell you—" I stopped typing, then started again. "Apology accepted. I'm never gonna be able to forget what you did, but I think I'm getting on the road to forgiving. Good luck with everything."

I sent it before I could have second thoughts.

Then I went downstairs and unlocked the door to Rebekah's old apartment.

It was time I cleaned the damn place out.

ON MY PATREON (HTTP://PATREON.COM/KRAD), I HAVE BEEN DOING monthly vignettes featuring my original characters. Fifteen of them thus far have taken place in the milieu of Coursers, whether Bram Gold, Yolanda Rodriguez, or Valentina Perrone (a Courser working out of the Atlantic City area, featured in my *Systema Paradoxa* book *All-the-Way House*). A large number of them have been conversations during the Sunday night Courser drink-ups at the Kingfisher's Tail, though there are others as well. There are also several that are holiday themed.

Here they are for the first time for non-patrons. Please note that they take place at varying points in the timeline, many of which are prior to *A Furnace Sealed*.

If you wish to read these vignettes as they're written, and also get monthly TV and movie reviews, weekly excerpts from my works in progress, a constant stream of cat photos, and/or first looks at my first drafts, please consider supporting me on Patreon.

Enjoy!
—Keith R.A. DeCandido

Sunday Night at the Kingfisher's Tail

"WAIT, YOU'RE FROM KENTUCKY?"

"Is that not allowed?" Abby Cornwell smiled at me from the next table over.

"No, I just didn't realize. Thought you were local."

Brushing a lock of blonde hair from her face, Abby said, "Nah, I didn't come to the Big Apple until about five years ago. And even then, I was in Brooklyn. I moved up to City Island after that."

I nodded. City Island was off the east coast of the Bronx, and I first met Abby when I was trying to wrangle a nixie there. That got out of hand real quick.

Dahlia Rhys-Markham and Eddie Mohapatra were sitting with her, while Sal Antonelli was next to me. There were only a few others around — sometimes it was quiet on Sunday nights. People were busy or working or just had other plans.

Eddie was sipping a Coke. "Abby was about to tell us about her first job on her own."

"In Kentucky?" I asked.

Abby nodded and took a sip of her bourbon. "It was a coal mine. They kept digging where there was supposed to be coal, and all they'd get was dirt. The guy who trained me went to school with the guy who owned the mine, so he was willing to believe that a supernatural creature was involved."

I smiled. "How'd that go over with the miners?"

Sal snorted. "I'm bettin' those yokels thought it was the devil's work or some shit." He took a quick gulp of his red wine.

"Actually," Abby said, "most of them figured the mine was cursed. The boss told his workers that I was an exorcist."

I winced. "Really?" Coursers were hunters — we didn't do magic. We left that to the specialists.

"Yeah, it was gonna be a problem if they expected me to actually perform an exorcism." Abby smiled. "Luckily, it never came to that. I went down into the mine — which was disgusting, by the way, I still have asthma because of that trip — and I found a kobold."

"Oh, fuck," Sal said, "those things are damn near impossible to kill."

Abby stared at him. "Good thing I wasn't there to kill it."

"Why the fuck not? I'm guessin' it was the one that turned the coal into dirt, right?"

I gave Sal a look. "So that's a good enough reason to kill the thing?"

Sal just stared back at me, and he looked like he was struggling. "I guess?"

"Let me guess," Dahlia said, "one of the miners was rude to the kobold?"

Abby nodded. "Yup."

"I knew it." Dahlia slammed a hand on the table. "Kobolds are notoriously prickly."

"Yeah, but all I had to do was get the miner to apologize."

Eddie chuckled. "'All,' eh? Was it really that simple?"

"Well, no." Abby sighed. "It took all my charm to get him to do it."

Grinning, I asked, "How'd you pull it off?"

"I told him that if he was scared of the kobold, then the little girl could go take care of it for him."

I shook my head. "Somehow, I'm not surprised that worked."

"His apology was awful, mind you, but the kobold was willing to accept it and turned the dirt back into coal. I left Kentucky a week later — can't stand the air there."

"Yeah, well, coal's nasty stuff," I said.

"Oh, not just that — the miner I had to convince to apologize asked me out! And was really confused and surprised when I said no."

After sipping my beer, I said, "Hey, c'mon, you saved the day. People always want to date the hero."

"I guess." She grinned. "But I gave him the kobold shoulder."

The Principle of the Thing

"WAIT, AN ACTUAL ZOMBIE?"

"Yes, Bram, an actual zombie," Eddie Mohapatra said as he sipped his Coke.

"So not just a stoner with bad posture whose parents have seen too many George Romero movies and just assume their kid is a zombie?"

Kaela Provoncher turned to stare at me. "Has that actually happened to you?"

"More times than I can count. Not always parents — once it was a reverend at a local church, but the people weren't zombies, they were just having their life force drained by a lamprey."

"I hate when that happens," Kaela said with a smirk.

"May I please continue my story?" Eddie asked.

I gave him a "go on" gesture and gulped down the rest of my beer. The bartender, Sheehan, started pouring my next beer without me having to ask for it.

I love having a regular bar. Especially one that caters to Coursers every Sunday.

"It turns out," Eddie said, "that someone was digging up graves in cemeteries all over the Bronx and lower Westchester. But they kept finding the bodies right next to the graves."

"Didn't the cops look into it?" I asked.

"Yeah, but they didn't have any leads — I did." He smiled. "It was a gentleman named Jarel Broxton. It was his sister, Camilla, who hired me. She said he was obsessed with turning José Pérez into a zombie."

"Who's José Pérez?" Kaela asked.

Eddie shrugged. "Camilla had no idea. And it turned out that every grave Jarel dug up belonged to someone named José Pérez. I finally tracked him down at the Holy Sepulchre Cemetery in New Rochelle, just as he was casting the spell on his latest José. As I got there—this was at about two a.m., he'd broken in—he was asking the zombie where the money was."

"Zombies carry money?" Kaela asked.

"Not usually," I said, "unless they're buried with it."

Kaela chuckled. "I thought burying your wealth with you went out with the ancient Egyptians."

"In this case," Eddie said, "he wanted to know where the money was hidden. It turns out that Jarel had lent money to someone, but they'd been arrested, and entrusted the money to pay Jarel back to José Pérez, who then died. Jarel had no idea which José Pérez it was, so he just kept digging them up and animating them until he found the right one."

"Was it the guy in New Rochelle?" I asked.

Shaking his head, Eddie said, "No. And I confiscated his spell components and had him sanctioned so he can't get any more. Also I informed the state police that he was desecrating graves, so he's incarcerated."

"Now he'll never get his money." Kaela sounded almost sad.

Eddie grinned. "He never would have anyhow. I did a little digging, and the José Pérez in question was cremated after the autopsy was done. Can't animate a pile of ashes."

"Actually, you can," I said, "but it takes way more mojo than a loser from lower Westchester's likely to have. And you need components that he could only afford if he actually got the cash he'd lent out back."

"Not likely," Eddie said. "It was only two hundred dollars."

I nearly snarfed my beer. "Wait, that's it? The stuff you need to animate a corpse costs more than that!"

"I know. I asked him that right before he was arrested. You know what he said?"

"What?" Kaela asked, rapt.

"He said, 'It's the principle of the thing'."

"That principle got him arrested," Kaela said.

"I never said that his words were smart ones."

"Good thing," I said. "And hey, you got a fee out of it."

Eddie nodded. "Which came out of the same bank account, since Jarel and Camilla share theirs. So they lost even more money to fail to get their two hundred back."

I raised my glass of beer. "To incredibly moronic clients."

We all drank to that.

"No," DAHLIA RHYS-MARKHAM WAS SAYING AS I ENTERED THE Kingfisher's Tail, "Jesus Christ was *not* born on the 25th of December."

Sal Antonelli shook his head. "That's just some fuckin' blasphemy right there."

Behind the bar, Brendan Sheehan poured me my pint of beer without my having to even ask for it. By the time I landsharked my way through the tables in the small pub, the pint was ready for me to drink.

Sal was looking over at John McAnally. "Johnny, you're a good Catholic, back me up here."

"I *am* a good Catholic, Salvatore, which is how I know that Dahlia is precisely correct. The notion of Christmas did not truly start until many centuries after the birth of Christ."

Dahlia sipped her wine, then said, "Exactly. It was after Christianity became a mainstream religion instead of an oppressed one. They started co-opting holidays and figures from other religions. They decided to celebrate Christ's birth around the winter solstice."

"That's some bullshit," Sal said.

"That's truth, and you're the one blaspheming now, Salvatore," John said.

"All I said was bullshit. That ain't blasphemin'."

I grinned. "Well, technically, it is if you're Hindu. That's gotta be a violation of the whole sacred cow thing."

Everybody in the bar groaned. A few threw peanuts at me.

"The point is," John said, "that the winter solstice is a popular time for festivals of birth and renewal. That's why many pagan religions celebrate true solstice as that's when the sun is renewed."

"Also," Dahlia added, "why the calendar flips at this time of year—it's when the sun starts over."

"And truthfully," John went on, "Christmas was not an important Christian holiday for some time. Indeed, there was a long period where it was considered a minor celebration at best, one to be discouraged, as there was a great deal of gluttony associated with it. Easter was the far more important holy day."

"Until the 19th century, in any case," Dahlia said. "It became a major celebration then and has remained so."

"Yeah," Pete Guthrie said, "thanks to the Coca-Cola Company and Chuckie Dickens, anyhow."

John frowned. "What is that supposed to mean, Peter?"

"Well, I know St. Nicholas is a real saint and all, but the whole idea of Santa Claus as a fat old white guy in a red suit was entirely made up by Coke for their ads back during the Depression. And it was the popularity of 'A Christmas Carol' that played a big part in making Christmas a big deal in the 19th century."

"I am not entirely sure I accept that," John said.

"All right, hang on," Sal said. "I get why Yule and Christmas and the new year and even Kwanzaa and all that is this time'a year. What about Hanukkah? Isn't that about lighting candles or something?"

Everyone turned to look at me.

I sighed. I was the only Jew in the bar, plus my aunt's a rabbi, so I guess I was supposed to be the expert.

"Basically, Hanukkah is about celebrating the rededication of the Temple in Jerusalem. The Greeks outlawed Judaism, there was fighting, then we got the Temple back, and we lit candles, but there was only one container of oil left. Somehow, it lasted eight days."

"It's a miracle!" Pete cried out.

I pointed at him. "Exactly. It was a miracle, and we weren't illegal anymore, so we celebrate by lighting candles, giving each other gifts, and eating a lot of food. Which is most Jewish holidays, when you get right down to it."

"So what's it got to do with renewal and all that other crap Dahlia and Johnny're talkin' about?" Sal asked.

"Nothing. It just happens to fall in the winter, so it kinda got lumped in with Christmas. Honestly, if it wasn't for being so close to Christmas, nobody'd know about it who wasn't Jewish. It'd be in the same 'which one is that again?' column as Purim and Tu B'av."

"What the hell is Tu B'av?" Sal asked.

Pete chuckled. "Wasn't he the Vulcan dude on *Star Trek: Voyager*?"

"Nah, Tu B'av is basically Valentine's Day," I said, "except without the massacre."

"So Hanukkah's got nothin' to do with the sun renewing itself?" Sal asked.

"Nope. Just us saying, 'They tried to kill us, they didn't, let's eat'."

Dahlia said, "I actually rather like that philosophy."

I raised my beer. "So Happy Hanukkah."

Pete raised his glass. "Happy Kwanzaa."

Raising his glass, John said, "Merry Christmas."

"Blessed Yule," Dahlia added.

I grinned. "And a happy Jew year."

We drank, and then they threw more peanuts at me.

Don't Have a Cow, Man

"Hey, you guys hear about the cow?"

I come in on the best lines. I had just entered the Kingfisher's Tail, and as soon as I shut the big blue door behind me, I heard Sal Antonelli say those words. I headed to the bar, where Sheehan was already pouring my beer from the tap.

"You'll need to be more specific," Eddie Mohapatra said with a chuckle before sipping from his Coke.

Siobhan Gleeson placed her Jameson's on the table as she said with her Irish lilt, "I can't imagine there are *that* many cows within the five boroughs. Beyond the zoos, in any case."

"Wait," Yewhala Chatwal said, "you mean the one on the Deegan?" He put his margarita down and started fondling his smartphone.

"Oh, right," Eddie said, "I saw the story on News 12."

"Crazy, ain't it?" Sal shook his head and gulped down some of his Chianti. "Damn Guernsey gummin' up traffic. Like the Deegan needs somethin' *else* backin' up traffic, am I right?"

"Yeah," Dahlia Rhys-Markham said quietly, "that wasn't a cow."

Sal frowned. "'Course it was a cow. I *saw* it."

"As did I," Eddie added.

Yewhala was holding up his phone—he'd already found video online and his phone's display was showing it. "Sure looks like a cow to me."

"Oh, he absolutely *can* look like a cow, yes," Dahlia said with a sigh and a quick sip of her mojito.

The proverbial light bulb went off over my head. "Oh for crying out loud, did Danny get out *again*?"

"Who the fuck is Danny?" Sal asked.

I sighed and took a long gulp of my beer. "Bogdan Helmold. He's a domovoy—and he's also rather severely bipolar." I looked over at Dahlia. "He got out of BPC again?"

Dahlia nodded, while everyone looked confused at me.

"Sorry," I said, "Bronx Psychiatric Center."

"He was committed?" Eddie asked.

"Committed himself," I said. "Meds were managing it for a while, but turns out a shape-changer's metabolism burns through meds faster than usual."

"Wait," Sal said, "a domovoy can change into anything—and this asshole changes into a fuckin' *cow*?"

I shrugged. "He likes cows."

Dahlia added, "And he can change his shape into any number of animals. Including a snake—can't hold it for very long because he has to fit a hundred and fifty pounds of mass into a three-foot-long snake."

"But that makes it easy to break out of your cell when you're on a manic phase."

Yewhala shook his head. "So what did they do with him? News said he got sent to a place upstate."

Dahlia shook her head. "That's the cover story they gave to the press. I got him back to the hospital."

"Thanks for that," I said emphatically. "He's a good friend."

Sal grinned. "Surprised they didn't call you, Bram, you bein' his friend."

Dahlia sheepishly said, "The hospital has me on retainer. Danny is *far* from the only supernatural being who has been admitted there."

I chuckled. "Isn't that where they put that kappa?"

Shuddering, Dahlia said, "Don't remind me. Every other month that thing gets out. I have to take three showers when I'm done."

"What's a kappa?" Sal asked.

Eddie said, "Japanese slime demon. I encountered some when I visited Japan many years ago, but was unaware that there were any here in New York."

"Just the one so far," Dahlia said. "I refuse to say anymore until I've had at least three more of these." She held up her mojito and then gulped a large amount.

"Y'know," I said, "the trick to luring a kappa is to shout, 'fie!' over and over again."

"Say what?" Sal asked.

Dahlia gave me a side-eye. "Shouting 'fie!'?"

I nodded. "Absolutely. Try it some time, and you'll see 'fie!' bait a kappa."

Everyone threw their peanuts at me.

"Hey, Miriam!"

"Hey, Bram. Thanks for coming over so fast."

"No problem. He awake?"

"The spell hasn't worn off quite yet."

"But any minute?"

"You never know with Sternquist. Could be in five seconds, could be in an hour."

"Why'd you cast Sternquist?"

"Because I tried Zipser and it didn't work."

"Okay. So we just have to wait?"

"Yeah."

"Great. Wanna try to get your revenge in the Street Name Game?"

"Hell yeah. You broke my streak."

"Two wins in a row is not a streak, Mimi, it's a statistical anomaly."

"Don't call me Mimi, and it is too a streak."

"Yes, dear. Still, I won last time—"

"When you broke my streak."

"—so I go first. Delafield. You get a D."

"Yes, Bram, I know how to spell 'Delafield.' Dyre."

"Eastchester."

"Riverdale."

"Another E. Um—Esplanade. Which, I gotta say, is a really pretentious street name."

"I agree. And it gives me another E. Einstein."

"Good one. Netherland."

"Dreiser."

"Sheesh, Mimi, you just gonna keep using Co-Op City?"

"Why not? You owe me an R."

"River. Now you owe *me* an R."

"Rochambeau."

"Nice. Underhill."

"Laconia."

"Allerton."

"Noble. You get another E, Bram."

"Dammit, I can't remember any of the names in Section 5 of Co-op City beyond Einstein Loop. Um… Oh! Yeah. East 149th!"

"Wait a minute, Bram, you can't—"

"I can, too, Mimi! Rules are street names in the Bronx. East 149th is very much a street name in the Bronx."

"And now I'm stuck with a 9! There's no street that starts with a 9!"

"Technically, the last letter is an H."

"Oh, right. Good point. Fine, Hull."

"Lafayette."

"That's in Manhattan."

"And also in the Bronx—runs parallel to the Bruckner in Castle Hill."

"Fine, then another E. And unlike you, I remember the street names in Section 5: Elgar."

"River—no wait, crap, I did that. Um—Rosedale. Gonna need to pull another Section 5 street outta your ass."

"Erdman."

"Netherland. No, wait, I did that already. Um, Naples."

"Sedgwick."

"King. And before you ask, it's on City Island."

"Already knew that, but thanks. Grand."

"The Concourse, or Grand Avenue?"

"Does it matter?"

"Guess not. Okay, gonna pull a you and do a Co-op City street: Darrow."

"Then I'm gonna pull a you and do West 242nd."

"Aaaaand I don't remember the other D's in Section 4 of Co-op. So I'll have to go with De Reimer."

"Radcliff."

"Fordham."

"Mosholu."

"Another U. Nice one, Mimi."

"Don't call me Mimi. Are you giving up on getting a U?"

"I am not. Um—I know there's another one. Aha! Undercliff! You owe me an F."

"I can think of something that begins with F, but it's not a street name. Fairfield."

"Oy, another D. Digney. I need a Y."

"Um… Dammit. Yankee?"

"There's no actual street that has 'Yankee' in it, just the stadium. I know because you've pulled this *every other time* we've played this game and I gave you a Y. C'mon, Mimi, it's easy."

"*Don't* call me Mimi, and I'm drawing a blank. This happened last time, didn't it?"

"Yup."

"Oh, hey, look, he's waking up!"

"So you're giving up? I win! I guess that means I have a streak now?"

"Don't be silly, two in a row isn't a streak, Bram, it's a statistical anomaly."

The Worst Case

I'D NEVER SEEN QUITE THE LOOK ON ABBY CORNWELL'S FACE AS SHE entered the Kingfisher's Tail.

On her entrance, Sheehan immediately reached for a bottle of Sancerre to pour for her, but Abby held up a hand and said, "Bourbon, neat."

Sheehan frowned. So did I. Abby *always* drank white wine.

"What happened?" I asked.

Abby didn't answer until after she'd taken a gulp of the sipping bourbon Sheehan had poured.

"Oh, fuck, I needed that."

Another indication that something was up: Abby never used profanity. She was from the south and was raised by Christians who did not approve of foul language.

"Just had the worst case of my life."

Bernie Iturralde snorted. "What, worse than that hellbender that got loose in St. Mary's Park?"

"Much worse."

I winced. The hellbender was basically a giant snot-demon, and it made a real mess all over the park and the buildings on 149th Street.

It was pretty light in the bar this particular Sunday night—just me, Bernie, and Sal Antonelli, and the two of them were starting to get on my nerves, so I was glad to see Abby, as she would've provided a nice antidote to the macho idiocy of the other two.

So Abby sat at the same table as the three of us. It was crowded, but it seemed silly for her to do otherwise.

"I was hired by a woman over on Sedgwick and 197th."

"Wait," Sal said, "was it a Latina woman—Patricia something?"

"Vazquez," Abby said without hesitating. "Yes."

Sal rolled his eyes. "She pull the same thing on you she pulled on me? Tried to pass off her husband as some kinda monster?"

Abby nodded and slammed down the rest of her bourbon, then signaled Sheehan for another.

I sighed. People tried that kind of nonsense all the time, hiring Coursers because we deal with supernatural things—but the monster in the closet, or wherever, turns out to be something harmless and ordinary.

"Sorry she wasted your time," Sal said.

But something felt off to me. Abby wouldn't be slamming back bourbons if it was just the usual bullshitters.

"What is it?" I asked gently.

"I tracked the husband for a bit, to make sure, you know?" She nodded at Sheehan as he brought her a second bourbon. "He propositioned half a dozen women on the street, wolf-whistled at a few more. He works construction, so I got to see him work on a building down by Yankee Stadium, and he kept ignoring his female supervisor and doing everything his male supervisor told him to do."

"So he's an asshole," Bernie said, "so what?"

"Then I followed him to a restaurant where he met up with Patricia. They had dinner, and he spent the *entire fucking time* talking down to her, belittling her, telling her she was stupid, not letting her eat or drink what she wanted, and then doing the same to the entire staff— all women, by the way. When he saw a male manager, *then* he was polite, but even then, he was a dick. Oh, and he made sure to interrupt Patricia every time she tried to talk and make sure she knew that he thought she was stupid."

"I repeat," Bernie said impatiently, "he's an asshole. So what? We ain't the cops, this ain't our fuckin' problem."

Abby gulped more of her bourbon.

I decided to risk a comment. "You know, you're supposed to sip that."

She just glowered at me, and then I held up both hands. "Never mind."

"I followed them home after that. I didn't get to see in the apartment, but I found a place in the courtyard where I could hear what was going on."

Rather than continue, she slammed back more bourbon.

"What was going on?" I asked.

"I heard the very distinctive sounds of an open hand striking flesh."

I winced. So did Sal. Bernie just shrugged and sipped his beer.

Abby continued: "I set up a meeting with her over coffee the next day and told her that this wasn't what I did, that her husband wasn't a supernatural creature, just a more garden-variety monster. She *begged* me, she told me she'd called the cops, but there was no evidence of abuse, and every time the cops did come by, he was polite and nice and sweet, and then as soon as they left, he beat her some more. But it was always just enough to humiliate and hurt, not enough to leave much bruising, and he never broke a bone or left a scar."

"Shit." Sal gulped down his red wine the same way Abby'd been mainlining her bourbon. "I had no idea, seriously."

"So what did you do?" I asked in a ragged whisper.

Abby let out a long breath, took an actual sip of her bourbon this time, and then said, "She *begged* me to do something. So I got in touch with someone who owed me favor who could get his hands on a metallivore."

"Oh, shit," Sal said.

I saw where this was going. A metallivore was a creature that ate metal.

"Fuck, Abby," Bernie said, "metallivores are shit we *stop*, not shit we *use*."

"I listened to him beating her!"

In all the years I'd known Abby, I'd never heard her raise her voice like that.

"She'd tried everything," Abby continued, "and he wouldn't stop. She was at the end of her rope. And why the hell do we *do* this if it isn't to help people?"

"It ain't our job."

"No, it's the cops' jobs, and they couldn't do it. I could. So I did. The metallivore ate through a beam at the construction site, it fell on him, and now he's in the hospital with a leg shattered in twelve places and a broken arm."

Sheehan spoke for the first time since Abby came in. "You realize that, technically, what you did is a violation."

"It absolutely is," Abby said. "It violates the oath I took as a Courser, it violates the law, and I would do it again every day of the week and twice on Sunday. If any of you wants to report me to the wardein, go right ahead. I won't stop you. I'll stand by what I did. But I'm not sorry I did it."

On the one hand, I wanted to say that what Abby did was wrong. She hurt another human being and used a supernatural creature to do it. That's completely antithetical to what we're supposed to be about. We're supposed to protect people from supernatural creatures who would harm them—and, to be fair, also protect those supernatural creatures from people who might harm them, as well—not use them like this. People who do what Abby did are who we're supposed to stop—

—in the abstract.

I had no idea what to do. Every instinct screamed to report her, and every instinct screamed to buy her another drink and congratulate her.

Bernie finally said, "I don't tattle to teacher. You did what you hadda do. I ain't gonna bitch about some asshole gettin' what he deserves."

"Me either," Sal said.

"Me three." I held up my beer. "To lousy cases."

Abby held up her bourbon. "To Patricia Vazquez. Let's hope she finds some peace."

"Yeah."

"The game is Murder. High hand splits with high spade in the hole, Queen of Spades up resets the game, Queen of Spades in the hole is wild."

I just kinda stared at Yolanda Rodriguez when she called that game. "You're kidding, right?"

Yolanda smiled. "What? It's a perfectly normal variation."

"Your definition of 'normal' varies wildly from mine." I sighed and threw a red chip into the center of the table, as did the other three players.

The five of us were all sitting in the Dyckman Farmhouse Museum. The oldest farmhouse in Manhattan and one of the oldest structures in the city that was still intact, the old farmhouse had only one issue: once a year, on the anniversary of when the original farmhouse was built back in 1785, the ghosts of every single member of the Dyckman family went crazy and tried to wreak havoc. Sometimes you could reason with them, but sometimes they needed to be dealt with.

And there were enough dead Dyckmans floating around the aether that it took five Coursers to deal with it.

But *when* they showed varied from year to year, so the five of us were on call—which, in real terms, meant we were bored shitless until something happened.

Yolanda dealt two down cards to everyone. I was hoping I'd have the Queen of Spades in the hole because 1) it meant I had a wild card and 2) it wouldn't come up and reset the game. Every time I played this stupid variant, I'd have a great hand, the Queen of Spades would come up, and on the re-deal, I'd get a stinky hand.

I didn't, but I did get the Jack of Spades, which *might* have been high enough to get half the pot. I also had the Jack of Diamonds, so I was starting out pretty good with a pocket pair.

Then Yolanda dealt the first set of up cards. I got an Ace of Hearts, Eddie Mohapatra got a King of Spades, Abby Cornwell got the Ace of Spades, Bernie Iturralde got the Two of Diamonds, and Yolanda dealt herself the Three of Clubs.

Now my Jack of Spades was looking better for high spade in the hole.

Yolanda looked at me. "First Ace bets, Abe."

I tossed another red chip in. "I open with one."

Eddie and Abby both called. Bernie said, "This is some *bull*shit," and folded.

"Dealer calls," Yolanda said, tossing in a red chip of her own.

We each got another card. I got a Jack of Hearts, meaning I had three of a kind *and* a likely high spade. I liked my chances.

But then Abby got the Ace of Diamonds, which gave her the best hand showing. Eddie got a Nine of Hearts, and Yolanda gave herself a Seven of Clubs.

Abby threw three red chips in for her bet. I couldn't really blame her with two Aces showing.

Eddie folded, but Yolanda and I stayed in.

Two more rounds of up cards, and I still had three Jacks, only one of which was showing. Abby's up hand didn't get any better than two Aces, while Yolanda had the Three, Six, and Seven of Clubs all showing.

Abby checked this time, and Yolanda bet three. We both called.

I figured Yolanda had the straight or the flush.

The last card was down, and I got an Ace of Clubs to go with the Ace of Hearts I had up. Suddenly, I had a full house. This was way better.

Abby bet five, which meant she either had the Queen of Spades in the hole to give her three Aces or she had another pair — or even trips — underneath. Still, my full house was pretty strong.

Yolanda called, and so did I.

Flipping over a pair of Twos, Abby said, "Two pair. I don't have any spades in the hole."

"Boat," I said, showing my cards. "And I've got the Jack also."

Then Yolanda flipped over the Queen of Spades in the hole, which was better than my Jack, so she got half the pot.

"Nice," I said. "I guess we split?"

"Not quite," Yolanda flipped over the Four of Clubs and the Five of Diamonds. With the Three, Six, and Seven of Clubs, it gave her a straight.

I frowned at her. "I've got a *boat*. A straight doesn't—"

"Straight *flush*, Abe." Yolanda was smiling sweetly.

"What? Oh, hell." I looked down at the Queen of Spades, which was a wild card, and could substitute as the Five of Clubs, giving her a straight flush and the entire pot.

YOU SHOULD HAVE FOLDED.

We all stood up suddenly.

NO, NO, DO NOT CONCERN YOURSELVES. WE HAVE LEARNED OUR LESSONS. THIS HOUSE IS NOW A MUSEUM AND WE DYCKMANS MUST RESIGN OURSELVES TO THAT.

I breathed a sigh of relief. Fighting ghosts was always a pain in the ass.

Bernie, of course, couldn't just let it go. He stood up, hoisting his shotgun, which was filled with buckshot made with goofer dust. "You sure 'bout that? 'Cause we ain't takin' no shit here, Dyckman."

COMPLETELY SURE, SIR. WE HAVE NO WISH TO CAUSE ANY FUSS.

"Good." Bernie sat back down and put his shotgun on the floor.

HOWEVER, PERHAPS YOU COULD DEAL ME IN?

And that, my friends, is how I lost fifty bucks to a guy who's been dead since the eighteen hundreds.

THERE WERE TWO PEOPLE IN THE KINGFISHER'S TAIL FOR THE USUAL Sunday night drink-up that I hadn't seen in there before. I knew them both, but they worked, respectively, Manhattan and upstate.

The Manhattan one wasn't a surprise, as I'd been telling Yolanda Rodriguez about the meet-ups since we first met years ago.

The upstate one was. I'd last seen Olivia Casey during the most recent eclipse when it was all hands on deck to round up the basilisks that escaped through the portal in the Botanical Gardens that *always* opened during an eclipse.

She was in the midst of telling a story as I came in, so I gave her and Yolanda both a silent wave as I went to the bar, where Sheehan was already pouring my usual pint.

"So I hop in my car," Olivia was saying after sipping her pink-colored cocktail, "and drive into the middle of nowhere in Hopewell Junction to the orchard."

That got my attention. "Wait, you went to the Kizior Orchard?"

Olivia smiled. "You know it?"

I nodded. "They've got a stand at the farmer's market—they've got the best apple cider."

"Wait," Sal Antonelli said, setting his red wine down, "is that the place that has those apple cider donuts covered in powdered sugar?"

"Those are addictive," Yolanda said before taking a sip of her mojito. "They got a booth at the farmer's market on 175th."

"So what'd they hire you for?" I asked Olivia.

Chuckling, she said, "I already explained that—a whole bunch of their apple trees fell over. But they weren't cut down, they were knocked down. It was hurting business. Too many bruised and busted apples that are hard to sell."

"And they hired you to find out?" I asked.

Olivia nodded. "I almost didn't take the job, because it was probably something mundane, but it also could've been Asftr!kyos'amma."

Sal chuckled. "Come again?"

"I just call him Sam." Olivia grinned. "He's a hugag, and he usually stays around Mohonk, but I guess he got to wandering, and started hanging out at the orchard."

I asked, "Was he the one knocking over the trees?"

"Yeah. He just wanted some apples, y'know? So he went over there to get some because he heard some tourists in Mohonk talking about how they had the best ones, and he fell asleep on one of the trees."

Sal asked, "That was enough to knock it over?"

"Hugags can't lie down—their knees don't bend."

"Like elephants," I added.

Olivia gave me a look. "Right. And so they fall asleep leaning on trees, and sometimes they knock them over because hugags are very big, and apple trees aren't the sturdiest trees in the forest."

"So what happened?" I asked.

"You didn't hurt him, did you?" Sal asked.

"Of course not!" Olivia was aghast. "Sam's a sweetheart! He just has a tendency to get fixated on things, and this time he wanted apples, so he started lurking at Kizior. I told him he was causing too much trouble, and I promised to make sure he got apples sent to him."

Sal was shaking his head. "Wait, how'd you swing that? Hugags don't usually have mailing addresses..."

"How do you know," I said cheekily, "you didn't even know they couldn't lie down until a minute ago."

"Fuck you, Gold," Sal said with a smile.

"He's right, though," Olivia added, placing her now-empty cocktail glass on the table. "But the folks at the Mohonk resort will take stuff to him, so I worked it out with Kizior. They'll ship him a pound of apples every week."

"Who's gonna pay for that?" Sal asked.

"Hugags aren't exactly picky eaters," Olivia said with a chuckle, "and the orchard'll just send the badly bruised apples that they can't sell anyhow. They usually just toss the ones they don't put into cider or pies or donuts or things."

"Nice," I said.

From the bar, Brendan asked, "Another?"

Olivia grinned. "Nah, I think I'll have an apple-tini."

"The worst was when we hit 2000, okay?"

I walked into the Kingfisher's Tail just as Hugues Baptiste said those words.

Brendan Sheehan said as he poured my beer, "I remember that particular end-of-year nonsense well."

Dahlia Rhys-Markham smiled. "What, were people asking you to solve the Y2K bug?"

"The what, now?" Yewhala Chatwal asked.

At that, Brendan rolled his eyes. "I'm surrounded by children."

"The computers they made in the olden days," Hugues said, "they were programmed with dates that were set up with two digits each for the month, for the day, and for the year."

"So what?" Yewhala asked.

Chuckling, Dahlia said, "It meant that on the first day of the new millennium, the computers would think the date was 01/01/00."

"That wasn't the new millennium!" Abby cried out. "The new millennium started in 2001. The same way every decade starts in the year ending in 1 because there's no year 0. Sorry," she said, grabbing for her wine glass, "I was a math major in college, and that always made me crazy."

"Well, technically, there wasn't a year 1, either," I said. "They didn't start dating from Jesus's birth until the year 500 or so. Anyhow, you guys all got it wrong, anyhow, since the year 2000 was really 5760."

"The point is," Dahlia said, "the computers would read 01/01/00 as 1900. These computers were mostly programmed in the 1970s and 1980s, and they weren't thinking that far ahead."

"A lot of people were panicking about it back then," Brendan said, "but it turned out to be a tempest in a teapot. No big deal at all."

"Actually," Hugues said, "it was a *huge* deal, okay? My uncle was a computer programmer on the Wall Street, and I heard chapter and verse from him on the subject. The reason why it *seemed* like not being a big deal was because programmers like my uncle worked their asses off for months to fix everything, okay?"

Holding up both hands, Brendan said, "All right, all right. It just didn't seem like a big deal then."

"Because people did their jobs right, okay?"

I smiled. "Kinda like us. Most people don't know who we are or what we do, and that's because we do our jobs right."

"Mostly," Hugues added with a glare at me.

"Hey, *you* trained me, so if I suck at the job, it's your fault."

Yewhala asked, "So what happened in 2000?"

"Everybody was convinced that it was the end of the world, okay? People who normally think like they rational people were being beyond stupid."

"Plus," Brendan added, "everybody thought that the flipping to a new millennium was a time of great power."

"Power's got nothing to do with the calendar," Dahlia said, "it's an human-made setup."

Hugues glared at her. "Yes, thank you, Dahlia, I wasn't aware of that, not having been a Courser for thirty-five years, okay?"

I chuckled. Most spells and rituals and stuff were tied to things like phases of the moon and the equinox and the solstice and other natural events, not arbitrary constructs like a calendar date.

"My favorite," Hugues said, "was the Swedish family who had put together components for the spell to be bringing the end of the world. They were planning to commit Ragnarök at midnight on the New Year's Eve."

"Wasn't that a Thor movie?" Sal Antonelli asked.

"It's the end of the world in Norse mythology," Dahlia said. "I heard a rumor that it almost happened in Key West recently, in fact."

Saladin Cruz snorted. "No way the end of the world happens in Key West."

"Why not?" I asked.

"That's way too depressing a thing for that island. When the end of the world happens it'll be somewhere like East St. Louis."

Laughing, I turned to Hugues. "I'm curious—what exactly are the spell components for Ragnarok?"

"According to them, mistletoe, ice, fur from a wolf, a fingernail, and a stick from an ash tree."

Dahlia added, "According to reality, nothing. You need actual Norse deities to bring about the twilight of the gods."

"So the spell didn't work?" I asked.

"Obviously, child, since we're all still here, okay? But I did my job— I was hired to stop them bringing ending to the world, and I stopped them doing that."

I smiled. "And if you hadn't stopped them, nothing would've happened, right?"

"Maybe, maybe not, but why risk it, okay?"

"I can beat that," Saladin said. "It was right after I started apprenticing with Pedro. Some guy tried to hire us to perform an exorcism of the Lord Jesus Christ when he returned, which he said was gonna happen as soon as the clock struck midnight and it was the year 2000."

"So let me get this straight," I said, after sipping my beer thoughtfully, "your client wanted you to send Jesus right back where he came from after the second coming?"

"Yup."

"He say why?"

"Yup. He said the world sucked, and Jesus would be *real* disappointed, and he didn't want to take the chance that Judgment Day would just destroy everything."

Hugues gaped at Saladin. "What did you tell the man?"

"That we don't do exorcisms, and that he needed a priest. That's when he told us he was a deacon in his church, and he'd already asked the priests. Big shock, they all said no."

"Look at us," I said. "Coursers are the best. Here we've got the end of the world, the second coming, *and* the Y2K bug, and we stopped all of them!"

"We didn't stop Y2K, child," Hugues said with a glower.

I shrugged. "It was your uncle, close enough." I held up my beer. "To surviving the year 2000!"

"Been more than twenty years, and you're toasting that now?" Yewhala asked.

"Why not?"

"Fair enough." Yewhala raised his rum and Coke. "Happy new year."

"Happy new year!" everyone shouted, and we all drank.

Valentina Perrone was just about to close up her storefront office on the corner of Atlantic Avenue and North Carolina Avenue when the potential customer walked in.

He wore a suit that cost more than Val's monthly rent on this place. The sunglasses he removed as he walked through the glass door were Ray-Bans, and the watch on his wrist looked like a genuine Rolex. His dark hair had just enough product in it to keep it from ever being in motion.

"Can I help you?"

"Maybe." The man slowly walked into the tiny office, looking around at everything. "You Valerie Perrone?"

Chuckling, Val said, "Valentina, actually, but you can just call me Val."

"I know a guy who said that you're someone who might be able to help with a problem."

"And you got a problem?"

"Maybe."

Val had been on her way to the tiny restroom when the door opened, but now she sat back down at her metal desk, indicating the guest chair facing her. "Why don't you have a seat and tell me what your possible problem is?"

"Yeah, okay." He took a seat, pulling a small card case out of the inside pocket of his suit jacket. "My name's Rocco Amalfitano. I'm the head of security at the Atlantic Resorts Casino."

That didn't surprise Val all that much. From the moment he walked in, it was pretty obvious that he worked for one of the hotel/casinos that dominated Atlantic City. He handed her the card.

"I got thirteen different people—including two of my employees who are not exactly what I'd call nutjobs, if you know what I'm sayin'—who say there's a ghost in the elevator."

Val nodded. "Okay."

"Now, look, I hear people talkin' 'bout ghosts all'a damn time. But this is different."

"How?"

"All thirteen people gave me the *exact* same description'a the thing. Young guy, red hair, Army uniform, blood on his chest. And it's only been in the new south elevator."

Recalling that Atlantic Resorts recently renovated, Val prompted, "New?"

"Yeah, we put a new wing'a rooms on the south side'a the hotel."

Again, Val nodded. "Okay. How much you know about the history of the land your hotel's on?"

"The fuck do I need to know about that for?" He winced. "'Scuse my language. It's been a day."

"It's okay. The reason I asked is that Atlantic Resorts was built in the 1950s. What used to be there was the Royal Oaks Casino and Resort, and during World War II, Royal Oaks was taken over by the U.S. Army as a field hospital. Lotta the restless spirits in AC are soldiers from back then."

"All right, so you really believe this crap?"

Val grinned. "Don't you?"

"No, I don't, but I don't believe that two tourists from Minneapolis, a family from the Bronx, three Chinese businessmen, a little old lady from Perth Amboy, a lawyer from D.C., and two guys I worked with for a combined twenty-two years would all have the same crazy-ass hallucination, y'know what I mean?"

Conceding the point, Val then asked, "They find anything when they did the renovation work?"

"Nothin' important that I know of. I mean, we got archeologists who go in to check it out if we find anything weird, and they didn't find nothin'."

"All right, I'm gonna have to check it out myself—assuming we can come to terms, anyhow."

Val quoted a figure of payment. As was her usual, she quoted a price twenty percent higher than she would have for any client who *wasn't* a casino.

"That's a little high, ain't it?"

Shrugging, Val said, "You don't like it, find someone else to get rid of your ghost."

"How do I even know you're legit?"

Holding her hands out palms-up, Val said, "Mr. Amalfitano, you came to me. I can take care of your ghost problem. Look, for first-time clients, I only ask for half the fee up front. You don't like what I do, then you don't have to pay me the back half."

"But I'm out the front half."

Val snorted. "You ain't out anything, Mr. Amalfitano, your employer is, and let's be honest—my entire fee, much less half of it, is a rounding error in your casino's budget."

Holding up both hands, he said, "All right, all right, I surrender. And it's 'Rocco.' Mr. Amalfitano is what people call me when they got problems. I'm the one with the problem here."

◄—THE BRONX—►

It took Val two days.

First, she checked out the south elevator and the area around where it was built, but found nothing specific. She did, however, see the ghost in question, briefly. Definitely a World War II-era uniform the spirit was wearing. She also imprinted the ghost on a Barker charm.

Then she did a deep dive into the records of who was at the old Royal Oaks when it was conscripted to be used as a hospital. That took most of a day, but she eventually found a likely candidate for the ghost: Corporal Frederick McGraw, wounded in action in France, died of an infection while being treated at Royal Oaks.

Then she talked to the construction crew, and found out that one of them, a man named Torbert Malinsky, did find something on site that he didn't report to his bosses: a gold wedding ring. He'd lost his and had been wearing the one he found. He did, however, refuse to give the ring up. "My wife'll kill me."

Using the Barker charm verified that the ring had belonged to Corporal McGraw.

Val had a couple of options, but she decided to go for the one that would both satisfy the client and give a bit of comeuppance to Malinsky.

The next day, the ghost of Fred McGraw was no longer haunting Atlantic Resorts. It was, however, now haunting Torbert Malinsky, wherever he went. She wondered how long it would be before Malinsky — or his wife — hired her, or another local Courser, to get rid of the ghost.

It took another two weeks before Rocco finally paid the invoice she'd sent — which included not just the second half of her fee, but also the cost of both the Barker charm, which she'd now have to replace, and the Fitzpatrick Stone, which she'd used to reunite McGraw's ghost with his wedding ring. He wanted to make sure there were two weeks' worth of no ghost sightings before paying up.

Rocco sent a text with the confirmation of the money transfer: "Guess you *are* legit, huh?"

I WAS JUST SWINGING BY MIRIAM'S PLACE TO PICK HER UP FOR OUR USUAL Friday night dinner at the fancy burger place when her phone rang with a call from Yolanda Rodriguez.

"Why is Yolanda calling me?" Miriam asked when she saw the name on the display. It was a legit question, as Yolanda lived in the Washington Heights neighborhood of Manhattan, and Miriam was the Wardein of the Bronx. If Yolanda needed her local wardein for something, it would be Damien van Owen, who was in charge of Manhattan.

"Well," I said, "the easiest way to find out is to answer the phone."

She stuck her tongue out at me — about the response that deserved, honestly — and answered the phone on speaker.

"Hey Yolanda — I'm with Bram Gold and I've got you on speaker."

"Did I interrupt something?"

"We're just heading out to dinner. What's up?"

"Well, I got this guy who wanted to hire me, but I think it's more your thing than my thing. He lives in my building, actually, but the thing he wanted me to deal with is up there."

"Okay."

Yolanda took a breath. "His name's Pedro, and Pedro was all worried about the hurricane that came up the coast last month, right? So he's got this brother, Alejandro, and Alejandro says there's this store on Jackson Avenue where he can get magickal charms and that kinda thing."

Miriam frowned. "There are no magick shops on Jackson Avenue."

"Yeah, I kinda figured." Yolanda sighed heavily. "I told Pedro he shoulda checked with me first. I woulda sent him to Kawtha's on 207th, but he went ahead and went to Jackson Avenue, and he said he wanted somethin' to keep the hurricane from comin'. The guy in the store, he sold him Balaguer's hat."

"Oh, no," Miriam said, "not Smitty again."

"Who the hell's Smitty?" Yolanda asked.

Miriam had her head in her hands. "Izzy Smith. Grifter who opens up fake magick shops. He's been doing it for years, different neighborhood each time, but always somewhere in the five boroughs or Long Island. He's got a brother-in-law who can get him hats wholesale, and every time there's a storm threatening, he tries to sell people Balaguer's hat."

I said, "I've never heard of Balaguer's hat." Given that I had a pretty decent knowledge of most of the common magickal items out there, I wasn't just—you'll pardon the expression—talking out of my hat.

It was Yolanda who replied. "Joaquin Amparo Balaguer Ricardo. He was the president of the Dominican Republic back in the day. Every Dominican kid heard the story of how President Balaguer had a magick hat. Long as he wore it, the DR wouldn't get hit with no hurricanes. When he died back in 2002, everyone figured the island was gonna get destroyed or something."

"Yeah," Miriam said, "but he was buried with his hat to keep the island protected."

"Wait," Yolanda said, "the hat really worked?"

Miriam winced. "No one really knows for sure, but nobody wanted to take the chance. Either way, though, this definitely sounds like one of Smitty's grifts."

"Whatever," Yolanda said, "point is, Pedro bought the hat, and then those storms hit last Friday, and he went back to Jackson Avenue on Monday and the store was gone. Pedro wanted to hire me to track this guy down, but I didn't even know where to start."

"You do now," Miriam said with a grin.

I hated to be a downer, but I had to say, "Yeah, but what's she gonna do with him when she finds him? I mean, Miriam here can sanction him, but it's not like he gives a damn about the rules anyhow, and I can't see any city cop arresting him for fraud when what he's claiming to sell is a magick hat."

"Actually," Yolanda said, "Pedro's aunt claims to be a bruja. I never used to believe it before I became a Courser, but now? Maybe. And Pedro says he wants to introduce this guy to Tia Maria."

"Officially," Miriam said slowly, "I can't condone that particular course of action." Then she grinned. "Unofficially, the deal between you and your client is your business. I've also got a file on Smitty that I'm more than happy to e-mail to you."

I heard Yolanda chuckle over the tiny speaker. "You're the best, Miriam. Glad it was in the South Bronx and not around here. No way van Owen's as cool as you."

"Thanks, Yolanda. Take care."

"You, too. Enjoy your dinner!"

As Miriam ended the call, I gave her a look. "You're really gonna hand Smitty over to a bruja?"

"Smitty's cheated tons of people out of their money, most of them poor people who just want some kind of magickal advantage in a shitty life. I can't stop him, and like you said, the cops can't stop him. What else do you suggest?"

I relented. "Fair point. Let's go get us some burgers."

I SHOVED THE BIG BLUE DOOR TO THE KINGFISHER'S TAIL OPEN, WALKED IN, and then just stood there for a moment, letting the cool air being pumped in through the bar's HVAC system wash over me.

Once the sweat started to evaporate, I focused on the rest of the bar, and noticed that it was surprisingly empty for a Sunday night. The only ones present were the owner, Brendan Sheehan, as well as Yewhala Chatwal and Pete Guthrie, Yolanda Rodriguez, and Sal Antonelli.

"Jesus, Gold, you look like shit," Sal said.

"Thanks, Sal," I said as I nodded to Brendan, who immediately got up and went behind the bar to get my usual beer.

Yolanda playfully punched Sal in the arm. "Ignore him, he looked like shit when he walked in, too."

"We all did," Pete said. "It's hotter than Hell out there, and I should know because—"

"YOU WERE BORN IN HELL," we all said in tired unison. Pete was born and raised in Hell, Michigan.

Sheepishly, Pete said, "I've been telling that joke too much, haven't I?"

"Just a lot," I said.

Yewhala patted his husband on the head. "It's all right, I still love you anyhow."

"Besides, who can come up with new jokes in this heat?" Brendan asked as he brought over my pint and put it in front of me. "It's after dark, and it's still above ninety out there, and the humidity's about two thousand percent."

In a mock-aside, Yolanda asked, "He knows that humidity can't get above a hundred percent, right?"

"It's his bar, he gets to math however he wants," I said, and then gulped down about a third of my beer. "What a day."

"You too?" Yewhala asked.

Sal said, "Mutt and Jeff here were just tellin' us about a yuki-onna they had to rescue up in Playland."

I stared at Pete and Yewhala. "What's a snow-woman doing in Rye in the middle of summer?"

"That was our question," Yewhala said, "but our client wasn't forthcoming with details, he just wanted her rescued."

"The fun part was driving the truck," Pete said with a chuckle. "Freezer trucks handle differently than U-Hauls, it turns out."

Yolanda asked, "So what was *your* crappy day, Abe?"

"Someone spotted a cherufe in Claremont Park."

Sal gestured at me. "See, *that* makes more sense than a yuki-onna."

I held up one finger. "You'd think that, wouldn't you? Cherufes usually live in volcanoes, after all. Hasn't been one seen around here in decades. I found him lying down in one of the tennis courts. And you wanna know what this creature of volcanoes who eats lava and comes from the tropical land of Chile said to me when I found him there laying down near the net?"

"What?" Yolanda obligingly asked when my pause went on too long.

"'It's too damn hot here.'"

Everyone just stared at me for several seconds, during which I finished my beer.

Brendan got up to get me another, and Yolanda finally said, "Nah, he didn't say that."

"He absolutely did. I got him to get up and go over to the pool to cool off, but I think we're officially in crazypants territory when the volcano creatures say it's too hot."

"I'll drink to that," Brendan said, putting one beer down in front of me and holding another. "To functioning air conditioning."

Pete said, "And to freezer trucks!"

I added, "And to community pools!"

Grinning, Yolanda added, "Saving us all from two thousand percent humidity."

We all drank.

The Courser's Apprentice

EVERY FIVE NEW MOONS, THERE'S A PORTAL IN FERRY POINT PARK THAT might—*might*—open up and let a whole host of demons out into the world. Since I became a Courser, it's only actually happened twice, but there's no real pattern to it.

But every five new moons, the wardein hires three Coursers to sit all night in Ferry Point Park and make sure the portal *doesn't* open, and if it does, deal with what comes through.

Which most of the time means we get to sit around and babble at each other. On this particular occasion, it was me, Saladin Cruz, and Kaela Provoncher.

"So I just got an apprentice," Kaela said with a sigh.

"What's with the heavy sigh after that?" Saladin asked. "I haven't been in for five years yet, but I'm lookin' forward to it so I can have an apprentice."

Kaela looked at him like he had two heads. "Why would you *want* some dumb kid following you around asking you stupid questions all the time?"

Saladin grinned. "I got a six-year-old, I'm used to it." The grin fell. "'Sides, training with Pedro was the best. I learned a lot from him, and I always said I'd try to train my apprentice the way he trained me."

Shuddering, Kaela said, "Well, if you want to take Ahmed, you're welcome to him. He will *not* shut up."

I grinned. "You should do what Hugues did to me when I asked too many questions—and bear in mind that in Hugues's lexicon, 'too many' is the same as 'more than zero'."

Kaela laughed, and then asked, "What did he do?"

"Say, 'Shut de hell up, child,' and then make me do some really annoying task."

Saladin gave me a look. "That was a *terrible* impersonation of Hugues."

I shrugged. I'd been hearing Hugues Baptiste's voice ever since I was in college, but I couldn't mimic his Haitian accent to save my life.

"The problem," Kaela said with a sigh, "is that some of his questions are good ones. And, yeah, he won't know what to do if I don't tell him, but—there's just so *many*."

Saladin said, "Maybe you should ration him. Only let him ask one question per day?"

"And if he asks more than one, make him do some really annoying task," I added with a grin.

"I guess," Kaela said.

Looking at me, Saladin asked, "How did you learn anything if Hugues wouldn't answer any questions?"

"Well, I was lucky. Miriam Zerelli was my best friend growing up, and I was always hanging around with her and Mike, so I picked up on a lot of stuff. I was already pretty knowledgeable by the time I apprenticed with Hugues. Which was good, as he wasn't interested in teaching me a damn thing, except to sit down and shut up."

Shaking her head, Kaela asked, "Why'd he even take you on as an apprentice?"

"Because if he didn't, Mike was gonna sanction him. Coursers *have* to take on at least one apprentice at some point in their careers, and Hugues had been putting it off for ages."

"Interesting," Kaela said. "Miriam didn't give me the option of putting it off. She said it was mandatory."

I chuckled. "Yeah, Miriam tends to take the direct approach more than her father did…"

"I'm surprised," Saladin said, "that you didn't send him down here for portal duty, since it's pretty light, usually."

"Honestly, I told him it was too dangerous for an apprentice."

I snorted. "What, you worried he'll get splinters in his butt from sitting on this bench all night?"

"No, I just wanted to get *away* from him for a night. And besides, I love portal duty. I hardly ever make it to the Kingfisher's Tail on Sunday nights, so this is my best chance to gossip."

"You should bring Ahmed to the bar one night," Saladin said. "Let him see the fun parts of being a Courser."

I added, "Just make sure it's a night Bernie isn't there."

Kaela shook her head. "Bernie's half of why I don't make it, to be honest. The other half is that I'm usually busy Sunday nights. But we'll see. Hey, Bram, when're you gonna get an apprentice?"

I sighed. "One of these days." In truth, I'd been putting it off, myself, and I had an easier time deflecting Miriam by dint of my long friendship with her.

At least for now. Eventually, I'd give in—but that's another story…

"Hey, Miriam."

"Hey, Bram, what's up?"

"I'm gonna need you to sanction someone. Guy named Giancarlo Manzanillo."

"You're kidding."

"No, that really is his name."

"I believe you—except I've already sanctioned him. In fact, you're the third Courser to ask me to sanction this jackass in the last month."

"Oy."

"Oy, is right. Where'd you find him?"

"At a restaurant on 187th near Third Avenue. He was trying to cast some kind of exorcism, I think. And now that I think about it, it makes sense that you sanctioned him."

"Why?"

"'Cause his spell components were all things you can get at a grocery store: sage, a pestle, a regular candle. He didn't have any proper magick stuff."

"You sure it was an exorcism?"

"I'm not, actually—he refused to say what the hell he was doing, but the restaurant owners were grateful to me for getting him outta there."

"Two weeks ago, Saladin Cruz got called to a supermarket on Brook Avenue and 149th. Manzanillo was performing some kind of ritual then, too, using a pestle, sage, a lighter, and string. And four weeks ago, Hugues called in from a house on Rochambeau near 206th, and he had a full bunch of magickal items, including an Obsidian candle and a Palmieri Charm."

"Wait, that doesn't make sense."

"What doesn't?"

"A Palmieri Charm? Those things are functionally useless. Palmieri was a scam artist."

"Actually, they do work, just not the way Palmieri wanted them to. It works if you want to summon a spirit."

"Oh crap."

"What crap?"

"Miriam, I think I may have figured out what this guy's been doing. The supermarket on Brook and 149th, that used to be a speakeasy run by the gangster Dutch Schultz. Another gangster, the head of the Lucchese family until he got face shot off, was Gaetano Reina, who lived in a house on Rochambeau near 206th. And the restaurant I found Manzanillo in used to be a community hall. It's where Sal Maranzano held the meeting that formed the five families of the American Mafia."

"So you think—what?"

"He was trying to summon the spirits of some of the Bronx's most famous wise guys."

"Okay. Why would he do that?"

"Gotta ask him."

"All right, I'm officially hiring you to track this guy down and bring him to me so we can find out what he's trying to do."

"Track him down?"

"Yeah."

"I'm not a PI, Miriam."

"No shit, Sherlock—and this isn't a huge priority. All this guy's doing is making a nuisance of himself, and it's not like he *actually* can summon these spirits with the spice rack he's using. Just do what you can."

"Or we wait until he hits Jake LaMotta's house or something."

"LaMotta was a boxer, not a gangster."

"Yeah, but he fought a lot at the old Bronx Coliseum, and boxing was rife with gangster activity back in the day."

"Isn't the Coliseum a bus depot now?"

"Yeah. And if Manzanillo follows the pattern, he'll be there in two weeks and will try to resurrect some fight fixer or other."

"Great. Good luck with that. Hey, can you bring the spell components by?"

"Why, it's not real magic stuff."

"Yeah, but I'm out of sage, and I want to make chicken tonight…"

"TRICK OR TREAT!"

Bram Gold had set up a lawn chair and a small card table in front of the three-story house he owned in the Riverdale section of the Bronx. Bram was dressed in a flowy black cape with a red lining, worn over an old suit, and had fangs in his mouth.

The latest kids to approach were a boy dressed as the Mandalorian from *Star Wars* and a girl dressed as Izzy Moonbow from *My Little Pony*. Bram stood dramatically, making sure his cape billowed properly, then reached into the large plastic pumpkin in which he kept a bunch of small candies he'd bought at CVS and handed some to each.

"Thank you!" Izzy said. For his part, the Mandalorian just took the candy and ran off to hit the next house.

Shaking his head, Bram said, "You're velcome" in a terrible eastern European accent.

The next person to approach the house was dressed as Gimli from the *Lord of the Rings* films, complete with an impressive replica axe.

"Treat or trick," "Gimli" said.

Bram started, "That is a wery good costume, litt—" Then he cut himself off and spoke in his normal voice. "Dmitri? That you?"

Shaking his head, the karzelek grumbled, "Shoulda realized that was you in that cape, Gold. I didn't know you lived here, I woulda skipped it."

"You *do* get that trick-or-treat is for *kids*, right? You're, what, two hundred years old?"

"Two hundred and twelve. Hey, free candy is free candy, y'know? And everyone *thinks* I'm a little kid the other three hundred and sixty-four days a year, so I may as well take advantage the one day it works for me."

Chuckling, Bram reached into the pumpkin and grabbed a small handful of candy bars. Dmitri was only four feet tall, and he was unusually tall by the standards of karzeleks, who averaged three-and-a-half feet. "Fine, here you go."

"Thank you," Dmitri said as he took the proffered sweets and dropped them into the drawstring bag he had tied to his belt. "Also, that accent you're using is *terrible*."

"That's on purpose."

"You just keep telling yourself that. Happy Hallowe'en, Gold."

"You too, Dmitri."

◄━THE BRONX━►

"Trick or treat!"

As little Eduardo Rodriguez—dressed as the Black Panther—said those words to the old woman who opened the door to Apartment 5C, his mother, Yolanda Rodriguez, held the Laveau Charm tightly.

The old woman grinned, placed two candy bars in Eduardo's bag, and said, "Wakanda forever!"

Eduardo crossed his arms and said, "Yibambe!" in response, and the woman and Yolanda both laughed.

"Happy Hallowe'en," Yolanda said.

"You too," the old woman said, and she closed the door.

The Laveau didn't glow at any point.

They moved on to 5D, but nobody answered, and the Laveau didn't glow when they were standing in front of the door.

A beautiful young man opened the door to 5E, and Eduardo said, "Trick or treat!"

The Laveau started to emit a blue glow immediately.

The man winced. "That is a wonderful costume, young man, and I admire your choice. But I am afraid that I have no candy for you. I gave the last of it to a young girl dressed as one of the Power Rangers. I would rather have given it to you, as T'Challa is a far greater role model."

Yolanda stepped forward. "I'm sorry, but—" She sighed. "Supprimer."

Now the Laveau's glow changed to red. And the person who opened the door suddenly straightened, his limbs going rigid. Then his arms shrunk, his legs started to fuse, and after a few moments, a large snake was coiled in the doorway.

The snake hissed very loudly and asked, "What have you done?"

"Revealed your true form, Dumballah. My name's Yolanda Rodriguez, I'm a Courser, and your wife Aida-Wedo hired me to find you."

Another hiss. "I should've known she'd try to find me. I needed a break."

"Maybe, but she misses you."

"I'm sure she does. I guess I do, too, I just—" He hissed again. "I'm a spirit of optimism, and it's been difficult to maintain. I needed a break."

"Well, break's over. Because if you don't come with me, Aida-Wedo will come after you herself."

Yolanda had never seen a snake shudder before.

"All right, then. Let me just make some arrangements. Come in, please."

They entered the apartment. Yolanda looked down at her son. "You okay, baby boy?"

"Yeah, I'm good, mamí."

"You're not too freaked out?"

"Nah." She could see, even under the full face mask, that Eduardo was smiling now. "It's his own dumb fault for not havin' no candy for me."

◄—THE BRONX—►

"Trick or treat!"

Valentina Perrone was sitting on the front porch of the small house she owned in Hammonton, New Jersey. As usual, she had made a huge batch of chocolate chip cookies from scratch and had wrapped them in Saran Wrap. Each kid who came trick-or-treating would get one cookie.

The first few years, she'd had issues with parents who were hyperworried about stranger danger and didn't trust homemade items, but Valentina's reputation for superlative baking spread around the town pretty quickly, and now it was rare to find a kid who didn't eagerly grab one of her cookies.

The two teenage girls who approached now, though—one dressed as a flower, with the petals radiating out from all around her head, the other dressed as Sailor Moon—were faces she didn't recognize, and she steeled herself for the complaints about how their parents told them not to take "risky" candy being given out.

Grabbing two shrink-wrapped cookies, Valentina said, "Here you both go."

"Thank you, Ms. Perrone," the flower said with a familiar voice.

She frowned. "How'd you know my—" Then she placed the voice and pulled back her hands. "Jesu, Giuseppe, Mari, are you two trying this nonsense *again*?"

The flower and Sailor Moon exchanged glances. "What do you mean, Ms. Perrone?"

"I've never seen your faces before, but you know my name."

Sailor Moon smiled. "Everybody knows you, Ms. Perrone, you're the one with the great cookies!"

"Uh huh. And I know both of you, Maria Elisabetta and Anna Domenica."

Suddenly, both teenage girls' skin became more wrinkled, and liver spots appeared on Sailor Moon's legs and upper arms.

The flower—Maria Elisabetta—sighed and said, "Every year, she gets us."

Anna Domenica shook her head, the big blonde Sailor Moon wig almost falling off. "One of these years, we'll fool her like we did the king."

"Again with the king?" Maria Elisabetta said. "Can't we go five minutes without you reminding me about the king you fooled into marrying you because he thought you were a teenager?"

Valentina interrupted the inevitable argument, which they got into every single time she saw the two crones. "Will you two please get off my lawn, so I can give my cookies to *real* trick-or-treaters."

They wandered off, Maria Elisabetta muttering, "Next year, we'll get her, you'll see."

"Damn right…"

Cryptid Christmas

"MERRY CHRISTMAS!"

Valentina Perrone said those words to Quinque Tredecim as she opened the door to the cabin in the heart of the Jersey Pine Barrens. Val was holding a big box wrapped in colorful paper with a bow stuck to the top and offered it to the tall creature with leathern skin and wings who answered the door.

"Ms. Perrone. You do know that we don't *all* celebrate Christmas here, yes?" Quinque asked the question in her usual harsh tone, while not actually taking the present.

"Maybe, but I do, and a big part of the season is giving gifts. This one's for you. Will you take it, please, so I can grab the others?" There was a shopping bag behind her filled with more wrapped boxes, as well as a few gift bags.

With a raspy sigh, Quinque took the proffered present. "I suppose you should come in."

Grinning, Val reached down to grab the shopping bag and followed the creature she knew as Quinque, but most of the rest of the world thought of as "the Jersey Devil," into the cabin.

There in the living room sat most of the rest of the occupants of the cabin, which Quinque's ancestors had created as a refuge for creatures like her who were different from mainline humanity, ostracized for it, but who never actually did harm to anyone. As Quinque had said the first time Val came to this cabin in her capacity as a Courser—a supernatural hunter-for-hire—there were no monsters here, only people.

Sitting on the couch were two giant creatures: Walter (an orange-furred sasquatch) and Nukilik (a white-furred yeti). Nguyet, a big spider, was hanging from the ceiling via a web over an eight-candle menorah, with three of the candles lit. Laying down across the floor in front of the roaring fire was Isembi, a mokele-mbembe (pretty much looking like a giant mallosaur). Four more were standing around a Christmas tree, hanging decorations from the branches: a chupacabra named Armando, a howler named Billy-Bob, a bunyip named Eleutheria, and a giant monkey named Munish. The only occupants of the house not present were Jimmy and Maria, two moth creatures. Maria preferred to be in Hawai'i during the winter, and Jimmy usually spent the holidays with her.

Upon Val's entrance, they all looked over at her, except for Isembi, who seemed to be napping. Armando asked, "What you doin' here, Val? Ain't you got family to be with on Christmas Eve?"

"I'm heading up to Fort Lee to do the Seven Fishes at Nonna's after this, but I wanted to give you all presents."

Walter's black eyes went wide, and he got up from the couch. "You got us presents?"

"Yup. Not too many people know about you guys, and you are supposed to kinda be in hiding, so I figured you didn't get too many gifts."

Munish hung a red ball on the tree and said, "I do not celebrate holidays."

Val chuckled. "And yet, here you are decorating the tree."

"As a favor to my housemates," Munish said.

Billy-Bob grinned, showing his large fangs. "And we're mighty grateful—there's a shit-ton'a decorations here…"

Quinque said. "I've always followed the tradition of the Quakers who raised my great-great grandfather. They especially do *not* celebrate Christmas, as they find it vulgar."

"They ain't wrong about that," Val said with a grin. "You gonna open your present, or what?"

"Very well." Using her talons, Quinque easily shredded the wrapping paper, revealing a box with a bright red KitchenAid inside it. "Thank you, Ms. Perrone."

"You said you needed one after the last one broke, and I figured your new one should be red."

"As I recall," Quinque said dryly, "you believe everything should be red."

"True." Val reached into the bag and pulled out a gift bag with a Star of David on it. "Nguyet, this is for you. Sorry I don't have the full eight gifts for you." She walked over to the menorah and handed the bag to the giant spider, who remained hanging from the wall.

"Few people even remember that I converted to Judaism in the Nineties." Holding the bag with two of his legs, he pulled the top apart with two others, and yanked out a tissue-paper-wrapped gift with a fifth. It revealed a very tiny yarmulke, with colorful beadwork also in the pattern of a Star of David.

"I got that from a craftsperson in Hammonton. She's got an Etsy shop if you want more. I had her make it so it would actually fit on your tiny head."

Nguyet started to excrete with happiness. "Thank you, Valentina. It means a great deal."

She continued to give out the gifts, including high-end conditioner for Munish, Walter, and Nukilik. "It would've been better," Nukilik said, "if you gave us food for Quviasukvik."

Walter added, "That's the traditional Inuit new year's celebration, which is a big feast. And stop being a jackass, Nuke, I for one could go with some less tangled fur in the new year. So thanks, Val."

"Yeah," Nukilik said reluctantly, "thanks."

"I'm also grateful," Munish said, "and would love to know where you got this."

"Different craftsperson in Hammonton. She does *not* have an Etsy store, but she lives two doors down from me. I'll get her information for you guys—assuming the stuff works as advertised anyhow."

"Excellent," Munish said. "My gratitude, Ms. Perrone."

Val then gave Armando and Billy-Bob their presents. From, respectively, Central America and Arkansas, both were hardcore Christmas celebrants, and very much loved the DVDs Val got them: a boxed set of Phase 1 of the Marvel Cinematic Universe for Armando and a boxed set of all the *Die Hard* movies for Billy-Bob.

"Only winter holiday I celebrate," Eleutheria said before Val could give her her gift, "is Survival Day, and that won't be until next month."

"Just take the present, Ellie," Val said as she held out another gift bag.

"And I hate that nickname," Eleutheria said as she took the bag and removed a handheld battery-powered sander.

"For your teeth," Val said. "You're always complaining about how toothbrushes never do the trick and what you really need is a sander. I got a cousin who's a contractor, and he said that little portable jobbie'll work perfectly on enamel."

"I don't know what to say." Eleutheria sounded stunned.

Quinque gave another raspy chuckle. "I believe an expression of gratitude is traditional."

"Yes, thank you, Val."

"And finally, I got something for Izzy. Think he'll wake up?"

In a deep, resonant voice, Isembi said, "I am awake. Merely resting my eyes while laying by the nice, warm fire." Raising his head and his long neck, Isembi said, "Like Nuke and Walt, my preferred solstice celebration is the harvest festival of Umkhosi Wokweshwama."

"Yeah, I know, that's why I got you this." She handed him a wrapped box.

Sitting himself up—which meant he now blocked the fire from the rest of the cabin—Isembi set the present down on the floor in front of him and tore the wrapping open to reveal a box, which he also tore open. Inside that was something wrapped in tissue paper, and under that wrapped in bubble wrap.

"How many layers must I endure?" Isembi asked.

"The bubble wrap's it." Val said with a chuckle.

Once he ripped off the tape securing the bubble-filled plastic, it was easy for Isembi to unwrap it, and it revealed a green glass sculpture that was in the gourd-like shape of a calabash.

"Oh my goodness," Isembi said almost reverently. "It's a calabash. The dashing of a calabash is how the end of the harvest festival is signified." He looked over at Val. "This is beautiful, where did you find it?"

"Commissioned it from the same woman who did Nguyet's yarmulke. Glad you like it, Izzy."

"Thank you, Valentina, I will treasure this. So much so that I will not even object to you calling me 'Izzy'."

Eleutheria asked, "What is your obsession with nicknames, Perrone?"

"These are all extremely generous," Quinque said. "But we have nothing for you. I can offer you to stay for the evening meal—but no, you said you were on your way to a family event."

"I am, yeah, and Nonna'll kill me if I don't show up, and I still got an hour-and-a-half drive to get up there. But hey, don't worry about it. Honestly, just seein' the looks on all your faces is the best gift you guys coulda got me. Look, it doesn't matter if it's Hanukkah, Kwanzaa, Christmas, Survival Day, Umkhosi Wokweshwama, Quviasukvik, Soyal, or just a celebration of the winter solstice, we're all doing the same thing. This is when the sun renews itself and the days get longer again and we're grateful for a new year, a new harvest, whatever. And a great way to celebrate that is to give presents—at least for me. And you guys got a rough life, having to hide in this cabin so other Coursers who ain't as nice as me don't get hired to kill you. Plus, you guys are *happy* here. That's the important part. I just hope these gifts make you a little bit happier."

Quinque—who was still holding the KitchenAid box in both taloned hands—bowed her head. "Well said, Ms. Perrone. A joyous holiday to you."

"Happy Hanukkah," Nguyet said.

"Merry Christmas," Billy-Bob said.

Val grinned. "And to all a goodnight!"

KEITH R.A. DECANDIDO HAS LIVED IN THE BRONX FOR MOST OF HIS LIFE — born here, raised here, educated here (Fordham University, Class of 1990, go Rams!), and still a proud resident of the northernmost of the five boroughs. He worked for the U.S. Census Bureau from 2009-2010 working in the Bronx, which was the inspiration for starting this series with *A Furnace Sealed* in 2019. He's hard at work at the as-yet-untitled third book. His other fiction in Bram Gold's world includes a short story in *Liar Liar*, two stories featuring Yolanda Rodriguez in *Bad Ass Moms* and *Devilish and Divine*, and a novella featuring Valentina Perrone, *Systema Paradoxa: All-the-Way House*, about the secret origin of the Jersey Devil.

Keith has written more than sixty novels, more than a hundred short stories, more than fifty comic books, and more nonfiction than he's comfortable counting. His work includes a great deal of media tie-in fiction in the worlds of TV shows (*Star Trek, Supernatural*), movies (*Alien, Cars*), games (Dungeons & Dragons, *World of Warcraft*), comic books (Spider-Man, Thor), and classic literary characters (Sherlock Holmes, She-Who-Must-Be-Obeyed). His extensive work as a writer and editor of licensed fiction has earned him a Lifetime Achievement Award from the International Association of Media Tie-in Writers, which means he never needs to achieve anything ever again.

He's also written in plenty of universes of his own devising beyond the world of Coursers: the forthcoming fantasy series *Supernatural Crimes Unit*, about the division of the NYPD that deals with crimes involving magic and monsters; the long-running "Precinct" series of fantasy police procedurals, the latest of which is *Phoenix Precinct*; one novel (*The Case of the Claw*) and several shorter works featuring the Super City Police Department, about cops in a city filled with superheroes; and urban fantasy stories set in Key West, the latest of which are collected in the newly released *Ragnarok and a Hard Place: More Tales of Cassie Zukav, Weirdness Magnet*.

Other recent and upcoming work includes *Manticore Precinct*, the next book in that series; the *Resident Evil: Infinite Darkness* prequel graphic novel *The Beginning*; short stories in multiple issues of *Star Trek Explorer*, in several installments of the *Sherlock Holmes: Cases by Candlelight, Thrilling Adventure Yarns*, and *Phenomenons* anthology series, and in *Weird Tales: 100 Years of Weird, Joe Ledger: Unbreakable, A Cry of Hounds*, and *The Good, the Bad, and the Uncanny*, as well as in two anthologies he also co-edited, *The Four ???? of the Apocalypse* (with Wrenn Simms) and *Double Trouble: An Anthology of Two-Fisted Team-Ups* (with Jonathan Maberry).

Keith writes nonfiction about popular culture for the award-winning webzine Reactor Magazine (formerly Tor.com), for his own Patreon (patreon.com/krad), and for essay collections published by Sequart, Becky Books, ATB Publishing, and Crazy 8 Press.

In addition to writing, Keith is an editor of many years' standing (though he usually does it sitting down), a musician (currently percussionist for the parody band Boogie Knights), and a martial artist (a fourth-degree black belt in karate, which he also teaches to both kids and adults). He may do some other stuff, which he can't recall due to the lack of sleep. Find out less at his web site at DeCandido.net.

Abigail Reilly
Alex Jay Berman
Andrew Kaplan
Andy Holman Hunter
Anthony R. Cardno
Aysha Rehm
Bailey A Buchanan
Barry Nove
Benjamin Adler
bill
Bill & Kelley & Kyle
Brendan Coffey
Brian D Lambert
Brian Klueter
Brooks Moses
Buddy Deal
Caitlin Rozakis
Candi O'Rourke
Carla Spence
Carol J. Guess
Carol Jones
Caroline Westra
Cheri Kannarr
Christine Lawrence
Christine Norris
Christopher Bennett
Christopher J. Burke
Coats Family
Colleen Feeney

Craig "Stevo" Stephenson
Crysella
Dale A Russell
Danielle Ackley-McPhail
Danny Chamberlin
Denise and Raphael Sutton
Doniki Boderick-Luckey
Donna Hogg
Duane Warnecke
E.M. Middel
Ef Deal
Ellen Montgomery
Emily Weed Baisch
Erin A.
"filkertom" Tom Smith
Frank Michaels
Gary Phillips
Gav I
GhostCat
GraceAnne Andreassi
    DeCandido
Greg Levick
Ian Harvey
J.E. Taylor
Jack Deal
Jakub Narębski
James Aquilone
Jamie René Peddicord
Jennifer Hindle

Jennifer L. Pierce
Jeremy Bottroff
Joe Gillis
John Keegan
John L. French
John Markley
Jonathan Haar
Judy McClain
Karen Palmer
KC Grifant
Kelly Pierce
Ken Seed
kirbsmilieu
krinsky
Lark Cunningham
LCW Allingham
Lee
Lee Thalblum
Lisa Kruse
Liz DeJesus and Amber Davis
Lorraine J Anderson
Louise Lowenspets
Lynn P.
Maria V Arnold
Marie Devey
Matthew Barr
Michael A. Burstein
Michael Barbour
Morgan Hazelwood
Mustela
Niki Curtis
Paul Ryan
pjk
Rachel A Brune
Raja Thiagarajan
Reckless Pantalones
Rich Gonzalez
Rich Walker
Richard Fine
Richard Novak
Richard O'Shea

Rigel Ailur
Robert Greenberger
Robert Ziegler
Ronald H. Miller
Ruth Ann Orlansky
Scott Schaper
Shawnee M
Shervyn
Sheryl R. Hayes
Sonia Koval
Sonya M.
Steph Parker
Stephen Ballentine
Stephen W. Buchanan
Steven Purcell
Subrata Sircar
Susan Simko
The Creative Fund by BackerKit
Thomas Bull
Thomas P. Tiernan
Tim Tucker
Tom B.
Tracy Popey
Tracy 'Rayhne' Fretwell
Will "scifantasy" Frank
'Will It Work' Dansicker
William C Tracy
wmaddie700

eSpec Books Titles by Keith R.A. DeCandido
(Available in print and ebook)

The Precinct Series

978-1-942990-82-6	Dragon Precinct
978-1-942990-84-0	Unicorn Precinct
978-1-942990-86-4	Goblin Precinct
978-1-942990-88-8	Gryphon Precinct
978-1-942990-92-5	Mermaid Precinct
978-1-956463-17-0	Phoenix Precinct
978-1-942990-90-1	Tales of Dragon Precinct

The Bram Gold Series

978-1-956463-41-5	A Furnace Sealed
978-1-956463-43-9	Feat of Clay

Miscellaneous Titles

978-1-949691-71-9	All-the-Way House
978-1-942990-62-8	Without a License

with David Sherman

978-1-949691-55-9	The 18th Race Omnibus Edition
978-1-942990-46-8	To Hell and Regroup (book 3 in the 18th Race Trilogy)

Anthologies

978-1-949691-03-0	Footprints in the Stars
978-1-942990-38-3	The Best of Defending the Future
978-1-942990-03-1	The Side of Good / The Side of Evil
978-1-956463-01-9	Best Laid Plans
978-1-949691-47-4	Devilish and Divine
978-1-942990-50-5	Best of Bad-Ass Faeries
978-1-956463-31-6	A Cry of Hounds

www.especbooks.com

* 9 7 8 1 9 5 6 4 6 3 4 3 9 *